"I wonder who that could be?"

Brianna went to the door, opened it and was shocked to find three men in business suits standing on the porch.

"Brianna Wells?"

"Yes..."

The man nearest the door flipped open a leather wallet revealing a badge. "Federal Bureau of Investigation, ma'am. We have a warrant for your arrest."

Brianna looked at Nick, who was standing at the doorway to the kitchen. He did not seem surprised.

"What's this all about," she said to him. "Why are they arresting me?"

Nick looked at her glumly. "I hope you know a good lawyer" was all he said.

What in the world had she gotten herself into?

ABOUT THE AUTHOR

Janice Kaiser thinks the Caribbean is one of the most romantic spots in the world. No wonder she and her husband have spent so much time there. Among Janice's other passions is antique jewelry, and she fell madly in love with the black pearls in St. Thomas. She decided that if she couldn't own a black pearl, the next best thing was to write a story about them. Once a full-time lawyer and now a full-time writer, Janice lives in California with her husband and two children. Her fifth Superromance is coming out this spring, and her second Intrigue promises to be a lot of fun.

THE BLACK PEARL

JANICE KAISER

Harlequin Books

TORONTO • NEW YORK • LONDON
AMSTERDAM • PARIS • SYDNEY • HAMBURG
STOCKHOLM • ATHENS • TOKYO • MILAN

For Edris Smith Bender,
whose love of beauty and whose love
have been a source of strength and inspiration.
Thank you, Mama.

Thanks to Patti Cadby Birch,
owner of Circe in St. Thomas,
whose black pearls and
works of art inspired this book.

Harlequin Intrigue edition published January 1987

ISBN 0-373-22058-8

Prologue

The child stared out the window of the train, hoping to see more of those funny looking llamas, but all she saw was the deep chasm that seemed to drop into the bowels of the earth. As the railroad cars snaked along the side of the mountain, she could see the gray smoke from the stack of the ancient engine drifting out across the canyon, where it seemed to mingle and blend with the wispy mountain vapors.

The train slowed as it climbed, and the engine, which had disappeared around another bend, whistled mournfully. This funny old Peruvian train was not at all like the trains or subways at home. Brianna decided she would have to tell all the kids in Mrs. Morganstern's third-grade class about the ride she had taken on it high into the mountains to this mysterious town where nobody lived and all the houses and stores had fallen down.

During their trip to Peru the girl's father had purchased a number of pieces of stone statuary, ancient necklaces, bracelets and other pre-Columbian artifacts for his gallery in New York. This little outing from Cusco to the Inca citadel of Machu Picchu was more for educational purposes than for any other, though the girl was too young to appreciate most of what Howard Wells and his Peruvian friend, Señor Gustavo Solari, had told her about the place.

Brianna looked at the Peruvian professor's worn leather briefcase on the seat opposite them and thought of Señor Solari's great big mustache that wiggled when he talked. The man had been gone for five or ten minutes, and the little girl wondered if he might have gone forward to talk to the engineer. He seemed very important and could speak the language of all the people in Peru, which was very convenient because he could also talk in English to her and her father, though his words sometimes sounded very strange, even when Brianna understood them.

The train whistle called out again from behind the next curve just as Gustavo Solari entered the car. His linen suit looked rumpled, and the thinning wisps of his black hair stood out, making him seem disheveled alongside her father, who was always meticulously groomed. But Señor Solari smiled as he approached, and his friendliness more than made up for his funny looks. Brianna liked him.

Taking his place opposite her, he leaned over to speak with the little girl. "Well, Miss Brianna, are you ready to see the wonderful, magical city of Machu Picchu?"

She nodded.

"Good, because it won't be so long, and we will be there." He smiled and glanced at Howard Wells before looking very deeply into Brianna's eyes. "You are a very fortunate young lady to be able to visit thees wonderful place."

Brianna Wells looked at her father, then at the Peruvian. "Is it really magical, Señor Solari?"

The man laughed, his brown eyes crinkling at the corners. "Not like in thees fairy tales, no, *señorita*, but it es a very special city."

"Are there princesses there?"

"You will be the first in a very long time."

"Because nobody lives there now?"

Solari grinned. "Do you remember all the things I told you about thees town, *señorita*?"

Brianna nodded again.

"If you like it, I will tell you more stories about thees town and the ancient peoples that lived there, Miss Brianna."

The child smiled.

Gustavo Solari looked out the window, thinking. After a moment he turned to her, his broad grin causing his mustache to bend at the ends. "You know, I have told you about the history of the Incas in Machu Picchu, but I haven't told you about their legends, *señorita*. Would you like that I tell you thees?"

Brianna looked at her father.

"Legends are like fairy tales, darling. They are stories that are told to each new generation of children." Howard Wells stroked his daughter's head, liking the feel of her black silky hair, remembering her mother and the painful loss and grieving he and the child had gone through together over the past months.

Brianna looked at the two men in turn, feeling very important. Her father squeezed her hand.

"What kind of a story do you want?" Solari asked.

"About a princess," Brianna replied.

The man laughed. "Oh, how fortunate you are. By chance I happen to know a story about a princess who became a queen. Would you like a story about an Inca queen?"

Brianna's eyes brightened, and the professor leaned back comfortably in his seat. The girl could see a little smile touch his lips as he stared out at the mists drifting across the face of the mountain.

"Not many people outside of Peru know thees," the professor began solemnly, "but before the Incas there was another race who lived in our country. They were a very fair people with white skin, like you. Some of thees people even had blond hair like your father's. We do not know where thees people came from, but for a long time they ruled the Andean region.

"Then, suddenly, many years ago they decided to leave, going first to the coast where they built rafts and sailed toward Polynesia, never to return."

"Is that why nobody lives now in the magical city?"

"No, not exactly, Brianna. You see, after thees fair race left our country, the Incas became the rulers of the Andes. But before they left, the legend says that the king of the white-skinned people left behind his young daughter, a princess, to live with the Incas."

"Didn't he love her?"

"Oh, I think he must have loved her, but he was the king, and a king must do the best thing for his peoples—he had to leave the girl with the Incas so that one day she would become queen. So you see, thees girl stayed behind, and all the others left. She grew to be a woman and married the Inca king."

"Was she sad?"

"I think she must have been sad when her family and friends went away, but because she was the daughter of the white king, she was treated well. So I believe she was happy."

"What was her name?"

"Thees I do not know. But she became an Inca queen and lived for many years. Still, her people did not forget her, for the legend says that even after much time a small group of the white people returned across the Pacific to bring gifts to the queen and her Inca husband, the king."

"Presents?"

Solari chuckled. "Yes, presents, little one. In fact, the legend says that the messenger from the white king brought to thees daughter who was left behind the most wonderful gem in all the world—a black pearl!"

"A black pearl?" Howard Wells asked with curiosity.

"Yes, the legend es a very interesting one, *señor*. We know that it es of ancient origin, from the time long before the precious black pearls of the South Seas became known to the rest of the world. Although thees idea of a pearl being black might be from the imagination of a storyteller, thees legend might also have some basis in fact."

"The notion is an appealing one, isn't it?" Howard Wells smiled gently. "I've never seen a black pearl, though I've heard of them. Have you see one, Gustavo?"

"No, *señor*, they are very rare in nature, and thus most precious—much more even than the most precious diamond."

"Where do they come from? Are they aberrations of regular pearls, or are they from a special oyster?"

"My understanding es the latter. They are from a rare black oyster found only in the waters near certain islands in Polynesia. They are rarer still by the fact that thees oyster es not so likely to make the pearl like the other species. To find one es a rare prize indeed."

Brianna moved to the edge of her seat. "But the queen got one?"

"Yes, Brianna, the white queen of the Incas got a beautiful black pearl from her father. The legend says that it was large, like a marble, and perfectly shaped. There was none other like it in the world."

The child looked at her father, her eyes wide.

"What do you think of that, darling?"

"I think the queen was very lucky."

The professor laughed. "Indeed, *señorita*, she was very lucky, and her father was very generous, don't you think?"

Brianna nodded.

"How about you, little one? Would you like to be a white Inca queen and have your father send to you a beautiful black pearl?"

She looked up at the man at her side. "I don't want you to go away, Daddy, but when I grow up, I want to have a beautiful black pearl, just like the Inca queen."

Solari and Brianna's father exchanged looks. The Peruvian smiled. "I think, *señor*, the daughter has the taste for beauty and the sense of adventure of the father."

Howard Wells put his arm around her shoulder and squeezed the little girl against him. "You may be right, Gustavo, you may be right."

Chapter One

Nick Severin leaned against the railing and stared across the runway at the rocky *morne* covered with tropical vegetation. His mind drifted from the chilly streets of Paris he had left behind to the balmy soft wind blowing off the Baie de St. Jean. The French West Indies were a long way from France, but he could hardly complain. A few days on the island of Saint Barthélemy in the warm wind and sea wouldn't hurt at all, not one little bit.

Severin looked at his watch then at the saddle in the mountain to the west end of the runway—Brianna Wells's plane would slip through the notch before dropping down onto the dangerously short strip of pavement the pilots euphemistically called a runway. The plane was due in any minute, and the clerk inside the tiny terminal had said the flight from St. Thomas was on time. Severin knew it wouldn't be long now.

He smiled to himself, thinking about the arduous month and a half since his initial meeting with Anthony Havergill in London. During the intervening weeks he had carefully worked his way down the list of people they had compiled, the task taking him first to Milan, then to Jerusalem, after that to Antwerp and now St. Barts. The more likely candidates—Rugieri, Weiss and Kessel, all men in their fifties and sixties—hadn't panned out. Now he was pursuing the lone woman in the group.

Though he had never met Brianna Wells, he had already bet himself a bottle of Bollinger Brut that she would not be the one, either. Severin had questioned Havergill on the choice of Brianna Wells. "Why a jewelry designer from the U.S. Virgin Islands, and a woman—a young one—to boot? Isn't that stretching it a bit?"

"The more unlikely, the more likely, Mr. Severin," Havergill had replied. "Besides, you haven't seen her work."

Still, they had agreed there was no substitute for proven criminal talent, so Severin had begun his search in Milan with Rugieri, who had several years of prison time on his record. Having come up empty-handed there, as well as in Israel and Belgium, he had left Paris for the Caribbean to test the most unlikely candidate of all.

Though he doubted anything would come of it, the trip wouldn't be a total waste. Severin already had one day on the beach under his belt, and had the company of a young American woman to look forward to. Even if she turned out to be a bore, it would be a change of pace from the suspicious and deceitful old men.

Looking again at the sky over the mountain, Severin wondered what she'd be like and, more importantly, how she'd react to his little surprise. In a way, he felt a twinge of guilt for having enticed the woman with a gem, but they had discovered that black pearls were her weakness, and the information was just too good not to use against her. Besides, this was not child's play. Brianna Wells was a clever woman, and they could take no chances with her. He'd be a fool not to use every weapon, every trick, at his disposal.

Severin smiled at the empty sky over the mountain. Villainy at the expense of others could be such fun, he thought. The smile became a grin and broadened farther until he began laughing to himself at his own black humor.

BRIANNA WELLS GLANCED at the pilot in the seat in front of her, feeling slightly irritated by the cavalier manner in which he sat, his arms folded across his chest, only his right knee touching the controls. Except for the fact that he would reach over from time to time to adjust the throttle or props, she half expected he might drop off to sleep.

Brianna felt that he was a competent pilot. She had flown around the Caribbean long enough to know that it took skill to hop from island to island, landing on airfields the size of postage stamps.

The casual way of life in the Caribbean was something that Brianna herself had come to prefer, but whenever she was in an airplane, she appreciated more professional behavior. Though one had little choice but to be trusting, she found herself looking around at the cloud-dappled skies, feeling better that someone—if only herself—was alert to danger.

Out the starboard side of the plane, Brianna saw the hazy profile of a large island that she judged to be St. Martin. Knowing that St. Barts was not far, she craned her neck to look over the high control panel and out the windshield of the craft. They were on the glide path, slicing through puffy white clouds that obstructed the view ahead.

The pilot had grown more alert. He had taken the microphone in his hand and was speaking to someone, probably the control tower on the island. As she watched and listened with interest, the clouds broke open and dead ahead a small emerald green island with sharp jagged peaks appeared.

For an inhabited island St. Barts was small, only about nine square miles in area, but Brianna had heard it was lovely. Nice hotels and restaurants had recently sprung up in response to tourist interest, but it was still considered relatively "undiscovered," though that, she had heard, was rapidly changing.

It was Brianna's first trip to the French Antilles, though she had wanted to visit them for a number of years, and she was looking forward to it. It was that, almost as much as Nicholas Severin's story about his fantastic black pearl, that had induced her to accept the invitation for a meeting with the mysterious gentleman.

Brianna had been suspicious when he had insisted that she meet him in St. Barts. And when he had refused her suggestion to come to St. Thomas, she had very nearly decided not to meet with him at all. But he had thrown so many familiar names at her—people her father had known and dealt with before his death—that she had wavered.

"Oh, why don't you go?" her shop manager, Sylvie Voirin, had said. "It might be interesting for you, no? And it's true you could use a little break."

And so Brianna had accepted Nicholas Severin's invitation.

Her last conversation with him on the telephone—in which he had informed her of the arrangements he had made for accommodations—had been very cryptic. But the man had once again employed the abundant charm he had used in convincing her to meet with him in the first place.

"I suppose," she had said, "since you're flying all the way from Paris to meet with me, I can go as far as St. Barts. But I really don't see why you don't come to St. Thomas. It may lack the same sort of charm, but it does have its virtues."

"I'm sure it does, Miss Wells, but it's important that I remain on French soil. You'll understand after we've had a chance to talk a little."

"I wish you'd be a little more explicit about this pearl of yours, and about what sort of business dealings you have in mind."

"I will later. I assure you."

"You may as well know in advance that if you've got something unsavory or illegal in mind I'm not interested."

"Of course you aren't," he had replied in his low, silky voice. "If you were, I wouldn't even be talking with you."

Brianna hadn't believed Nicholas Severin for some reason, but she had decided to meet with him, anyway. The pearl sounded too good to be true, but she *had* to know for sure. Permitting her curiosity to get in the way of her judgment was probably just what Mr. Severin had been counting on, but Brianna couldn't help herself.

Besides, being familiar with the man's principal reference, Lucien Pillet, had eased her concern somewhat. Though she didn't know Pillet personally, her father had respected him greatly and had done business with him before the well-known French art dealer had retired to quieter pursuits.

Brianna had tried to call Pillet to check up on Nicholas Severin, but he was traveling and not available to answer her questions. His secretary did confirm that Mr. Severin was an American living in Paris and was known to Monsieur Pillet, so she decided that all she had to lose by accepting the mysterious American's invitation was a couple of days on St. Barts.

The plane was nearing the island, and Brianna found herself scanning it warily. The steep mountains seemed to rise directly out of the sea and no place for an airstrip was immediately apparent. It must be on the other side of the island, she concluded.

The passenger seated next to her was an elderly Frenchwoman wearing a straw hat. She seemed as uncomfortable as Brianna. In the rear seat was an American couple from Connecticut, tourists who had been chatting excitedly during much of the flight. The copilot's seat was vacant, giving Brianna a clear view of the island ahead that seemed no more than a few miles away.

The small plane bounced a little in the bumpy air. The pilot made no sign of banking in either direction to circle the island—they continued straight toward the mountainous wall rising from the sea. Brianna found herself leaning forward to get a look at the pilot to make sure that his eyes were still open. He was awake, fortunately, his hand now resting casually at the bottom of the controls.

Just to the south of their point of approach she saw the tiny port of Gustavia rimming a horseshoe inlet filled with pleasure craft. The red roofs of the buildings of the town were in stark contrast to the white concrete structures and the deep green of the surrounding countryside.

Again Brianna looked anxiously out the windshield at the mountain. They seemed to be heading for a gap along the ridge line between two higher peaks. Then at a distance of a half a mile or so out, she was able to see a narrow runway on the far side of the gap, apparently starting right at the base of the mountain. She looked at the pilot, unbelieving for a moment that they were actually going to fly through the notch and land on the little strip of pavement.

The airplane was only a few hundred feet above the water and below the elevation of the highest promontories. The ridge line was dead ahead, only the narrow gap below the elevation of the aircraft.

Brianna felt her breath wedge in her throat as the plane glided through the narrow passage then dropped precipitously, the wing tips seeming to skim the bushes as they coasted down the far slope of the mountain. An instant later the landing gear touched down and the pilot quickly braked the craft to a halt, just a couple of hundred feet from the end of the runway.

Brianna glanced at the old woman seated beside her and, seeing her glazed expression, let her own breath slowly escape from her lungs. The unexpectedly dramatic landing behind her, she now could turn her thoughts to the objective of her trip—Nicholas Severin, the mysterious stranger from Paris who had sought her out.

THE PIPER APACHE TAXIED back toward the small terminal building, and Nick Severin glanced at his watch. It was three minutes past four. The girl had been right; the flight was on schedule.

The warm wind was blowing in from the Atlantic across the small half-moon of the Baie de St. Jean, ruffling Severin's stylishly cut blondish-gray hair. He dropped his sunglasses back down onto his nose from where they had been resting in his hair and leaned back against the wooden railing. His arms were folded across his chest, his bare legs protruded from his safari shorts and were crossed at the ankles.

The girl who had been acting earlier as reservation clerk inside the building was now standing nearby with the outgoing passengers and a dolly loaded with their baggage. Like Severin, she was watching the plane, which was nearly at the terminal building. From where he stood, none of the faces of the passengers was visible, and Severin felt both expectation and curiosity about Brianna Wells.

He had no idea what she would look like and knew little about her except that she was about thirty, divorced and an extremely talented designer. With the death of her father she had come into possession of one of the most remarkable collections of ancient jewelry and objets d'art in private hands. She owned a gallery in New York in addition to her shop in Charlotte Amalie on St. Thomas and divided her time between the two places.

Most important for Severin's purposes, Brianna Wells's talent was such that she could reproduce priceless pieces of ancient jewelry—necklaces, bracelets, rings—with remarkable accuracy. It was a rare, and invaluable, ability, which certain persons were willing to reward with many, many dollars. Severin was determined to find out just how receptive to his plan Brianna Wells herself might be.

When the plane had stopped on the apron and the twin propellers had come to a halt, the door opened and the pilot exited, followed by the passengers whom he helped down the wing that doubled as a boarding ramp. First there was an elderly woman in a straw hat, probably one of the island's inhabitants.

Following the older woman was a slender young one with glossy black shoulder-length hair. She wore a short-sleeved yellow blouse, white cotton pants and espadrilles. Severin scrutinized her closely, thinking she might be Brianna Wells. He glanced at the last two passengers exiting the plane—a man and woman in their late forties, seemingly together—and concluded that the attractive dark-haired woman was his target.

The airline representative had pushed the dolly out to the plane and addressed the milling passengers, directing them back toward him, his eyes scanning in particular the young woman he presumed to be Brianna Wells. She had taken the arm of the elderly woman and was saying something to her. The tall brunet seemed thoughtful—a quality he'd hardly expected. Severin smiled.

They were near enough that he had a good look at the young woman's face. Her eyes were large, wide-set and light in color, perhaps gray. Her mouth seemed a little large for her face, and because she was so tall and thin she seemed coltish, though her reedy figure was imbued with a gracefulness. There was something sensuous about her, as well.

When she was near the door of the building and just a few steps from where Severin stood, she looked up in his general direction and smiled, perhaps at something her elderly companion had said. He liked her mouth. It was warm, sensuous, happy. Though she wasn't beautiful in the classic sense, he decided that the overall effect was most pleasing.

When the passengers had entered the building, Severin went back inside through another door to the small waiting room just beyond the lectern of the passport control official. The elderly woman's documents were being examined by the khaki-clad customs officer when Severin entered. Behind her was Brianna Wells.

When the older lady moved on to the welcoming embrace of relatives, Brianna stepped to the lectern, though she was still fishing through the large shoulder bag she carried. Severin watched as she unconsciously tucked her long, silky hair behind one ear, then looked up at the official with a broad smile, handing him her passport.

She watched the officer as he slowly opened the document, glancing first at her picture in the passport, then at her. The slightest smile touched his lips, and she wondered if he disliked the photograph as much as she. Without comment he thumbed through the pages of the booklet until he found a place for his stamp, which he proceeded to imprint with a ceremonious and deliberate motion. Then he handed her the passport. *"Merci,"* he said blandly.

Brianna returned the document to her purse, stepping away as she did. After fastening her bag, she looked up to find a man in front of her, with a smile on his face. His eyes were masked by dark glasses, and his skin was deeply tanned, handsomely contrasting the beigy-champagne color of his hair.

"Miss Wells?"

Hearing her name on the attractive stranger's lips surprised Brianna. She glanced briefly at his tanned bare legs and the open neck of his faded blue epaulet shirt.

"I'm Nick Severin," he said, extending his hand.

The man's casual appearance and imposing good looks did not correspond with her expectation, so Brianna was a little stunned by the revelation. "Oh, Mr. Severin," she said, taking his hand, "I didn't expect to see you here."

"I couldn't let you walk."

He was grinning, and she looked at him, still a bit taken aback. "I could have found a taxi."

"That would have made for a rather cold and impersonal welcoming."

She saw Severin's lip curl slightly beneath his thick mustache. A funny feeling washed over her. The reaction was based on the scantiest of evidence, but Brianna instantly concluded that the man considered his charm and good looks to be formidable weapons. What's worse, it was apparent he intended to use them on her. Instinctively she recoiled, feeling defensive. "I thought the purpose of this trip was business."

"It is. I just thought it would be much friendlier if I were to come and pick you up."

Brianna watched Nick Severin lift his sunglasses and push them up over his forehead and into his hair. His eyes were a soft brown color and seemed to smile right along with his mouth. Brianna noticed how the pale mustache seemed so perfectly to belong over the man's smiling lips. He was exceedingly attractive, his skin smooth and soft. The tan and the angular contours of his face gave his beauty an acceptably masculine cast. She couldn't ever remember seeing a better looking man in her life.

"Is the hotel very far, Mr. Severin?"

"Nothing's very far on this island. Les Castelets is on a mountaintop above Gustavia. A very nice hotel. I think you'll like it."

Brianna was aware of Nick Severin's eyes on her, and her guard went up. "I'm sure it will be fine," she said, trying to maintain a cool visage.

The couple from Connecticut finished with the passport control and squeezed past Brianna and Nick Severin. Feeling the urge to move on herself, she started walking across the small reception area toward the exit.

"Wait a minute," Nick said, taking her arm. "Don't you have a bag? I mean, you didn't squeeze everything in that purse, did you?"

"Oh! No, I forgot..." Brianna flushed with embarrassment. "I do have a suitcase." He hadn't let go of her arm, and she was very aware of his hand on her bare flesh, annoyed by the uninvited familiarity.

"I believe they'll be bringing it around here," he said, pointing to a platform at the end of the room. "The baggage should arrive in a minute or two." He saw Brianna looking at his hand and released her, smiling as he did. "Would you care to sit and wait?"

Without a word she went to a chair and sat, feeling very uncomfortable in the man's presence. He had stepped over to the baggage bay to look out onto the field. Brianna eyed him warily.

Severin was about six-two, a good five inches taller than she and, in addition to being almost too good-looking, he was nicely built. His tanned legs were well shaped, covered with thick beige hair, as was his chest, which was easily visible through the opening in his shirt.

He walked to where she sat waiting and dropped down beside her. "The bags are on the way."

"Good."

In the ensuing silence, she found herself glancing down at Nicholas Severin's bare legs.

"Please forgive my informality, Brianna, but we're rather casual here—even more so than in the Virgin Islands, I think."

It was bad enough that he had to catch her looking at him, but it was patently rude to comment on it. "It wasn't that, Mr. Severin. I was—"

"Please, it's Nick."

"All right, *Nick*. I was wondering where you got your tan if you're coming from Paris."

He smiled at her. "You're the suspicious type, aren't you?"

"I'm not particularly comfortable coming here to meet you, to be perfectly frank."

"In good time we'll have a nice long talk and get to know each other better."

Before Brianna could respond, a couple of suitcases thumped onto the platform nearby. She followed him to the place where the luggage had been deposited. The couple from Connecticut was already there, and the man picked up two bags and followed his wife out.

"It's the small black one," Brianna said over Nick's shoulder.

He already had it in his hand. "Yes, I'd guessed."

When he turned, looking pleased with himself, their eyes met, and Brianna could feel the charm emanating from him. Despite herself, she smirked, turning toward the door. He was at her side, then stepped ahead to hold the door. Brianna groaned silently at his exaggerated solicitousness and walked by without looking at him.

Just as they neared the exit to the small terminal building, the reservation clerk came running toward them.

"*Ô, voilà!* Miss Wells, you are still here. I was afraid that I had missed you." The young woman glanced at Nick Severin, then back at Brianna. "There is a call for you from St. Thomas."

"Now?"

"Yes, they are on the line. The lady is from your shop. She said it is very important. Come this way, please."

Brianna followed the clerk to the reservation counter, and Nick Severin trailed along behind. After stepping over the scales, the girl took the telephone receiver and handed it to Brianna.

"Hello..."

"Oh, Brianna, I'm glad I got you."

"Sylvie..."

"A cable came for you from Tahiti. I thought you might like to know before you met with Mr. Severin." The young woman's soft French accent was more pronounced than usual, as it always was when she became excited or emotional.

Brianna glanced at Nick Severin, standing not three feet from her. "Yes. That would probably be a good idea," she said in a measured tone.

"Do you want me to open it and read it to you?"

"Yes, please."

As Brianna waited, her eyes met Nick's. He gave her a little smile. She looked away.

When the rustling of papers stopped, Sylvie came back on the line. "It is from your friends on Marutea."

"Yes..."

"I will read it. 'Brianna: I regret to inform you that I have no information on this Nicholas Severin. The distributors also are not familiar with him. It is difficult to believe he is a merchant of black pearls, and we do not know him. Unless he can prove some indirect source, I would be suspicious and careful. *Amitié*, J.'"

Brianna's eyes flickered over Nick Severin's unsuspecting face, and she felt her stomach tighten. She forced a pleasant expression on her face. "Is that all, Sylvie?"

"Yes, Brianna. There is nothing more."

"Well, thank you very much, then. There won't be a reply."

"What are you going to do? Will you meet with him?"

Brianna tried not to look at Nick. "No reason why I shouldn't, is there?" she said, turning away from him.

"Perhaps there is something wrong. I don't feel good for you."

Brianna had to smile at Sylvie's concern. She pictured the cocoa smoothness of the young woman's pretty face, the large dark eyes that were doubtlessly very round just then. "It's all part of doing business, Sylvie." She wanted to say more, to be a little more reassuring, but she couldn't risk saying something that would tip off Nick that he was the subject of discussion.

Brianna glanced at him again. The man seemed to be listening with more than just casual curiosity, or was it just her imagination?

After a few more ambiguous words, Brianna hung up.

"Problems?" Nick asked, his voice almost sounding tinged with irony.

"Usual little tempest in a teapot. Whenever the owner of a shop goes away, every little development seems like a crisis to whomever is left in charge."

Nick didn't say anything, but the little twist at the corner of his mouth meant something—she just wasn't sure what. After a moment he extended his hand toward her.

"No need to worry then, is there? Shall we go?"

Brianna stepped toward the outstretched hand that, as she passed, settled firmly and warmly on her elbow. She walked from the terminal building with Nick Severin, wondering somewhat more anxiously with each step if there wasn't more to Sylvie's concern than she had allowed.

Chapter Two

Brianna watched as Nick Severin put her bag in the back of a funny little Jeep with a canvas top and no doors, and sensed she was getting into something she ought not to be involved with. He turned to her.

"Transportation is a little informal around here, too. But you'll see why. Jump in," he said, and went around to the driver's side of the vehicle.

When he climbed in beside her, she looked again at his perfect face. The man didn't seem dangerous, but something kept telling her that he was and that she should be careful. "You make this seem more like we're going on safari than to a hotel."

"No wild beasts, I promise you."

"Not even of the two-legged variety?"

He grinned and started the car.

Moments later they were driving up a narrow lane-and-a-half-wide road toward the gap in the mountain Brianna's plane had skimmed through a little earlier. They passed several vehicles like their own, a motorbike or two, and a Chevy pickup that looked monstrous, taking up most of the roadway.

"What is this thing?" Brianna asked, gripping the flimsy support bar as the wind whipped about her face.

"It's called a Mini Moke. Very practical for the roads they have here."

"So I see."

Nick laughed. "No, this is one of the good roads—an extra half lane in width. Wait till you see the others."

"I don't know if I want to."

He grinned at her, his white teeth gleaming. Brianna studied the man's profile, liking what she saw in spite of the way she felt about him. Whatever the cause of her misgivings, she decided Nick Severin certainly was friendly enough.

When they arrived at the gap in the ridge line where the airplane had passed through, Brianna saw that two roads intersected at the spot. "Good heavens, what happens if a car and an airplane arrive here at the same time?"

He laughed. "I think the aircraft have the right of way."

"Lord, I wish I'd known before coming. They ought to warn the fainthearted."

"Wouldn't be good for tourism."

"I imagine not."

After he had negotiated the turn, Nick patted Brianna's knee in a friendly sort of way. "Don't worry, the planes take off out over the bay. Less exciting to leave St. Barts than to arrive—unless you can't swim."

She stared at the hand on her knee, uncertain whether to push it away or ask him to remove it, then Nick took it away himself. Was he insensitive or just presumptuous about taking liberties? Brianna glanced at him warily, but Nick was smiling, a happy expression on his face, oblivious to the offense.

She eased to the outer edge of her seat. "Did you have the sense to come by boat, Mr. Severin?"

"It's Nick. No, I flew in via Guadeloupe."

Brianna studied him, thinking how he seemed to be a little too blasé, a little too confident. The tan, the mustache, the devastating smile, it was all a little too much. And why was he so knowledgeable about St. Barts? "Judging by your tan, I'd have thought you lived here in the Caribbean rather than Paris."

He gave her a quick glance. "You have a fetish about tans or something?"

"No, but I find it curious. It hasn't been sunning weather in Paris for a while, has it?"

"I spent most of September in Morocco."

"On business?"

"No. Pleasure."

The way he pronounced the word, Brianna immediately had the image of a beautiful young woman on his arm. Between his looks and charms, he undoubtedly was popular and successful with the ladies.

"I've spent some time in the Middle East recently, as well," he added. "*That* was business, but I managed to get in a little time in the sun."

"Your work seems to take you around the world, Nick. What is it, exactly, that you do?"

"I buy and sell things. But let's talk about that later, if you don't mind." The assertive words were softened with a charming little curl of his lip. *God,* she thought, *the man is just too good-looking!*

They were coming down the mountain toward the town of Gustavia. At a wide horseshoe bend in the road Nick pulled over and stopped.

"This is one of the nicest views of the harbor," he said, looking back up the road in the direction they had come. "If you like, get out for a moment and have a look."

Brianna glanced back up the road, too. She saw nothing but another small vehicle like their own that had pulled to the side of the road several hundred feet back. After another look at Nick, she got out of the Moke and went to the stone wall rimming the roadway. "It is lovely," she said, peering down at the harbor. "Mind if I take a picture?"

"No, be my guest."

She stepped back to the vehicle to get her purse and saw Nick again looking over his shoulder. "Is something wrong?" she asked.

"Do you have any friends on St. Barts?"

"No. Why?"

"Don't look now, but there's a lady back there in a Moke who's been following us since we left the airport. I thought she might be a friend of yours."

"Of mine?"

Nick shrugged.

Brianna sneaked a peak at the suspicious vehicle, then began searching through her purse. "More likely a friend of yours, since you seem to know your way around, *and* it's a woman." Finally she pulled out a small camera. After giving him a knowing smile, she returned to the wall.

Severin watched her climb up on the wall, her slender body in profile as she peered down at the town and harbor below. "I know my friends very well," he called at her. "She's not one of them."

"Maybe she has aspirations," Brianna said, looking through the viewfinder of her camera.

He smiled at her pluck and admired the silhouette she offered. Her bust line was modest, but her waist was very thin and her hips nicely rounded. One hand held the camera and shielded her eyes from the sun, which was sinking in the western sky. The other unconsciously pulled her lank silky hair behind one ear.

He could see that Brianna's ears, which were slightly large, were amply utilized to manage her tresses when she wanted them out of the way. Yet the mannerism appealed to him, and the ears he liked because they were nicely shaped and seemed to suit her well. In fact, her overall appearance pleased Severin greatly. Each little idiosyncrasy, like the gentle downward curve at the end of her nose, her high, angular cheekbones, or the broad, full mouth that he had noticed immediately, seemed to work harmoniously and with charming effect.

When Brianna had taken her picture, she looked in the Moke at Severin, then glanced up the road at the other vehicle, which was still parked. "Shall I take your girlfriend's picture? It might discourage her. Or would you prefer to *en*courage her?"

"No, just get back in."

"One more picture of the harbor, Mr. Severin."

He smiled, amused at her stubbornness, finding the quality unexpectedly appealing. There was an air of combat between them, and he knew she preferred it that way.

Brianna clicked the camera again, then jumped down from the wall, lifting her long legs, one after the other, into the Jeep. Her perfunctory smile was laced with irony. "Cute place. Looks like it fell off a charm bracelet."

Nick started the vehicle, and they headed down into the town.

"Your friend still following us?" she asked after a while.

He glanced in the rearview mirror and gave a big sigh. "Yeah, she's still there."

THEY HAD DRIVEN through Gustavia, its narrow streets crowded with vehicles and shoppers, the tiny harbor a flotilla of pleasure craft, when Nick Severin stopped at the base of a steep hill at the far edge of town. He put the Moke in first gear and started up the grade. Brianna clung to the frame as the vehicle groaned and whined its way up the incline.

"Thirsty?" he asked good-naturedly after a few moments.

"No, but if we keep going up like this, I'm likely to get a nosebleed."

Nick chuckled. "We'd best stop for a rest, then." He pulled over at the entrance to one of the low buildings terraced on the side of the mountain. "This is the Hibiscus, the best place to have a drink and watch the sunset."

Because of the slope it was difficult to get out of the vehicle. He came around to help her out.

"Just so we don't lose anything," he said, taking her suitcase from the back seat, "I'll take this in with us."

"Afraid your friend is a thief?"

"Whoever it was, is not my friend," he replied a bit irritably. "And besides, she didn't follow us through town. Maybe it was just a coincidence."

"Oh, come on," she chided, "I bet this happens to you all the time."

Nick pointedly took her arm. "Considering how hard I've tried to get this started on the right foot, you're certainly being very difficult."

Brianna smiled to herself as they walked into an open-air lounge and terrace overlooking the town. There were a couple of people sitting on stools at the bar, chatting with the bartender, but the place was otherwise deserted. Nick waved to the man, who greeted him. *"Bon soir, Nick."*

A small swimming pool surrounded by lounge chairs occupied a sizable portion of the deck. Brianna immediately went to the railing and looked out over the harbor at the sun sinking into the Caribbean Sea beyond.

There was a steady warm breeze blowing in, and she smiled at its soothing caress, tucking her fluttering hair behind her ears. "This is magnificent."

He joined her at the railing, leaning casually against it, his shoulder and arm just brushing hers. Brianna turned to him, easing herself a few inches away as she did, rather than recoiling from his touch. They looked at each other. She saw both good-natured bonhomie and seduction on his face. What was the man up to?

"Don't you ever take those sunglasses off?" she said irritably.

Nick removed the glasses and dropped them into his shirt pocket. "Sorry. Hadn't noticed I still had them on."

Brianna realized she had let her discomfort show, but when she looked at him once more, she could see he wasn't a man easily deterred. She trembled involuntarily.

Nick looked down at her, seeming to notice the goose-flesh on her arms. "You can't be cold; the air's warm."

She colored at his insistence on pointing out her every reaction to him. "No, I'm not. It's a nice breeze. Sometimes I just shiver for no particular reason."

The wind had blown the hair on one side of Brianna's head across her cheek. Nick reached up, took the strands between his fingers and tucked them behind her ear. She froze at his touch.

"Maybe it's the breeze affecting you," he said in a low, seductive voice. "It can be very sensuous."

Brianna turned away, feeling his game was an intentional affront. She was nominally staring out at the harbor, but in her mind she was composing words of condemnation. The phrase "I wish you'd keep your hands to yourself" was forming on her lips when he broke the silence.

"What can I get you to drink, Brianna?"

She turned to him, prepared to have her say, but thought better of it, deciding she wouldn't give him the satisfaction of the response he was probably trying to evoke. His brown eyes were friendly and soft just then and didn't seem threatening in the least. Maybe it was all her imagination.

"What are *you* having?" she asked dryly.

He rubbed his chin. "Well, let me see. We could have one of those tropical drinks . . . but then you live in the tropics; there's nothing special in that. How about some champagne? Does that appeal to you?"

"Yes . . ." She was about to say that it seemed a little extravagant, but decided to let him have his way. "If you'd like some, I'll join you."

"Okay, you sit down and enjoy the view. I'll order the champagne."

Brianna sat in a chair by the pool and looked out at the town and harbor. Scattered lights were beginning to appear, and the red that had been in the sky only minutes earlier was masked now by dark clouds that had moved across the island. On the other side of the pool and under the protective cover of the roof, Nick Severin was chatting with the bartender in French. She didn't speak the language, but from the flow of patter Brianna judged him to be most fluent. He said he lived in Paris, so it shouldn't be surprising that he was.

She watched him, unsure whether his physical appeal had in fact gotten to her somewhat, or whether his unwarranted familiarity had offended her to a point of severe annoyance. Brianna realized to her consternation that it was equally plausible that she liked and disliked him.

A moment later Nick returned, glancing up at the sky as he sat down in the adjoining chair. "Looks like a little rain shower coming our way."

"Yes. The sky darkened rather quickly."

"I'm sure it'll blow over before long. It's usual this time of year."

She glanced at him warily. "You seem to know St. Barts well, Nick."

"I've been here several times. It's a favorite place of mine, but I must admit it's gotten a little touristy for my taste."

"You've been coming long enough to see changes, then."

"Believe it or not, twenty years ago donkeys were the primary means of transportation here. It was a bit before my time, admittedly, but it shows how much change there has been." He smiled in a polite yet seductive sort of way as the bartender came over with a bottle of champagne in an ice bucket and two flutes.

"Bon soir, mademoiselle," the man said, and placed the wine and glasses on the small table beside Nick.

"Laisse-le, s'il te plaît. Je veux qu'il glace," Nick said to him.

"Bien." The bartender withdrew.

"I thought we could let the bottle chill for a few minutes."

Brianna nodded. They looked at each other in silence for a moment. "So, is that why you were so anxious for me to come to St. Barts—because it's a favorite haunt of yours?" she asked.

"That's part of it."

"What's the rest?"

"Like I told you on the telephone, I preferred to stay on French soil."

She thought of the curious conversation they had had when he'd called from Paris. "Yes, that comment troubled me at the time, Nick. I can't imagine why it's important to you. You aren't even French."

"No, but it'll become apparent later."

"There seem to be a lot of things that you'll be clarifying in the vague, indefinite future. It's not exactly reassuring."

A strong gust of wind came up, blowing Brianna's hair across her face. Nick smiled.

"It looks like your poor ears are being put to the test."

"I beg your pardon?"

"Your ears. With the wind they aren't holding your hair in place."

Brianna blushed. "They're big enough. You'd think they'd do the job."

"You have lovely ears." He reached over, touching one of them with his fingertips. "I like them."

Once again his touch sent a little tremor through her. She tried to cover her reaction by moving on without acknowledging his comment. "When I was a baby, they mortified my mother. I had no hair until I was three. There was nothing to cover my ears."

Again the wind gusted, rustling the leaves of the potted palms that surrounded the deck.

"Perhaps I'd better open the champagne before it gets too windy to hold a glass."

As Nick opened the bottle, lightning flashed on the mountaintops at the west end of the island.

"We can move under the roof if the wind bothers you," Nick said as he popped the cork, sending it shooting high into the air and off the deck into the dense foliage below.

Brianna smiled at his cavalier manner. "No, it's very warm and pleasant. I don't mind it at all."

He poured the wine and handed her one of the flutes. "To us. And all that we do together."

She touched her glass to his, thinking the toast rather strange and wondering at the tone, which somehow sounded as though what he had in mind was more of a personal than business nature. "What *are* we going to do together, Nick? Or at least, what is it that *you* have in mind?"

"I thought that after the champagne we could go up to the hotel, get you settled, have dinner, and in the process get better acquainted."

She sipped her champagne and studied him, convinced now that some sort of seduction was the objective of his charm. But the question was, were his designs of a personal or business nature? "You really enjoy being evasive, don't you?"

"Evasive?"

"About the purpose of our meeting. About this pearl of yours and why you invited me here."

"It's not so mysterious. I want to do business with you."

"What sort of business? Sell me a black pearl?"

"That's not all."

"If you want to buy some of my pieces, you should have come to St. Thomas."

"I don't want to buy your jewelry."

"What then?"

"For the moment let's say I'm more interested in selling than in buying."

A knowing smile crept over Brianna's face. "Bottom line, Mr. Severin, is that you're a salesman." She drank some champagne. "I must say your technique is rather clever. But you may as well know that I'm satisfied with my suppliers."

"Every business person is interested in a better deal," he said dryly.

She poked her tongue in her cheek. "Obviously, you have a better deal."

He tilted his head rakishly, saluted her with his glass, then sipped his champagne. "Of course."

"Maybe we should discuss your 'better deal' now, Mr. Severin. I might be able to save you the expense of dinner."

"It's still Nick," he said easily, "and, if you'll permit the observation, I like the other Brianna better." Then he reached over and brushed her cheek with the back of his fingers.

Brianna leveled her eyes on him, this time unhesitating in her determination to let him know she didn't appreciate his liberties. "The *other* Brianna?"

"Yes, the less cynical one."

"I tend to be cynical when it comes to business, Mr...Nick, at least when I'm dealing with...obfuscation."

His eyebrows rose ever so slightly. He sipped his wine. Brianna did, as well.

"If it's a pearl you want to sell, why don't we talk about it now?"

"I'd thought perhaps we could begin negotiations tomorrow...unless, of course, that's not satisfactory."

"What's wrong with right now?"

They were staring into each other's eyes. He had remained calm, and Brianna struggled to hold her ground. Neither of them flinched, but their resolve seemed to ebb at the same time, and their expressions softened.

Nick drank from his glass, then put it down. "All right, *madame*," he said in a very formal tone, as though he were conceding, "I'd like to become your supplier of black pearls."

Brianna's mouth dropped slightly, and the smile faded instantly from her face. "My supplier?"

"Yes."

"Where would you get black pearls in quantity? There's only one source in the world."

"I have another."

"Impossible."

"But true."

"Cultured Tahitian black pearls? Marutea is the only place in the world they're cultivated, and Jean-Claude Brouillet is the only one who does it."

Nick took the bottle of champagne from the ice bucket and refilled their glasses. "I've heard that, too."

"It's true. And my father was a personal friend of Monsieur Brouillet. That's how I managed to secure a regular supply."

Nick sipped his wine and shrugged.

"If you're planning on reselling me some Marutean pearls, you're wasting your time. You can't possibly beat my price and make a profit."

"I'm not selling you Brouillet's pearls, and I can beat his price. By a very wide margin, I might add."

"Impossible."

"Yes, you said that. The trouble with you, Brianna, is that you're a skeptic as well as a cynic."

"You've been smoking something, Nick Severin."

"No, just drinking some very fine champagne... which you don't seem to be enjoying, by the way."

Brianna took a large sip, realizing he was right—she hadn't really noticed the wine, which was exquisite. She glanced at the bottle, noting that it was Bollinger. "Are you always this extravagant when entertaining customers?"

"No, I just thought I'd give myself a little treat. And you, as well."

"It'd have to be opium before I'd buy the cock-and-bull story you've given me." She looked at his handsome face, realizing for the first time that the champagne was beginning to affect her. "Forgive my bluntness, but it's true."

"Will you keep an open mind long enough to look at my wares?"

"Certainly I'll look at them, but from what you've said, I already know there's something wrong."

"You aren't impugning my integrity?"

"You may be convinced of what you've got, but frankly I'm skeptical."

He took her hand as the warm air swirled about them. "I enjoy the challenge of being persuasive."

This time Nick Severin's touch was pleasant and, despite herself, she couldn't help liking the feel of his hand on hers. Brianna knew it was a dangerous development, but she proceeded to do the exact opposite of what was wise—she took a very large sip of champagne and let Nick refill her glass.

Chapter Three

By the time they made their way back out to the Mini Moke, Brianna was feeling a little tipsy, but she tried hard not to let Nick Severin know just how dizzy she felt. She had let him have his way about tabling their business discussion until later. She had even managed to relax a little and enjoy the wine and the air.

Nick had been pleasant, hadn't pressured her, and Brianna had let down her guard a bit. While not exactly trusting the man, she had decided he might not be as pernicious as she had thought.

As he put down her suitcase and helped her into the vehicle, Brianna decided that she actually liked him more than she disliked him, which was probably a bad omen. Still she rationalized her feeling, arguing that other than touch her affectionately a couple of times he hadn't really done anything offensive.

He was walking around to the driver's side of the Moke, with Brianna watching him, when an earsplitting screech and the roar of a motor pierced the night air. An instant later a motorcyclist flashed past Nick, barely missing him.

Brianna twisted around as the unlighted missile hurtled down the hill and disappeared. Simultaneously Nick shouted an epitaph after the rider. *"Salaud!"* He muttered the word again as he pried himself from the side of the vehicle.

"Are you all right, Nick?"

He slid into the seat, shaking his head. "God, I nearly had my arm taken off."

"What an idiot! He scared me to death!"

Nick gave a little laugh. "Just be glad you weren't standing out in the road."

"What was he doing? No lights, no warning..."

"I don't know, but life on this island has certainly swung into high gear since you arrived."

Brianna looked at him. "You don't think it was intentional?"

Nick stared back into the semidarkness. "Probably not."

Thunder rumbled from the distant end of the island, and Brianna looked apprehensively at her escort.

He took a deep breath and exhaled, as if to put the incident behind him. "Maybe we should have left for the hotel a little earlier. On top of everything else that's happened, I'd hate to be responsible for getting us caught in a downpour."

"It won't be the first time I've gotten wet." Brianna forced a smile, her heart still pounding at the scare the motorcyclist had given them.

After a long, silent look, he started the Mini Moke and put the vehicle in gear. They began the climb up the steep grade.

The wind gusted in the side of the Jeep, rippling the canvas and whipping Brianna's hair about her face. She brushed it back and looked at Nick, thinking how nicely shaped the shadowed contours of his face were. He seemed unthreateningly gentle just then, despite what she had thought earlier.

She wondered about him, how he was affecting her, how the champagne might be clouding her judgment. She knew it would be far, far wiser to get her guard back up, to doubt his word, suspect his motives, question his intent.

"Tell the truth, Nick. Did you really think I'd buy your pearl story?"

"What do you mean 'story'?"

She grinned at him in the darkness. "You really thought I'd believe you had another source of Polynesian blacks?"

"I thought we were going to wait and talk business later."

"Come on, there's no need to play games. Sweet talk won't affect my judgment when it comes to business."

"What sweet talk?"

Brianna laughed. "You're cute, Nick, but you're kind of slow. Either that, or you think *I* am." She smiled when he glanced over at her. "I mean, how are you ever going to sell black pearls at bargain-basement prices if you underestimate the opposition?"

They came to the first sharp bend, and Brianna gasped as they went around it.

"You all right?" he asked solicitously.

"Yeah, but I think I left my stomach back there."

Nick put his hand on Brianna's knee, and she picked it up and placed it on his own leg. Then she looked at him, knowing there was no need to explain her actions.

"Sorry, I meant no offense."

There was a flash of lightning overhead as the Jeep continued grinding its way up the slope. She watched Nick in the darkness. "Are you married?" she asked after a while, ignoring how it might sound.

"No, are you?"

"I was. But I'm not now."

The road was exceedingly narrow, with thick foliage growing right to the edge of the pavement. Through occasional gaps in the vegetation Brianna was able to see the lights of Gustavia far below. They negotiated another turn, causing the champagne in her stomach to slosh, and she burped.

"What happened?" Nick asked.

"That's not a very polite thing to ask a lady. I can't help it if champagne makes me burp."

He laughed. "No, I was referring to your marriage."

"That was a mistake, too."

"Who was he?"

"A young Madison Avenue lawyer I met my last year of college."

"What went wrong?"

"The only thing we had in common was the bedroom," she replied honestly. "And that's not enough, believe me."

There was a clap of thunder overhead.

"Did you divorce him, or did he divorce you?"

"It was pretty mutual, actually. But it didn't help when Steve developed a taste for his secretary. I decided I'd be better off without a philandering husband. So we divorced. I moved to the Virgin Islands, started a career, and well . . . here I am."

Nick was silent, and Brianna watched the narrow strip of concrete illuminated by the headlights, feeling sobered by her last speech.

"What happens," she asked, wanting to change the subject, "if a car comes from the other direction?"

There was a flash of lightning and another clap of thunder. Nick chuckled. "There's your answer."

"You're saying I'm supposed to pray?"

Just then large splats of water began hitting the windshield.

"Damn, it's too late for that now," Nick muttered.

"I guess we can't roll up the windows, can we?" Brianna couldn't help teasing him.

"We haven't far to go, fortunately. We'll be at the hotel in a few minutes."

The road jogged back in the other direction, putting Brianna's side of the Moke windward, causing the rain to blow in on her. She squealed in surprise and slid over to the inside of her seat, nearly up against Nick. As he negotiated another turn, his arm brushed her breast.

Just then headlights appeared around the bend ahead, shining down the road at them. Nick stopped the vehicle. The pavement was not wide enough for two cars to pass and, where they were, the concrete dropped a foot off on either edge. Shrubbery abounded on both sides. "Damn," he said again.

"You're starting to repeat yourself, Nick."

He shrugged. "We would have been at the hotel in another minute or two."

"Well, at least this vehicle had the courtesy to keep his lights on and not run us down."

"Don't say that too loudly," Nick replied with a laugh. "You might give him an idea."

The car descending the mountain had stopped a hundred feet or so in front of them.

"I'm going to back down to that wide spot at the last curve. He may have too far to go to a suitable spot." Nick peered behind them into the darkness. "No back-up lights."

Brianna leaned out the Jeep and watched the road on her side. Nick began inching down the road as the rain started coming down in sheets. In seconds Brianna's right side was soaked. "You see, Nick Severin," she called over her shoulder, "I'd have been better off to take a cab."

"Thank God, it's a warm rain," he shouted over the roar of the water pelting the canvas top.

Brianna pulled her head back into the Jeep. "It's probably ten below in Minnesota right now. Think of it that way."

Nick was still hanging out of the Moke, slowly backing down the hill. "Still," he called to her, "a hot shower, a cognac and a nice warm bed sounds pretty good."

She looked at the back of Nick Severin's head, wondering why what he had just said sounded like an invitation. "What about dinner?" she asked.

He was at the curve now and stopped in the wide spot in the pavement. He turned and looked at her as the other vehicle came down the hill. Their faces were clearly illuminated by the oncoming headlights. "We can eat first, if you like," he said in the low voice that Brianna realized she had begun responding to.

Angry at her lapse, she stared up the road, knowing somehow that, had he continued his speech, he would have added "and then we can go to bed." She grimaced into the darkness, more upset with herself than with him.

The other vehicle squeezed past, leaving them looking at each other in the semidarkness.

"Well, are we just going to sit here?" she asked impatiently.

A faint sign of amusement touched Nick's lips as he put the Moke in gear and started up the road. Brianna wondered if he regarded her irritation as an indication of his failure or success.

BRIANNA WAS pretty well soaked by the time they arrived at Les Castelets. Her hair was plastered to her head, and her blouse clung to her like another layer of skin.

Nick went past the dozen or so vehicles in the little parking strip and stopped directly in front of the entrance to the main building.

"I'll run in and get your room key. You can register later," he said, and disappeared without waiting for a reply.

Brianna shivered a little from the dampness, though the air was still warm. If nothing else, the rain had sobered her up, and it was none too soon. She was determined to let Nick Severin know she had no desire to play games with him.

And why the games, anyway? Did he think she was too stupid to see what he was up to? Obviously he fancied himself a super salesman, though he was too slick for his own good. Black pearls at bargain prices! How naive did he think she was?

A few moments later Nick returned. "Damn," he said, getting into the Moke.

"Either you have a limited vocabulary, or this has turned into a bad day. What happened?"

"There was some confusion about your room. Somehow the maids and maintenance people didn't get the word that it would be occupied and left it undone for minor repairs. The manager assured me they would have it fixed up immediately...which means it should be ready for you after dinner."

"Wouldn't you know, just when I'm soaked to the bone."

"Well, it's all right. You can get cleaned up and changed in my room."

She looked at him, astounded. "Your room? There must be someplace else..."

"No," he said, starting the engine, "there isn't."

He was pushing things too far, and Brianna didn't like it one little bit. "There has to be!"

"I'm afraid not. They're fully booked." He started down the narrow drive toward the outbuildings scattered about the complex.

Brianna shivered, as much with annoyance as the discomfort of her wet clothing. She looked at the man for a moment, trying to decide whether she could trust him.

"There's no danger in borrowing my room to change," Nick said, as though he had been reading her thoughts.

Brianna felt herself giving in. St. Barts hardly seemed like a place to commit a crime and, though there was always the possibility, it was unlikely Nick Severin was dangerous.

They went by the first villa and stopped at the steps to the second. The rain had already let up, and by the time he had come around to the passenger side of the vehicle and taken her bag, it was only sprinkling.

Nick helped her up the steps to a wide covered porch that ran the width of the two-story building. The complex was fairly new, and the architectural style seemed more appropriate to alpine mountains than the tropics. Each of the scattered villas contained two or three suites.

While he fiddled with the key, Brianna turned and looked back at the view, which was a sweeping panorama of the entire west end of the island.

The rain clouds had moved out over the water for the most part, and the lights of scattered homes dotted the landscape like sparkling jewels. The moon partially shone through breaks in the clouds overhead. Perched on the mountain as they were, the feel was almost like that of an eagle's nest.

Nick pushed open the door, and they stepped inside. Just as he reached for the light switch, a woman's voice stabbed at them from the darkness.

"Ne bougez pas!"

Brianna gasped and Nick froze beside her. Across the dark room was the vague figure of a woman, motionless in the shadows.

"Ne bougez pas," she repeated, her voice lower, but hard as steel.

"Don't move," Nick whispered, and his hand tightened on Brianna's arm. *"Qui êtes-vous?"* he said to the woman.

"Silence! Je suis armée."

Her heart in her throat, and not understanding a word being said, Brianna stared at the shadowy figure, seeing the faint glint of a metal object in the woman's hand—a pistol.

"She's got a gun," Nick said under his breath. "Be careful. Don't move."

Brianna swallowed hard, her mouth dry. "Yes," she whispered, "I see it."

The woman snapped out several more commands, punctuating her words with movements of the gleaming weapon.

In response to the instructions, Nick eased Brianna inside and slowly closed the door behind them.

Brianna began shaking, and Nick held her firmly against his side, his motions very slow and deliberate. A brief conversation ensued between Nick and the faceless figure across the room. Then he started moving slowly away from the door, taking Brianna with him.

"Doucement!" the voice warned, and Nick slowed, barely inching his way through the darkness.

"She wants us to go upstairs," he explained.

Ahead Brianna could see the hazy outline of a staircase. "What's she going to do?" she asked in a trembling voice.

"Ferme ton bec!" the disembodied voice snapped before Nick could reply.

The words were so angry that Brianna expected a gunshot to follow, but all she heard was the even breathing of the man beside her. They had reached the stairs, and Brianna stumbled against the first step, though Nick supported her with his strong grip. She reached for the banister and slowly began mounting the stairs. Nick was right behind her.

After several steps Brianna risked a glance at the woman, who, she saw, was edging toward the door they had entered.

"Doucement!" warned the voice.

Brianna cringed, barely able to breathe.

As they neared the top of the stairs, which she could now see led to a loft area overlooking the large room below, the woman barked out several more commands in French.

"She wants us to go into the bathroom." Taking Brianna's hand, he led her across the loft, fumbled for the door handle in the dark and, finding it, pulled it open. They stepped inside and Nick closed the door, then turned on a faucet in the basin.

"What are you doing?"

"This is what she told me to do," he replied perfunctorily and stepped past her to the window, which he unfastened and swung open, admitting a bit of moonlight into the cramped room. He peered out.

"What, Nick?"

"Shh!" He craned his neck, then exclaimed, "Ah, there she goes!"

Suddenly he spun, pushed past Brianna and threw the door open. "Stay here!" he shouted over his shoulder as he rushed down the stairs, his feet thundering on the wooden steps.

Brianna stepped to the window and, rising to her tiptoes, peered out. A darkly clad figure was just disappearing up the drive, a shock of blond hair glinting in the cloud-filtered moonlight. A moment later Nick appeared below her, racing full speed up the drive in pursuit.

When he was out of sight, Brianna turned from the window only to find another woman staring at her wide-eyed in the gloom. Brianna gave a terrified scream before she realized it was nothing but her own reflection in the bathroom mirror. Feeling suddenly faint, she felt her way to the commode and sat down, resting her head in her quivering hands.

Brianna was shaken, but no longer felt in immediate danger. Still, she was light-headed and felt almost too weak to move. There must be something she ought to be doing, she knew, but she didn't know what. Go for help?

Outside, at some distance, a shot shattered the night, and Brianna's heart stopped as the echo died on the distant slopes of the mountain. An image of Nick Severin's felled body exploded through her mind, and a very real pain went through her.

Getting to her feet, Brianna fumbled for the light switch and flipped it, wincing at the glare, fighting the heightening surge of fear within her. The stark surroundings of the strange bathroom, together with her state of mind, made the circumstances seem otherworldly. Seeing Nick's toiletries laying about added to her sense of anxiety, and Brianna quickly stepped out of the room and made her way back down the stairs.

The front door remained open, admitting some light to the main room below. Only moments before Nick had rushed out that door, but where was he now? Was he hurt? Did he need help? Surely others had heard the shot. If she went out into the night, she would not be alone.

At the door she found the light switch and turned it on, briefly surveying the room before stepping out onto the porch. But before she had moved farther, Nick came walking around the corner of the building and started up the stairs.

"Nick! Are you all right?"

When he had reached the top step, she saw the side of his shirt, pants and leg caked—not with blood, but rather with mud. The expression on his face was one of exasperation, not pain. "Yeah, I'm okay."

"What happened? Was that a shot?"

"She wasn't pleased that I followed her. I think she was making a point."

They both looked at the mud covering one side of his body.

"I hit the dirt," he explained.

"And the dirt was wet."

He laughed.

"Nick, who was she?"

"I don't know."

She searched his face. "You don't?"

"No, do you?"

"Of course not."

He stepped past her and went into the room. Brianna followed him inside. "Why 'of course not'?" he said over his shoulder, then turned to face her.

"Why should *I* know her? This is your room. She spoke French."

"It might as well have been Chinese for all the difference it made. It obviously wasn't a social call."

"You don't think I had anything to do with this, Nick?"

"I don't have any enemies."

"Nor do I," she replied, eyeing him.

There was a man's voice outside the villa. *"Allô?"*

Nick returned to the door, and Brianna could see a man looking up inquisitively from the foot of the stairs. He appeared to be a hotel employee, perhaps a clerk. The two men spoke in French for a minute or so, then the employee retreated into the night.

Nick closed the door.

"What was that about?"

"He wanted to know what was going on."

"Did you tell him what happened?"

"I said I was out for a walk and a car backfired and nearly ran me down."

"You didn't tell him about the woman and the shot?"

"No."

"But why?"

"I want to find out why she was in my room first."

"Nick, that's crazy. You should report the incident to the police. That woman was up to no good. She might be back."

He shook his head. "I don't think so."

Brianna stared at him in disbelief, wondering why, having been assaulted, he wouldn't go immediately to the police. It struck her as fishy, but when she turned to challenge him, Nick was already moving about the suite, seemingly looking for clues.

Brianna glanced around the pleasantly appointed room. It was full of antiques, and the walls were covered with old prints and maps. To one side was a bar. A ceiling fan turned slowly overhead. The place seemed more like it belonged in Chamonix than in the Caribbean.

She watched as he surveyed the room, his eyes darting about. After a moment Nick went to the dresser, pulling at a half-open drawer before pushing it shut. He opened others, looked inside, then closed them.

Curious, Brianna walked over to him. "What's the matter?"

Nick turned and looked at the window, then retreated to the door without responding. He examined the lock, then glanced at her.

"What is it, Nick?"

"She's a pro. Picked the lock."

Brianna's mouth twisted whimsically. "Sure she didn't have her own key?"

"Very funny."

"Maybe it was your lady friend from this afternoon. She might have been more interested in you than you realized."

Ignoring her, Nick quickly went to an armchair, tipped it over and pulled back the corner of the undercover. Reaching inside, he removed a small velvet pouch.

"What's that?" Brianna asked as he walked back to the dresser and deposited the pouch in a drawer, closing it carefully.

"Never mind," he said, turning to her with a smile.

"Nick, what's going on?"

"I was concerned that the intruder had taken some of my property, but she didn't."

"You know what she was after, then?"

"Maybe. She didn't ransack the place, obviously. I think she was in the middle of a search when we walked in on her."

"She didn't get what she was after, apparently."

He looked at her quizzically.

"You seem relieved that your little bag was still here."

"Oh, that. Yes."

"Well, don't you think you ought to call the manager, or the police, or someone?"

"Not yet."

"You aren't concerned?"

"There's no reason anyone should be interested in me, unless it's because of my... friendship with you."

"Oh, this is my fault now."

"Fault, no." He smiled, letting his eyes drift up her body to meet her inquisitive gaze.

He seemed to be looking at her ears, and Brianna was sure they were poking through her wet stringy hair. Then he let his eyes drift down her again.

"I must look like a typhoon hit me," Brianna muttered as she turned to look in the mirror over the side table. She was horrified to see that her soaked cotton blouse was virtually transparent, exposing completely her braless condition. "God, I'm practically naked," she moaned and lifted the wet fabric off her skin in order to render it opaque again.

"Yes, I'd noticed."

She turned around to face him, the front of her blouse hanging from her fingers and clear of her chest. "A gentleman would have said he hadn't noticed."

"A liar would have said he hadn't noticed. You can dispute the fact that I'm a gentleman if you like, but I'm not a liar." They looked at each other for a moment, then Nick began laughing.

"What's so funny?"

"You look pretty silly, Brianna."

She glanced down at her billowing shirt and, through the gap at the neck, at her small, firm breasts and erect nipples that were swollen by the cold. Then she looked at Nick, who was a terribly good-looking specimen, even covered with mud and dripping wet. "If your pants had gotten a little wetter, *you* might look pretty silly, too."

He looked down at himself, and Brianna laughed.

"I don't know about you, but I'm getting out of these wet clothes," he said, and began unbuttoning his shirt.

Nick didn't turn away from her; he just stared brazenly as he jerked his shirttail out of his shorts and slipped it off. Brianna gaped at the light mat of hair covering his tanned, muscular chest.

"I think I'll go up to the bathroom," she said, knowing it was up to her to keep matters within the bounds of propriety.

"Aren't we going to flip to see who gets it first?"

"You *aren't* a gentleman."

"You're right. It would be ungentlemanly of me to leave you standing in that ridiculously modest pose while I went first."

Brianna grimaced, then defiantly let her wet shirt fall against her chest. "I suppose if you live in France and have been to the beach you've seen strangers' breasts before." She went over to where Nick had put down her suitcase by the door and picked it up. She threw back her shoulders and walked boldly past the smiling man.

THERE WAS NO LOCK on the bathroom door, which was louvered and afforded little privacy, but Brianna had managed to take a shower, wash her hair, dry it and slip into a V-neck lavender T-shirt dress without interference or impropriety on the part of Nick Severin.

She took her purse from the counter and removed a necklace of gold hourglass-shaped beads interspersed with medium-size black pearls. The design had been inspired by an ancient Sumerian necklace from her father's collection. Brianna slipped it around her neck and studied the effect in the mirror.

When she stepped out of the bath, Nick was lying on the king-size bed in a terry bathrobe, watching television. His hands were behind his head, his ankles crossed. He turned and looked at her, his expression immediately indicating delight at what he saw.

"Well, from drowned rat to beautiful princess in just—" he looked at his watch "—thirty minutes."

"Mr. Severin, you're a master at left-handed compliments."

"What's left-handed about that?"

"No woman wants to be referred to as a drowned rat."

"I thought I'd placed the emphasis on beautiful princess."

"My ears heard the drowned rat part." She walked over toward the bed, glancing at the television.

"Just watching the news," he said offhandedly.

Brianna listened to the unintelligible patter in French for a moment before looking back at Nick. "Have they said anything about a wild woman with a gun who runs around breaking into..." It was then that she saw a black velvet jeweler's cloth lying on the bed beside him. Poised in the center of it was the largest black pearl she had ever seen. Her mouth dropped open, and Nick Severin grinned.

"Gotcha!" he said and began laughing.

"Where on earth did you get that?" Brianna asked, not even trying to mask her amazement.

"I thought you might like to see my wares."

Brianna sat on the bed, oblivious for the moment of the man who reclined there with only a bathrobe between him and nakedness. She peered down at the pearl. "I've never seen a Polynesian black this big. My God, it must be eighteen millimeters. And a nearly perfect round." She glanced up at the man. "I'm beginning to see why it was so important for you to meet me on St. Barts. You didn't have to go through customs, did you?"

Nick's only response was a smile.

"Is it genuine?"

"You're the expert. What do you think?"

Brianna picked up the pearl, holding it between her thumb and index finger, moving it alternately to the side of her toward the light then away from it. She got up and went to the lamp beside the bed to examine the luster and color.

"What do you think?"

"Nicely shaped, but I still can't believe the size. And I'm not so sure about the color—the luster seems a little strange—but I'd have to see it in daylight."

"There's nothing wrong with the luster. There are easily several millimeters of nacre on that pearl."

Brianna thought she heard a hint of defensiveness in Nick's tone and looked up at him. "I would imagine so, given the size."

"So?"

"I've seen a few Burmese whites like this, Nick, but never a black."

"I abjure the ordinary."

She looked at him lying just a few feet from her, keenly aware now of his masculine aura. "Apparently you do."

Nick's eyes seemed to caress her, and Brianna self-consciously placed the pearl back on the cloth.

"Is it for sale?"

"For the right price."

"Which is . . . ?"

"The pleasure of your company for dinner, plus an unspecified sum of dollars." He rose from the bed to stand next to her.

Brianna looked up at him. "I take it you want the down payment before you divulge the rest of your terms?"

He swept the hair hanging down one side of her face behind her ear, then brushed her cheek lightly with his fingers. "I think I'll enjoy doing business with you, Brianna Wells."

She watched him saunter into the bathroom without looking back. When the door closed behind him, Brianna looked down at the pearl, which still lay on the bed. "Nick," she called through the louvered door, "you forgot your pearl."

"Watch it for me, will you?"

There was a casual indifference in his tone that made Brianna feel a little ill at ease. Somehow she sensed he was baiting her. But why? For what purpose?

She picked up the pearl again. It was beautiful, the shape exquisite, but there was something about it, just as there was something about its owner, that bothered her. Perhaps neither of them would stand up under close scrutiny.

Still the gem was impressive to look at, and she liked the feel of it in her hand. She looked down at it, wondering. Then she touched her cheek, aware of the fever Nick Severin had engendered.

This man had a way of lighting fires with his fingers, Brianna thought. She would have to watch him carefully, very carefully; there was absolutely no doubt in her mind about that.

Chapter Four

Brianna sipped her wine and gazed out the window at the black-shrouded night, knowing the Atlantic stretched endlessly into the darkness. The lights of a ship were faintly visible far out at sea, and lightning flashed occasionally on the distant horizon, the last evidence of the thunderstorm that had passed through several hours earlier. She looked at Nick across the table. He was watching her.

"It was a nice meal," she said simply.

"I enjoyed your company."

His flirtatious manner was not at all subtle. Brianna tried to ignore it. "But will you enjoy it when you find out I'm not interested in being a customer?"

"Man cannot live by bread alone."

"Yes, I've heard that before."

He grinned. "But you don't believe me?"

"I don't know you."

"We're in the process of correcting that, are we not?"

"We're having dinner as part of the ritual prior to talking business."

He sighed. "Obviously there's something about me that puts you off."

"Perhaps."

"What?"

She thought. "The unnecessary mystery you insist on cloaking everything in, for one thing." There was a good deal more to it than that—the woman with the gun, the danger that seemed to surround him—but Brianna wasn't prepared to go into the many things about the man that disconcerted her. Not yet, anyway.

"I don't know about the mystery, but what I've done is necessary."

"Then you're strange, Nick."

"And you don't like strange men, I take it."

"One tends to trust the known, not the unknown."

He gave her a quirky little smile, running the knuckles of one hand along his mustache. Brianna contemplated the mannerism, deciding the man knew full well how attractive he was.

"It'll all become known in due time," he said easily. "Then you can relax and perhaps enjoy this a little more."

"Business should be pleasant, but I associate enjoyment with pleasure. It's my policy not to mix the two."

"Is that an admonition?"

"Take it as you like. I'm just trying to be very frank."

He smiled over his wineglass. "You're a hard woman, Brianna Wells."

"I take my business seriously, if that's what you mean. There are other sides of me, but I don't expect you'll ever have occasion to know them." After she'd said it, Brianna realized she was resisting too strongly. He had to know there was a touch of insecurity behind her protest.

"You're trying to discourage me," he said wryly.

"Do you need discouraging?"

"Well, I like you, if that justifies discouragement."

Brianna smiled, amused at his undaunted spirit. She listened to the symphony of frogs through the open window nearby. The high, chirping sound fell somewhere between the clatter of a cricket and the singing of a bird. It filled the night air completely, though on balance it was rather soothing, pleasant.

"So, tell me," she said after a while, "why is it you aren't more upset about the fact that you were nearly killed tonight?"

"If that was her best shot, I think I'm pretty safe."

Brianna ignored his bravado. "What about the attempted burglary? I'd have thought that would be rather disconcerting considering your pearl."

"A hazard of my business, I suppose."

"Well, I'm in the jewelry business myself. If it had happened to me, I'd hardly be so blasé."

"Different people react differently."

She contemplated him, feeling uncomfortable with his flippant attitude.

The waiter came by and exchanged a few quick words with Nick.

"Care for some coffee? Or an after dinner drink?"

"No, thank you. I'm fine."

Nick asked for the check, and a few minutes later they were walking down the drive toward the villas. The air was nice, but the darkness brought thoughts of the intruder to Brianna's mind.

"I'll walk you to your room," Nick said, as though he sensed her trepidation.

"Perhaps I will let you stick your head in my door. I wouldn't want to have to confront that woman alone."

"I'm sure she's long gone, but if you didn't bring any valuables on the trip, you needn't worry, I'm sure."

"I have my personal jewelry, but I am wearing most of it. Still, the thought that someone has been lurking around is a bit worrisome."

They went up the steps of Brianna's villa.

"Do you think her motive was theft?" Brianna asked. "Perhaps she knew about your pearl."

"No one knew I was coming here with a pearl—except you."

Brianna looked at him, surprised. "You don't think I—"

"No, no. Of course not." He waited while she fished her room key from her purse, then took it from her, opening the door. He flipped on the light switch and glanced around the room. "Appears safe enough," he said, turning back to her.

Brianna was eyeing him thoughtfully. "If you don't think I had anything to do with the intruder, why did you bring it up?"

Nick grinned and pinched her cheek. "As I recall, you brought it up, not me."

"It was *you* who said I was the only one who knew about the pearl."

"You are."

"Well?"

"That doesn't mean I'm accusing you of anything. If it was an attempted theft, the burglar might have found out about it through an inadvertent disclosure."

"I didn't tell anyone, either, except my assistant, the manager of my St. Thomas shop, Sylvie Voirin. But she wouldn't—"

"Perhaps she mentioned it to a friend, or perhaps it had nothing to do with either her or you. It may just have been a coincidence."

Brianna smiled mischievously. "Or maybe you talk in your sleep." She started to walk past him into her room, but he blocked her way with his arm.

"If I do," he said, looking her square in the eye, "no one would know."

She gave a little laugh. "Mr. Severin, you have a habit of straining your credibility."

"Oh?"

Brianna ducked under his arm and stepped inside. She took the door, closing it partway as she smiled at him. "In other words, I don't believe you.'' With that, she closed the door.

NICK SEVERIN WOKE EARLY the next morning, not having passed a very restful night. He went downstairs and checked the door and windows, finding the threads he had placed over the latches still in place. No one had entered the suite during the night. He hadn't really expected that the intruder would return, but he couldn't be sure.

Severin went back upstairs to shave, shower and dress, content with the fact that his pearl was safe. Had someone returned during the night, it would have been very interesting to see if the armchair, in which he had first hidden the pearl, had been searched. Only Brianna Wells knew about the chair. But she and her cohorts were probably too smart for that kind of a mistake. After all, the pearl was only bait, though she would have no way to know that—not yet.

And there was also the woman who had followed them. Was she the same woman who'd broken in? The odds were that she was. Severin wondered if she could be involved with Brianna Wells. There had to be a connection between them, though he wasn't sure if Brianna herself was aware of it.

She seemed rather innocent regarding the incident, but then she could be a hell of an actress. The degree of her culpability, if any, couldn't be determined yet. He'd need more time.

As Severin shaved, he thought about the intruder. He hadn't really had a good look at her other than to have an impression of blond hair. Nor had he had a good look at the woman in the Moke, though she seemed in her twenties or thirties and was also blond. That was about all he could say for sure. He wondered if they had seen the last of her—or them, as the case may be.

After showering and dressing, Severin went out to walk around the grounds and enjoy the fresh balmy air. It was not yet seven, and the sun had only just risen over the blue-gray sea to the east. He encountered a gardener working on the periphery of the property, fighting back the natural vegetation that always seemed to threaten to reclaim its territory. They exchanged greetings, and Severin walked on.

Finally he ended up by the small hotel pool built against the mountainside and overlooking the coarse terrain of the island. Dropping into a lounge chair, he stared out over the vista and thought about Brianna Wells, wondering about her capacity for criminal behavior, her willingness to profit from a fraud. She seemed so self-righteous, but then it could be an act.

Severin sighed, realizing he didn't much care for the job he'd taken on. He didn't like dealing with Brianna, not under the circumstances that had been forced upon them. The truth was she fascinated him, and in a perverse sort of way he kind of liked her.

It wouldn't be easy to test her, to dangle that pearl in front of her nose and wait for her to bite, like a big fish after an irresistible morsel. And yet it was his obligation to find out if she would. Havergill was depending on him.

Severin knew where the problem lay. It was the woman in her, not the criminal, that interested him. It was a very untidy dilemma.

For a while he watched the fishing boats and other craft on the Caribbean side of the island where most of the activity was centered. St. Barts was a hell of a nice place. Severin wondered if he ought not to give it all up and come to an island like this—move to the tropics as Brianna Wells had done.

First, though, he'd have to get through this job, get it behind him. He forced his mind to concentrate on the problem. What was the next step? He knew he had her attention. That part had gone well, exactly according to plan.

Now he'd let her stew over the pearl for a while, tantalize her with it. If he were going to test her, he might as well test her to the limit. To be absolutely sure, he'd have to do his damnedest to seduce her—every way he knew how. And based on what he'd seen thus far, she'd be a formidable challenge.

Severin looked at his watch. He'd given her plenty of time for beauty sleep. He'd get her up, whether she wanted to or not. Rousing himself, he rose from the lazy comfort of the lounge chair and headed off toward Brianna Wells's villa.

BRIANNA WAS IN THE MIDST of a very sensuous dream, not exactly a sexy one, but very close, when she was awakened by a knock on her door. She blinked awake, not realizing for a moment where she was. There was another knock.

"Who is it?"

"Nick. Did I wake you?"

"Yes."

"Sorry, but we've got a big day ahead of us. You can't sleep it away."

What was it about his cheerfulness, Brianna wondered, that she found so annoying? On top of all his other failings, Nicholas Severin was apparently an early riser. *She* liked to sleep in. No wonder they were so incompatible.

"Okay, Nick, I'm getting up."

"Really?" he called through the door.

Brianna slid her leg off the bed and let her foot drop onto the tiled floor. "Yep, feet on the ground."

"Okay. I'll order breakfast on the terrace of my villa. How long do you need?"

She groaned, not liking to be put on the spot so early in the morning. "Half an hour."

"All right. You've got it."

Brianna heard him walking off the porch and pulled her leg back up onto the bed. She would have loved to drift back to sleep and recapture the dream that he had interrupted—it had been such a pleasant one—but it was too late now. She was awake.

Rolling slowly to the edge of the bed, Brianna sat up-right, trying to clear her brain of the numbness of sleep. She thought about the bizarre events since her arrival on the island—about Nick Severin and his pearl. She remembered the woman who had followed them the day before, the confrontation with yet another woman in Nick's darkened room, the chase, the shot, the candlelight dinner. But most of all Brianna thought about the handsome beguiling man who had such a keen interest in...in what? Her, or her business? She wasn't sure which.

BRIANNA DESCENDED THE STEPS of her villa and headed for Nick's. She wore a turquoise T-shirt with the words St. Thomas written across it, white cotton shorts and sandals. She rarely wore her hair up, but that morning she had pulled it back in a ponytail, rationalizing that he liked her ears, so she might as well let him see them.

She was twenty minutes late, and Nick Severin was already on the terrace, a copious continental breakfast of fruit, cheese, croissants, breads, jams and coffee spread out before him. He was wearing a white polo shirt and pants, looking very tanned, very handsome. It amazed her how his face was almost beautiful, though in an extremely masculine way. Nick's lips and pale mustache blended into a smile.

He seemed to be examining her feature by feature. Brianna knew the individual parts weren't sensational, but the composite worked well enough.

"You look ready for the beach," he said cheerily as he stood to greet her. "How'd you like to drive up to Anse des Flamands with me after breakfast? We can have lunch at the Taiwana Beach Club. A friend of mine owns it. Best food on the island."

"Sounds nice, but what about our business discussion?" she asked as Nick helped her with her chair.

"There's plenty of time for that later."

She glanced up at him as he sat down across from her. "Are you sure you're not Latin?"

"What do you mean?"

"It's always *mañana*, every time I ask you a question."

"Maybe you ask the wrong questions," he said with a sly grin.

She smiled sardonically.

Nick gestured. "If the coffee's cold, I can order more. I . . . was expecting you a little earlier."

"Sorry, sometimes I'm not very punctual."

"Perhaps you're the one who's Latin."

Brianna nodded. *"Touché."*

They ate breakfast, chatting amiably about all sorts of things except the reason they were there. For a while she let things drift, but it soon became apparent Nick had no intention of bringing up the pearl. Finally she lost patience.

"Do you still have your pearl, or was there a mysterious theft during the night?"

"No burglaries. No armed robberies. It's safely inside."

"Well, aren't you going to let me see it in the sunlight?"

"It *is* business before pleasure with you, isn't it?"

"Pleasant as this conversation has been, it's not what I came to St. Barts for."

"All right," he said, getting up, "I'll get it for you."

After going into his suite, Nick returned a minute later with the velvet pouch. He spread the jeweler's cloth on the table where Brianna had cleared a spot and set the pearl in the middle of it.

She picked the gem up, holding it so she could see it in the sunlight. Then she carefully rolled it on the tablecloth, bending over the pearl for a close look.

"What are you doing, checking the symmetry?"

"No, I'm testing it for 'wink'—indications of being too thin-skinned, not enough nacre."

He waited. "Well?"

ll me, then. What do you think of it as a dyed black?''

must say I'm impressed. It wasn't at all obvious. One
e best jobs I've seen.''

ou can still have it for forty thousand.''

e was watching her intently, more, it seemed, than just
n anxious salesman. Brianna wasn't so sure she fully
erstood him, after all. She shook her head. ''No,
nks.''

Nick looked surprised. ''Why not?''

''It's a nice gem, and maybe you could even get forty
ousand for it, considering the unusual size and the shape,
ut I just can't use it in my business.''

''Why's that?''

''I deal in genuine blacks. I've built a business and a reputation on them. If I start dealing in dyed pearls, how will
people really know? Sorry, but I'm just not interested.''

''Other jewelers deal in both genuine and imitation
gems.''

''I don't regard myself just as a jeweler. I like to think of
myself as an artist, or craftsman. I design everything I make,
and black pearls are among the materials I work with.
They've become my trademark. They're beautiful and
they're unusual. That's how I want my work to be regarded, too.''

Nick had a skeptical expression on his face. ''You're
trying to tell me the buck doesn't count?''

''No, it does count. But I believe you make money if your
workmanship is superb and your integrity sound. I've had
people buy something from my shop in St. Thomas, take it
home to Milwaukee or Boston or New York and have an ignorant jeweler tell them it's costume jewelry made of imitation materials.''

Nick's grin was wry. ''You mean not everybody trusts
you?''

''It's not a question of trust. Black pearls, even cultured
ones, are not often seen, and a jeweler's mind is by defini-

Brianna silently examined it before loo.
"What do you want for it, Nick?"

He contemplated her. "I'll let you have it
sand."

A slight smile touched her lips. "A genuine
black of this size and shape would easily comm
ures. If you knew pearls, you'd know that."

"I told you I was bringing you a deal."

"Do I look needy or something?" She shook h
"No, Nick, there's more to the story than you are t

"Like what?"

"Look," she said, leaning toward him, "if this p
genuine, why don't you take it to one of the large house
get what it's worth?"

"I get the feeling you're suggesting it's not genuine."

"What are you representing it as?"

"You tell me."

Brianna straightened her back. "All right, I'll tell you
what it is. It's a dyed pearl, not a cultured black."

"You sound rather sure."

"There are maybe a dozen people in the world who could
tell the difference by sight—without examining it in a lab. I
happen to be one of them."

He smiled. "My congratulations."

Brianna leaned back, thinking she was beginning to understand Nick Severin's game. She watched him.

"You aren't offended, are you?"

She shrugged. "Why would I be offended?"

"I never said it wasn't dyed, did I?"

"You never said it was."

"If I was ambiguous, it was because I was curious just
how well you know your business."

"What have you decided?"

His mouth lifted at the corners. "You're either very
knowledgeable, or it was a lucky guess."

"It wasn't luck," she replied matter-of-factly.

tion suspicious. Every time it happens, I have the customer take the piece to the Gemological Institute labs to have it examined. There have been a number of red faces around the jewelry business as a result. Why should I sell imitations, even good ones, when I can offer the real thing?''

"But if you buy a ten to fourteen millimeter pearl from me, you can save thousands over what you're paying now."

"Are you suggesting that I buy dyed pearls from you and represent them as genuine?''

"I'm not suggesting anything. You can represent them anyway you wish. I'm just showing you where there's an opportunity."

"Well, Mr. Severin," Brianna replied, feeling her anger rising, "if by opportunity you mean cheating people, you might as well know I'm not a crook. And if that's the purpose of this business proposition—to induce me to misrepresent my work—you can just take your French-dyed pearls and . . . and . . ." She got to her feet, but Nick took her arm.

"I didn't mean offense," he said calmly. "I just wanted to find out who I was dealing with."

Brianna stared at him, uncertain whether he was playing more of his games, or if he was sincere. "Presumably, you know now."

He nodded. "Come on. Sit down."

She reluctantly sank back into her chair. "We've established that I'm not interested in your pearls, so we don't really have anything else to discuss, do we?"

"Oh, I have a couple of other things up my sleeve," he said mysteriously.

"If they're anything like your last proposition, you can forget it," she insisted.

"Ah, but I haven't forgotten you agreed to go to the beach. Our discussion can wait. Why don't you run along and get your swim things for the beach. It's a shame to waste such a glorious day."

"You know," she said, shaking her head knowingly, "I don't think you're a salesman at all. You're a cat."

"A cat? Why's that?"

"You always seem to land on your feet." With that Brianna stood up. "I'll get my suit. Give me five minutes."

Nick gave a little laugh. "I'll be at the car in fifteen minutes, then."

She gave him a dirty look but couldn't help a smile. "You think you've got me all figured out, don't you, Nick Severin?"

He shrugged, and Brianna turned and strode purposefully off the terrace toward her villa.

A FEW MINUTES LATER Severin walked into the hotel office. The clerk looked up from his newspaper.

"Oui, Monsieur Severin?"

"I'd like to make an overseas call," he replied in French. "Do you have a private phone I could use?"

"Oui, monsieur. The director is not in; you can use her office. It's just through that door."

Moments later he had managed to get through to London.

"Nick!" Anthony Havergill said on hearing his voice. "How's it going? Have you managed to connect with the Wells woman?"

"Yeah, we connected all right."

"What's the matter, chum? Another dead end?"

Nick laughed. "More nearly a dead me."

"What happened?"

"There was a Frenchwoman with a gun in my room last night. She'd broken in and was searching the place when we walked in on her. She got away but I followed her. That's when she took a shot at me."

"Lord. What do you make of it? Could she have been after the pearl?"

"I don't know. She might be hooked up with Brianna in some way. But if she is, it's not at all obvious."

"Well, be careful. You aren't there to get your head blown off."

"Thanks, I'll remember that."

"So, how's it going with the Wells woman?"

"I'm not sure yet, Tony. I dropped the pearl on her nice and easy like I'd planned, but she didn't bite."

"What happened?"

"She spotted it as dyed almost immediately. Gave me this big speech about her integrity, then refused point-blank to deal with me."

"That doesn't necessarily mean she won't come around though, does it?"

"No."

"What's your impression?"

"I don't know yet. She's either suspicious of me or honest; I'm not sure which." Severin knew it wouldn't be easy to find out, either. He suspected his judgment was clouded by his own growing fascination with Brianna Wells. His desires might end up getting in the way of his coolheaded reason.

"Then you haven't eliminated her?"

"Not yet."

"What do you plan to do, Nick?"

"I'm going to give her a bit of slack. The pearl was a jolt. She needs time to get over that, and besides, it will take time to repair the damage."

"I take it you're not going to move immediately into phase two, then."

"No, not for a while. When the time is right, I'll try to catch her off guard."

Havergill chuckled. "What's she like anyway, mate?"

"Nice woman, actually. Likable, quick. She's got a little fire in her blood, which appeals to me."

"By your tone I take it she's attractive?"

Severin smiled, knowing his reputation was bound to get in the way at times. "Yeah, Tony, she's a good-looking woman."

"Just remember, it's your knowledge of the criminal mind that you're being paid for, not your talents with the fairer sex."

"Oh, I won't forget. Crime before pleasure. That's our motto, isn't it?"

"Well, do what you must to get the job done, but please, let's not have too many romantic dinners."

Severin laughed. "Face it, Tony. You're just jealous."

"Maybe so, but that never seems to stop you from having fun at my expense."

"If I pull this off, Tony, you owe me a bottle of Black Label."

Havergill chuckled. "Luck, chum. And do stay away from Frenchwomen with guns." He rang off.

Chapter Five

They had descended the mountain, passed through the town of Gustavia, driven along the narrow ribbon of concrete undulating through the hills to the Anse des Flamands, a secluded bay on the northwestern side of the island. Brianna looked back several times in route to see if they were being followed, but the pavement behind was always empty.

Just as they were dropping down to the sea, she glanced back a final time, and Nick noticed. "If you're looking for our lady friend, Brianna, she's back there."

"The one who broke into your room?"

"I don't know about her, but the one who followed us yesterday is back there."

"I haven't seen her."

"She's pretty far back."

"Are you sure it's her?"

"Not positive, but it looked like the same vehicle."

At the base of the incline Nick made a sharp right onto a dirt track surrounded by thick foliage. He stopped the Moke just off the road.

"What are you doing?"

"This is the drive to the Taiwana, but I wanted to wait here and try to get a look at our friend."

They sat for a moment, the engine idling, when through the undergrowth they could hear the sound of a vehicle coming down the highway. Looking back, they saw a green Moke speed by, with a blond woman at the wheel. The driver continued on toward the other end of the bay, oblivious to them. Brianna looked at Nick.

"Was it the same woman as last night?"

"Could have been. I really didn't see much in the dark. Does she look familiar to you?"

"No," Brianna replied. "But then I hardly saw her, either."

Nick put the car in gear, and they continued on through the forest of palms and shrubs down the track. "I'd say the one who just went by on the road was French, or at least European."

"How could you tell?" she asked.

"By the way she drives—fast."

Half a minute later they came to the small hotel-restaurant built right on the edge of a broad expanse of white sandy beach that rimmed the entire bay. They parked, took their things and went down the walk past the bungalows to the restaurant, a Spartan affair with a thatched roof and open sides. Several people were sitting at tables on the palm-shaded patio. One of them, a man, got up and walked toward Nick and Brianna.

"Nick! *Ça va?*"

Greetings were exchanged, and Brianna was introduced to the manager, a slender Frenchman in shorts with a thin, aquiline nose and very tan skin. He took Brianna's hand, smiling affably.

"Bienvenue, mademoiselle. Bienvenue."

Nick and the manager, Alain, chatted for a few minutes before the Frenchman summoned over a young man working behind the bar.

"Thees es Jean," Alain explained to Brianna in halting English. "He will show you to a room . . . where you . . . can change, if you like."

"Thank you."

Nick took Brianna's arm, and they followed the young man back toward one of the bungalows.

"The restaurant is so popular and the food so good that a lot of people just come for the day. In effect it's as much a beach club as a hotel," Nick explained. "We can change and have a swim before lunch."

They entered a bungalow consisting of a single large room with a four-poster in the corner. The bathroom was behind a partition that went only halfway to the high ceiling. Nick thanked the young man, who left them, closing the door to the room.

"An unorthodox arrangement," he said, looking around, "but there's enough privacy for changing. Do you want the bathroom, or would you prefer to undress out here?"

Brianna gave a little laugh. "Do I look like an exhibitionist? I'll take the bathroom." With bag in hand, she went behind the partition, pulling the curtain across the entry behind her.

Moments later she had changed into her bright yellow bikini and slipped on a filmy, royal-blue muslin caftan that she wore as a cover-up. "Safe to come out?" she called over the wall.

"All clear," he replied.

As she slid the curtain open and stepped out, Nick took her in with his eyes, noticing her wonderfully slim figure. Though her breasts were small, she was nicely curvaceous, her legs very long and attractive. Her wide mouth seemed most sensuous just then, or was it her state of near nakedness that made it seem so?

Nick had a large beach towel around his neck, and the skimpy European trunks he wore left little of his anatomy to the imagination. Brianna only briefly let her eyes sweep over him, taking in his rich, even tan and the mat of beige hair covering his chest and legs. He looked as though he belonged on the cover of an August issue of *Les Jours*.

He smiled at her behind his sunglasses. "Ready for some sun?"

The question seemed strangely vacuous. Under the circumstances it seemed much more appropriate for him to ask if she were ready for him. The honest answer would have been "Yes, but no thanks." Brianna groaned to herself, wondering why she had agreed to go to the beach with the man.

They walked out onto the sand where they were met by a pleasant sea breeze blowing off the water.

"Let's go on up to the other end of the bay," he said. "It's a little more private up that way."

They didn't talk a great deal; mainly they just enjoyed the sun, the air and the water. Midway around the bay they passed another small hotel. A few people were sunning themselves on the beach. The women—as was customary with the French—were topless.

The casual ambience struck Brianna as a rather unlikely circumstance in which to persuade Nick to talk business, and seeing the bodies around her made that fact all the more evident. After a quick glance at Nick, she felt the incongruity of the situation acutely. Still, there was not a lot that could be done about it now, so she tried to relax and go with the flow.

Soon they came to a nice spot and spread out their towels on the sand. About thirty yards or so away were three young women. Two of them were lying down, but one, a striking redhead, was combing her tangled hair. Her bare breasts were large and tan as a berry. Nick noticed Brianna staring at the girl.

"Don't feel you have to take off your top just because it's done here," he said casually. "Not if you'd feel uncomfortable."

It almost sounded as if he were daring her. "I'm not exactly a prude," she replied a bit pointedly, "but there's a time and place for everything. Our relationship is essentially a business one, and I intend to keep it that way." With that she plopped down on her stomach, unfastened the snap of her top behind her and tried to relax in the comfortable warmth of the sun.

Brianna's eyes were closed, but she could feel him watching her. She tried to act indifferent, nonchalant, but her heart was beating heavily. She could hear him arranging his towel beside her. Feeling very vulnerable just then, she wondered if he was leering at her, examining her body, thinking about her sexually. She tried not to let it bother her, but it did.

"You have a lovely figure," she heard him say softly, over the sounds of the wind and surf.

Brianna lifted her head abruptly, glaring in response to the offending comment, but he wasn't even looking at her. He was staring out to sea, his arms wrapped around his legs. The unexpressed anger on her face gradually began to fade. "Why did you say that?"

Nick turned to her. "I wasn't being impertinent. I was just saying what I thought. Is that bad?"

"Under the circumstances, it's inappropriate."

"If you didn't want me to notice, why didn't you keep your clothes on?"

Irritated, Brianna started to get up to challenge him, but remembered almost too late that her top was off. She instantly dropped back down onto her towel. "Because I came out here for the sun, not to be ogled by you!"

"I'm not ogling," Nick replied irritably. "If I was interested in that, there's plenty else to ogle."

Feeling duly chastened, Brianna turned her head the other way. She stared up the sandy beach, convinced entirely that it had been a mistake to come on the outing. As she thought about it, she became vaguely aware of a woman standing in the shrubs at the edge of the nearly deserted beach, fifty or a hundred yards farther along.

The woman had her hands to her face and seemed to be staring in their direction. Then Brianna saw wisps of blond hair fluttering in the breeze, and realized the voyeur was looking through binoculars.

"Nick, don't look now, but your blond girlfriend, the one in the Moke, is watching us through binoculars from the bushes farther up the beach."

So as not to be obvious, Nick slowly leaned back on his elbows, then rolled over on his side, facing Brianna and their uninvited guest. He took strands of Brianna's hair, tucking them behind her ear as he stared up the beach.

"What are you doing?" she asked, turning her head to face him.

"Trying to act as if I'm looking at you. Turn your head back again and see if you can spot something that might help to identify her."

"She's pretty well hidden. The blond hair is about all. She doesn't look too tan."

"Yes, I was noticing. She's not an islander."

"What are you going to do?"

"I'm not sure, but I think it's time the lady and I had a talk." Nick started getting to his feet. "I'm going to walk down that way and see if I can get close enough to confront her."

"What if she has a gun?"

"I don't think she'd try anything in broad daylight." He started walking casually up the beach.

Brianna watched him go, feeling trepidation. Almost immediately the woman lowered her binoculars, turned and disappeared back into the undergrowth. Nick immediately started running after her. With the excitement, Brianna sat up, forgetting completely about the top of her suit.

A FEW MINUTES LATER Nick returned. Brianna waited anxiously as he strode toward her through the sand.

"She got away," he said wearily and dropped down beside her. "All I saw was the tail end of her Moke disappearing up the road."

"Nick, I really don't think you can continue being so casual about this. If it's the same woman who shot at you, she's obviously dangerous. You should go to the police. I really think you should."

"I don't know what they could do. I can't prove anything, and following us is not a crime."

"What about breaking into your room? And the shot?"

"Well, we don't know for sure it was the same woman. It may not have been."

"Even so, she's bound to be up to something."

Nick absentmindedly tossed a handful of sand toward the water. "I don't know what."

"We can't just ignore her."

"For the moment there's not much else we can do."

They sat, letting the breeze caress them.

"It must have something to do with your pearl," Brianna said after a while.

"Why do you say that?"

"What else could it be? I imagine if she were a jealous lover you'd recognize her."

Nick grinned. "Do you think she has cause to be jealous?"

"Well, no. But you can never tell about wo—people."

"There's no need to worry. She doesn't even look vaguely familiar to me."

"Did you get a better look at her this time?"

"She has a nice body."

"I'm not surprised you noticed that. See any distinguishing scars or birthmarks?"

"Is that sarcasm?"

Brianna grimaced. "Sorry. I guess I don't like the idea of being followed. And if it is a jealous lover maybe next time she'll shoot at me!"

Nick smiled. "First you have to give her something to be jealous about."

Brianna felt herself color. "She could react without justification."

He looked at her, seemingly enjoying her discomfort. "Well, let's forget about her. Just relax and enjoy the sun. Would you like some oil on your back?"

His tone was innocent enough, so Brianna agreed without thinking. In a moment he was expertly massaging her back, deeply rubbing the oil into her skin with strong, sensuous strokes of his hands. Judging by his enthusiasm and the sensuous effect it had on her, she realized it had been a mistake.

"That's enough," she finally said, stopping him.

"Doesn't it feel good?"

"It feels too good."

"How can it feel too good?"

"Believe me, it can."

"All right, I'll take your word for it. Mind giving me a little?" He held out the bottle of oil.

Brianna looked at him, knowing she couldn't say no. She snapped her top back on and got up on her knees as Nick dropped down on his stomach. She poured some oil on his back and began plying his smooth, rich skin, feeling his muscles underneath.

"You're good," he murmured, sounding quite content. "No wonder your husband thought you were good in bed."

"What makes you think he did?"

"You said so."

"When did I say that?"

"Yesterday... when you told me about your marriage."

"I never said that. I said it was all we had in common."

"Then you weren't good in bed?"

"Of course, I ... I mean I ... Oh, never mind!" Brianna plopped down on her towel amid Nick Severin's laughter. "Beast."

"Don't be embarrassed," he said, recovering. "I already knew you were."

She got onto her elbows. "What do you mean by that?"

"Don't you know that an informed observer can tell?"

"Oh, you cannot."

"Sure you can."

"How?"

"Body language, personality, reactions to things."

Brianna felt herself blush. "I don't believe you."

"It's true."

"What is there about me that says I'm good in bed?"

"You want me to divulge my secrets?"

"Damn right. I'm not going to let you get away with a cock-and-bull story like that."

"Your mouth is a dead giveaway."

"My mouth?"

"Yep."

"How so?"

"It's sensuous. You use it sensuously. Mouths speak more than words."

The conversation made her feel ill at ease, but the perversity of it held a strange sort of fascination for her. "I still don't believe you."

"And the way you move, the way you hold your body, the way you respond to me."

"This is getting worse. How do I respond to you that suggests that I'm sexy?"

"That isn't quite what I said. I said you're good in bed."

Brianna felt herself turning red through her tan. "That's even worse."

"Of course it's not."

She realized she couldn't let him have his way with her so easily. "Just so you know being good and being interested are not the same thing."

Nick grinned. "I'm aware of that. Don't worry, your virtue is intact."

"I'm not concerned about my virtue."

He laughed.

"That's not what I meant!"

Nick laughed still louder, and Brianna, indignant, took a handful of sand and threw it over his freshly oiled back.

"Foul!" he cried and got to his knees. "Come on, young lady," he said, grasping her wrist and pulling her to her feet, "you're going to help me wash off."

He dragged her down to the water and marched with her into the surf, Brianna trying to resist, but to no avail. As they entered the water, it felt warm, yet refreshing. Though she stopped resisting, Nick didn't let go of her. He came to a halt when the surf was about waist deep. "How repentant do you feel?"

Brianna narrowed her eyes, then slashed at the surface of the water with her hand, splashing him in the face. Nick tightened his grip, and she spun around trying to free herself. Just then a big wave came rolling in from behind her, catching Brianna square in the back and throwing her against him before washing over them both.

Nick wrapped his arms around her, and she looked up at him as water ran from both of their faces. "Neptune's on my side, you see," he said through his grin.

Brianna squirmed to free herself, but he held her too tightly. When she looked again into his soft brown eyes, his face drew near hers, and he kissed her, fully, sensuously on the lips.

As the kiss ended, Brianna's eyes narrowed. "Nick," she said through clenched teeth, "let go of me." But before she finished saying it, he had released her. She backed away, her hands just settling on her hips when another wave came, and threw her against him again.

This time he leaned over and lifted her into his arms before trudging back up toward the beach.

"Put me down," she said when he was in ankle deep water.

He complied. "I didn't want a drowning on my conscience."

"Why did you do that?"

"I told you. I didn't want a—"

"No, why did you kiss me?"

"I was just confirming my suppositions about you. A woman's kiss is the definite clue."

Brianna's mouth dropped. She spun angrily on her heels and marched back toward the towels. Nick followed along behind her.

"I hope I didn't offend you," he said in response to her angry silence.

"No, your kiss confirmed my suspicions, as well," she said, drying herself with her towel.

"What's that?"

"That you're an arrogant, egotistical rake and womanizer!"

"Is that all?"

His teasing enraged her. "That's all that's fit to say!"

"I've been called worse."

"I'm not surprised." Brianna slipped her caftan over her head, the breeze billowing it from her body.

He looked crestfallen. "It was intended as good-natured fun."

"You were out of line."

"I'm sorry."

She picked up her bag, her expression cross.

He took her arm. "I *am* sorry."

Brianna pulled her arm free and began walking back toward the club. Nick was beside her.

"You did fire the first shot," he said a bit defensively.

"*I* did?"

"That's why you threw the sand on me, wasn't it? To get into a tussle?"

"Nick!"

He laughed, and she could see he was teasing again.

"You're nothing but an overgrown bully!" She swung her bag at him, but he leaped back. She tried again, and he danced away. In a moment she was chasing him down the beach, the wind filling her caftan like a sail.

They were out of breath and laughing when they finally stopped.

"I was afraid you were going to blow away like a balloon," he said breathlessly.

"It would have served you right."

Nick's white teeth gleamed beneath his smiling lips and mustache. He slipped his arm around her waist, and they walked together in the sun. It was precisely what she was intending to avoid, but Brianna rationalized it, thinking that Nick had—in the course of their play—become a friend.

AFTER SHE HAD SHOWERED and changed, she returned to the restaurant where she found Nick sitting at a table in the open terrace, chatting with Alain. The men rose as she neared, and the Frenchman withdrew.

"You look refreshed," Nick said, helping her with her chair.

"It was a nice shower."

By the time they had cleaned up and dressed, it was mid-afternoon and most of the luncheon crowd had left. Only a few customers remained. Alain returned with a chilled bottle of white wine and two glasses. He poured, exchanged a few words with Nick about their lunch and left.

"Alain said the steak was not wonderful today," he explained, "but the fish is fabulous so I ordered it for us. I hope that's okay."

"Fine. Sounds good."

For a while they watched the sea, enjoying the brisk but pleasantly warm breeze. Brianna really didn't look at Nick, but she was very aware of him. Their kiss and the horseplay on the beach had thrust their relationship onto a new plane, and she could tell that he was as uncertain about it as she.

Brianna wondered about him—what he was thinking, what he was really up to, who he really was. "Tell me about yourself, Nick. I really don't know a thing about you. How did you come to live in France and become a merchant of dyed pearls?"

"It's a long story." He smiled.

"Tell me anyway."

"You really want to hear?"

She nodded, sipping her wine.

"Years ago I was an army officer stationed in Germany. When my commitment was up, I decided to stay on in Europe. I've been there ever since, the better part of fifteen years."

"Doing what?"

"At first I got a job working for a concessionaire serving the American bases in Germany. Then I became a wholesaler and a jobber, trading various commodities. Nine or ten years ago I took part in some transactions involving gems and art. I found it fascinating, looked for more deals, eventually specializing. I finally settled in Paris, and...well, you know the rest."

"Now your thing is pearls?"

"Not really. It's just a sideline. Most of my business consists of supplying museums with ancient jewelry, artifacts and art objects."

Brianna's eyebrows rose. "Interesting. Do you have a shop?"

"No."

"A company?"

"Not really. I work alone."

He had slipped his dark glasses down onto his nose, and Brianna could feel him watching without being able to see his eyes. "Ancient jewelry, huh?" she mumbled, somewhat absently.

"We have more in common than meets the eye, Brianna."

She looked at him, sensing there was meaning in his words beyond what she understood. "You know, it's funny that your name hasn't come up before. You'd have thought we'd have run into each other, or at least heard of each other."

"Obviously I've heard of you."

"Why hadn't *I* heard of you?"

"I maintain a pretty low profile."

"Why?"

"I like to work that way."

"Why is it I get the feeling you always dance around my questions?"

His mouth compressed. "Haven't we had this conversation already?"

"Yeah," she said sardonically. "As I recall, the problem is my questions, not your answers."

He nodded as the waiter brought a plate of crudités.

"How is it you know Lucien Pillet? If you hadn't given his name as a reference, I probably never would have agreed to come to St. Barts."

"Thank God for old Lucien."

"Where do you know him from?"

"Didn't you talk to him?"

"No, he was out of town. I spoke with his secretary."

"I must confess I don't know Monsieur Pillet well. We've had dealings in the past—fairly limited ones, actually."

Brianna contemplated Nick, sensing that he was stalling.

"How well do *you* know him?" he asked casually.

"Not terribly well. But he and my father were fairly close in business at one time. They traded a lot. Of course, Monsieur Pillet's semiretired now, so I don't have much occasion to run into him."

Nick popped a carrot into his mouth and munched absently. Brianna wasn't sure why she was feeling uncomfortable about the conversation.

"Where do you know me from, Nick?"

He reached over and tweaked her chin. "Your black pearls have made you very famous."

She could see he had a knack for vagueness. Just then their lunch arrived, and they both ate with good appetite. It was a fabulous meal, very simple, but the flavors were magnificent, the cuisine deceptively refined. Brianna enjoyed it, but something about Nick continued to bother her. Something wasn't fitting. And the blond woman was beginning to trouble her, as well.

She looked at his handsome face and wondered what she had gotten herself into. Maybe the man should be checked out a bit more. Maybe she should try and reach Lucien Pillet again.

Looking into his sunglasses, Brianna saw two images of herself, one in each lens. It struck her as ironic, because in a way she had also been seeing two Nicholas Severins—one playful and charming, the other a little slippery, a little mysterious, and very uncomfortable about something. She wondered if it could possibly be that he wasn't really comfortable with himself.

Chapter Six

On the return trip Brianna had grown silent and thoughtful. At first none of the strange things that had been happening worried her much, but her growing interest in Nick Severin made them a little more relevant than they had been before.

When they were coming down the hill into Gustavia, Brianna touched Nick's arm. "Would you mind dropping me in town? I want to do a little shopping, take care of a few errands. I'll take a taxi back to the hotel later."

"Well, if you like. But I can wait for you . . . have a drink in a café while you shop . . ."

"No, you go on back. I'll be fine."

"Our friend was nowhere in sight on the way back, so I guess you needn't worry about her."

Brianna laughed. "No, she's probably busy ransacking your room."

"It's okay. My pearl's in the hotel safe."

"You should have kept it there from the beginning," she chided.

"How was I to know negotiating with you would draw such attention?"

They had entered the narrow streets that, after the heat of the day, had become congested with vehicles and pedestrians.

"Where do you want me to drop you off?"

"Anywhere is fine."

Nick stopped at a crowded intersection.

"I'll just jump out here."

Before he could say anything, she was out of the Moke. "Thanks for lunch and the swim," she said cheerily.

"When will you be back? I had an interesting little place in mind for dinner."

The traffic had begun to move, and a Jeep behind Nick honked when he didn't advance.

"I'll just grab a bite in town," she said. "You go on."

He rolled on a few feet, looking back at her. "No, I wanted you to see it," he protested.

The Jeep tooted, and Brianna stepped onto the curb. "Okay," she called after him. "Give me a couple of hours."

Nick waved his assent and moved on up the street. Brianna turned and joined the milling crowd on the narrow walk. She had decided to try to call Lucien Pillet in Paris, though it was already quite late there. His office was in his home, so it was possible she'd reach someone. Regardless, she felt the need to try. Reassurance about Nick Severin seemed to be getting more important all the time.

Nick was too well-known by the people in the hotel to make the call from there, so Brianna decided to call from the post office. It would be more secure.

She had remembered seeing the *bureau de poste* when they had driven through town before, and started walking in its general direction. On the way she paused briefly to glance in a few windows, feeling somehow obligated to window-shop, at least.

But as she moved through the streets, she found herself looking at faces in the crowd, not realizing at first that she was unconsciously searching for the blonde. Though she had no idea what the woman looked like up close, she scrutinized every fair-haired woman she encountered.

Brianna hadn't realized there were so many blondes in their twenties or thirties, but she was quickly able to eliminate the vast majority she encountered. By concentrating on those who were alone, looked European, had pleasing figures, medium-length hair and who were a little paler than most, she drastically reduced the possibilities.

Brianna knew the exercise wasn't such a foolish one, because it was a small island and there weren't that many people on it, even counting the tourists. Nevertheless, no suitable candidates appeared. And as best she could tell, she wasn't being followed.

When Brianna got to the post office, she found it jammed with people. The small building was not air-conditioned, and it was hot. There was a lot of jostling going on—orderly lines being unknown in her experience outside of the States and the United Kingdom—and Brianna had no desire to enter the fray. She saw that there were only two phone booths, though from the doorway she couldn't tell if they were occupied.

Deciding that since she was there she may as well find out, Brianna pushed her way across the tiny room to the *cabinets de téléphone*. One of the booths was occupied by a large man whose stomach was too big to permit the door to close. He was speaking very loudly into the receiver over the general din in the room.

She glanced into the other booth and saw that it was occupied by a young woman. The caller looked up at Brianna through the glass door, and just as Brianna was noticing her medium-length fair hair, the woman's eyes rounded slightly. They stared at each other for a moment, and Brianna could tell instantly that it was not meaningless recognition. It was the blonde.

For a moment she didn't know what to do but stare, etching into her brain the face that until now had been vague and featureless. But suddenly here she was. Was it the woman who had held a gun on her in the darkened room?

The one who had shot at Nick? The one who had been following them? As their eyes locked, Brianna felt curiosity as much as fear.

The blonde was actually quite attractive, her permed hair fashionably untamed and windblown, her makeup impeccable. There was a worldliness in the face that suggested guile rather than innocence. After a long moment of mutual recognition, the woman gave Brianna a look of annoyance and turned into the booth, as though she were showing contempt at being observed.

The loud man in the adjoining booth hung up and left, but Brianna still couldn't hear clearly the woman's words, though she could tell that she was speaking French. Was it the voice she'd heard in the dark? She couldn't be sure.

The blonde kept her face turned away, even sliding her hand alongside her cheek so as to hide her profile. Her fingers were slender, feminine, her red nails beautifully manicured. She wore no rings, but there was a gold slave bracelet above her elbow and a heavy gold collar necklace around her neck.

Though the woman didn't turn back, Brianna could still picture her attractive dark eyes. Through the glass she saw that the pale skin of her bare arms was a little pink from the sun. Her outfit was not entirely visible in the booth, but it appeared to be a cotton jump suit, cinnamon in color. She seemed sporty, elegant, and very fashionable. In just a few seconds Brianna had learned so much.

She looked around the crowded room, uncertain what to do. Her suspect was trapped. Eventually she'd have to come out. Brianna could confront her, but what would she say? And would it be safe? She could go to the police, whose headquarters were in the adjoining building, but, as Nick had pointed out, they really had no proof.

The blonde would undoubtedly act indignant at being accused. On a small island people keep running into one another—that was easy enough to claim. And it wasn't absolutely certain she was the one who'd been in Nick's room and fired the shot. The more Brianna thought about it, the more confused she became.

Perhaps it was enough that the woman had been discovered—that she had been seen up close. Maybe that would discourage her from more high jinks. As Brianna stood thinking, the patter continued inside the booth, though the voice was lower and more controlled.

Standing there, Brianna began to feel conspicuous. She could think of nothing else she might do. Perhaps it would be better to slip away and leave the blonde guessing.

Making her way out of the hot, stuffy building, Brianna returned to the street. She hadn't managed to make her call to Paris, though she had an interesting story. And considering she had come to town to find out what she could about Nick, spotting the blonde had turned out to be more ironic than satisfying.

Brianna had walked a block or so and found herself standing in front of Renier et Cie, an international jewelry chain with shops all around the Caribbean. It occurred to her that she vaguely knew the manager of the shop in Charlotte Amalie. Between that and her own business card, she might be able to persuade the manager to let her use the phone.

Brianna entered the shop, greeted by the soothing comfort of cool air. It was then that she realized she had been perspiring heavily. Between that and the afternoon at the beach, she probably looked a mess.

An immaculately dressed woman in a long-sleeved silk blouse and pearls approached. *"Oui, madame?"*

"Hello," Brianna said, suddenly feeling a little desperate. She searched her purse for a business card. "I was wondering if I could impose on you for a favor."

BRIANNA LISTENED to the telephone ringing across the Atlantic. It went on and on. She was about to give up when someone picked up the receiver at the other end.

"Allô, oui?" It was a woman's voice.

"Hello. Is Monsieur Pillet there, please?"

"Monsieur Pillet? No, I am sorry. He is not here. Who is calling, please?"

"Brianna Wells."

"Oh, Madame Wells. Yes, you called before. This is Louise Frachet, Monsieur Pillet's secretary. You are fortunate that I am here so late. It is only by chance. I came for something I had forgotten."

"Do you expect Monsieur Pillet to return soon?"

"Not for several days. Can I help you with something?"

"I'm calling again regarding Nicholas Severin. We're in the midst of business discussions, and I would like further information regarding his reputation."

"I don't know what more I can tell you, *madame.*"

"Do you know if Monsieur Pillet has had extensive dealings with Mr. Severin?"

"I am told they are acquainted, but I don't know more."

"Told?"

"Oui, madame."

Brianna thought it was a strange thing to say. "There's nothing more you can tell me?"

"About Mr. Severin, no."

"Perhaps there's someone else you can refer me to, someone who may have dealt with Mr. Severin involving antique jewelry or museum pieces, that sort of thing."

"Hmm. In Paris, no."

"Anywhere else, perhaps?" Brianna asked anxiously.

"I know there is a French gentleman living in New York who handles such matters. Monsieur Pillet knows him. They have had dealings previously."

"Who is it, Mademoiselle Frachet?"

"Henri Rosenthal. He is a dealer who does a lot of work for museums. I believe he has handled items for Monsieur Pillet, as well."

"Yes, Henri Rosenthal. He has a shop in New York. I'd forgotten about him, though we've met."

"*Oui, madame*, and he is in Paris often, as well, I believe."

"Perhaps I will try and reach him. You've been a great help, Mademoiselle Frachet. Thank you very much."

Brianna called New York information, finally getting the number of Rosenthal's shop. New York was an hour behind the West Indies, so she was optimistic about reaching him. She put a credit card call through.

"Brianna Wells! What a surprise to hear your voice. It's been a year or two since I've seen you, has it not? Where was it? An antique show? An exhibit? Someplace like that."

"I believe it was at the opening of an Egyptian art exhibit."

"Oh, yes, I recall. We spoke of your late father. He is very much missed in our business, *mademoiselle*."

"And I miss him, too." At times like these in particular, she thought.

"What can I do for you, my dear?"

Brianna explained her strange business encounter with Nick Severin.

"Nicholas Severin, you say his name is?"

"Yes."

"Hmm. And you say he is not French?"

"No, he's American but living now in Paris."

"It's strange that the name is not familiar. I thought I knew everyone of consequence in the business."

"Apparently Lucien Pillet knows him, though not well, I believe."

"Lucien? Did you speak with him about this Mr. Severin?"

"No, only his secretary."

"I see. Very strange. But you believe he deals in museum-quality pieces?"

"That's what he says."

"For how long?"

"My impression is for eight or ten years."

"It hardly seems possible. Surely I would have at least heard the name. Tell me, Brianna, did he want to sell you anything in particular?"

"Well, he showed me an enormous dyed black pearl and wants to become my supplier, but I turned him down because I use only genuine Polynesian blacks."

"Yes, Brouillet's pearls, as I recall. But if this Severin does antique jewelry, why is he selling dyed pearls?"

"That's what I've been wondering, too. He claims it's a sideline, but I don't know if I believe him."

"It sounds very, very strange to me. If I were you Brianna, I would be careful. The man's legitimacy is doubtful."

The words gave her a sinking feeling. "If Lucien Pillet has dealt with Mr. Severin, it is possible that he's all right though, don't you think?"

"Possible, yes. But I would talk to Lucien personally before drawing any conclusions."

Brianna recalled that Louise Frachet had been rather vague about Nick. Her own feelings of uncertainty grew. "What do you think I should do? Maybe there's someone else I might talk to."

"Perhaps I can help. Let me make some inquiries on your behalf. I will investigate this man. Call me again tomorrow. I may have news for you."

"That's very kind, Mr. Rosenthal, but I hate to put you to any trouble."

"No trouble at all. Besides, this Mr. Severin interests me. How can he work in my field, and I do not know him? Very puzzling, indeed."

Brianna could see the man's curiosity was aroused, and he did seem concerned, though he couldn't feel nearly so anxious over the matter as she. "Thank you for your help," she said, feeling somewhat at a loss. "Thank you very much."

THAT EVENING Nick took Brianna to Chez Tatie, a tiny restaurant in the country. He looked devastating in a white linen suit and opened neck blue silk shirt. They sat at one of several tables squeezed onto a wooden deck adjoining a small frame house. The structure contained the restaurant and living quarters of the proprietor, a corpulent Creole woman with a happy disposition and a wonderful menu of home-cooked food.

Brianna ate stuffed crab, curried vegetables and tropical fruits and watched her charming companion, his face bathed in candlelight. Nick couldn't know the grave doubts about him that Henri Rosenthal had elicited. He chatted away as though nothing was amiss.

Brianna was torn. She wanted to believe that Nicholas Severin was what he represented himself to be, but she was afraid that he wasn't. As regards business, she knew it really didn't matter a great deal—the purpose of their meeting, his pearls, was academic now. Nevertheless, she had grown to like Nick and hated to think he might be a phony.

For some reason her pride and judgment seemed to be on the line. It was important to know, one way or the other. Hopefully Henri Rosenthal would have some answers when she called the next day.

"You seem awfully quiet this evening, Brianna," Nick said with apparently genuine concern. "Are you all right?"

"Yes, I was just enjoying the setting, the air."

It was pleasant. All during the meal they had heard the bells of grazing goats in the surrounding fields and the ubiquitous singing frogs. Between the ever-present breezes, the pastoral sounds and the wine, Brianna had been lulled into a quiet, melancholy mood.

"I thought you'd like it." He sipped his wine.

"It's been a pleasant trip. I'm sorry in a way I can't stay longer."

"You weren't planning on going?"

"I was thinking of leaving tomorrow."

"You can't go so soon. Our discussions have only begun."

"So you keep reminding me. But frankly, Nick, I've got a business to run. I can't afford to wait on you much longer. If you've got an idea, a proposal, why not just come out with it?"

Nick looked around. "This really isn't the time and place."

"More stalling?"

"Brianna, you're so hard on me."

"You asked for it," she countered.

He smiled. "Maybe, but it's not entirely my fault. You see, it's the foreign influence. I've developed a taste for letting things develop slowly, for getting to know the people I do business with before entering serious discussions."

"What are you saying? That you haven't been serious yet?"

"Not as serious as I intend to become."

"Now that sounds ominous."

Nick laughed, his wonderful white teeth gleaming under his mustache. Brianna could see where his talents lay. He could squeeze out of a tight situation like an accomplished escape artist. She reflected. Maybe it wasn't just his skill. Perhaps the problem was that she wanted to believe him.

"You must admit," he said, "it hasn't exactly been your dull everyday business trip, now has it?"

"Oh, no, it's been delightfully unique."

"Sarcasm?"

"It's not been dull," she admitted.

"I don't deserve all the credit, or all the blame. Our little blond friend, for example, is none of my doing."

Brianna grinned. "*Your* little blond friend is no longer such a mystery."

Nick looked perplexed. "What do you mean?"

"I saw her today, in town, up close."

His face filled with surprise. "Oh?"

Brianna had waited expectantly to spring the news on him and was amazed at the apparent honesty of his reaction. Nothing in his eyes betrayed either foreknowledge or dismay. "Yes, I was in the post office, and I saw her in a phone booth."

"Really? How do you know it was she?"

"By the way she looked at me, primarily. And the way she reacted when I looked at her. I'm sure it was the same woman."

"Well, what did she do?"

"Nothing. Tried to ignore me after a while. But she knew that I knew. I'm sure of it."

"Did you try to talk to her?"

"No, I considered it, but I didn't see the point. I thought it might be enough to let her know she'd been exposed."

"Exposed as what? A voyeur or a lousy shot?"

"That's just it. We don't know about her for sure, but she's up to something. And it has to bother her that I've seen her face in broad daylight."

"I'm not so sure about that. She didn't sound like a pushover when she had the gun on us."

Brianna heard a hint of reproach in his voice and suddenly felt doubt about the way she had handled the matter. "Well, what was I supposed to do, call the police? You were the one who pointed out we have no proof against her."

"That may be true, but I think you should have grabbed her by the throat and given her what for."

She felt stung by his criticism. "Well, I didn't. Besides, she was French. It would have been easy enough for her not to understand me."

"I suppose so. I wish I'd been with you, though."

"What would *you* have done? Beaten a confession out of her?"

"Do I seem that sadistic?"

"Well, I think she's gotten to you." Brianna drank the last of her wine. "The whole thing seems crazy to me." She looked at him. "Including you, if you want to know the truth."

Nick called for the bill. "Come on, I think it's time to go home."

They drove back to Les Castelets mostly in silence. Brianna didn't feel good about their conversation, though she knew she couldn't really blame Nick. But even as she felt her resolve melting, she told herself to be patient, to keep up her guard. In twenty-four hours she would have talked to Henri Rosenthal again and would probably know whether it was even safe to talk to this man.

"HOW ABOUT A NIGHTCAP?" he asked when they had parked the Moke at the hotel.

"I'm pretty tired."

"I've got a nice cognac in my room. We could—"

"No, Nick. I'd rather not." She climbed out of the vehicle without waiting for him to come around.

They stood staring at each other in the moonlight. She could see him taking in her glossy black hair, her mouth, her eyes. There was regret on his face.

"Perhaps in the bar?"

He did seem to understand that it wasn't so much his company that was a problem. In public she could be with him, yet feel a measure of security.

"All right, then."

Inside they descended the spiral staircase to the bar. Except for an elderly couple in the far corner, the place was deserted. They sat by the window, and Nick ordered two Napoleon brandies.

"You really want to leave St. Barts?" he asked as they clicked their brandy snifters.

"I see no reason to stay."

"If the pleasure of my company isn't sufficient reason, perhaps I'd better try to entice you."

She smiled wryly. "Business seems to be your weapon of last resort, Nick."

"If so, it's only because of the personal friction between us."

"You're not used to having women resist, are you?"

"Is that what you think of me?"

"Frankly, I don't know what to think of you."

"It's an idle gesture to say so, I'm sure, but the truth is I'm rather fond of you. I'm just sorry it isn't a little more mutual."

He did seem offended. Or was it wounded pride? She suspected she liked Nick every bit as much as he liked her, but how could she admit that she didn't trust him, that she was half convinced he was a phony? Brianna sipped her cognac.

He gazed into her gray eyes, looking for all the world to be sincere. "Well?"

"Well, what? Am I supposed to be flattered?"

He laughed ironically. "I was hoping you would be."

"Don't beat around the bush, Nick. If you want to do business, you better tell me what you've got in mind."

He contemplated her. "All right. Tell you what. Let's compromise. I'll give you a general idea of the subject matter of my project, and tomorrow we'll go snorkeling at a secluded little beach I know. After a pleasant day in each other's company, we'll talk business."

Brianna looked at him, knowing instinctively it was the best she could hope for. "Okay, let's hear what you have to say. I'm not making any promises, though," she warned.

He looked her dead in the eye. "Brianna, you are interested in ancient jewelry. I know you inherited a fabulous collection from your father and that it is largely the inspiration of your creative work."

She waited, hearing the gravity in his voice.

"Actually, I don't give a damn about dyed pearls. That was only—shall I say—a test. My real interest is in museum-quality ancient jewelry. It's that common interest that brought me to St. Barts."

Brianna was confused by his statement. "Why didn't you come out and say so from the beginning? Why all the cat and mouse? I add to my collection from time to time. If you have some pieces to sell, why not just say so?"

"I don't want to sell, and I don't want to buy."

She shook her head. "What else is there?"

Nick regarded her. "Careful, Brianna. You're getting ahead of yourself. I've fulfilled my half of the compromise, now it's your turn. First we snorkel, then we talk . . ."

Brianna sighed in frustration. "Tell me, Nick, is there some method to your madness?"

He smiled. "What do you think?"

Chapter Seven

Brianna sat on the small sandy beach looking out over the water through Nick Severin's binoculars. Seventy-five yards or so out into the cove, near an outcropping of rocks, she could see his snorkel bobbing in the waves, then periodically disappear under the surface of the water.

Anse du Gouverneur was on the Caribbean side of the island at the foot of a steep cliff. They had driven partway there on a dirt track, but had descended on foot to the sea along a rocky path that was a discouragement to the faint-hearted. That explained why it was so unspoiled and secluded.

They had swum together for a while, but Brianna declined to go snorkeling, electing to sit in the sun instead. Nick had made one trip back to their camp on the beach, bringing her an assortment of gorgeous shells, then had returned to the water, leaving her to her thoughts.

They had talked briefly about the blond Frenchwoman, Nick conceding that the encounter with Brianna might have scared her away, after all. They hadn't been followed, he'd said, so she tried to put the woman from her mind.

Waiting for Nick, though, Brianna found herself scouring the cliffs with the binoculars. She observed the boats that passed by the cove, or circled into the mouth of it before heading back out to sea. One sailboat glided into the small bay, dropped anchor and spent a quiet half hour as the three young men on board ate a leisurely lunch on deck before setting sail again.

Brianna put down the binoculars and enjoyed the warmth of the sun, thinking about Nick's curious comment that his true interest was in ancient jewelry. What could he have in mind, if it wasn't buying and selling? What an unusual, beguiling man he was, and what a bizarre few days she was spending with him.

She couldn't help wondering what it might be like if he were just an ordinary fellow, a lawyer like her ex-husband, the owner of a hotel, a business executive or an airline pilot. What sort of relationship might they have?

Despite the peculiar events of the past two days, Brianna knew she was very attracted to him. There hadn't been much other than the kiss in the surf, but she had little doubt there would have been a great deal more if she had permitted it.

What rotten luck! Why had she been sent a man she neither understood nor trusted? Though she preferred not to think about it, much worse might be said of Nick Severin before her adventure was over. She looked at her watch and wondered if Henri Rosenthal had had enough time to have checked up on Nick.

Propping herself up on her elbows, Brianna noticed that a small motorboat had moved into the cove and was approaching the rocks near where Nick was snorkeling. Picking up the binoculars, she focused on the craft and could see that it had a single occupant—a woman—though Brianna couldn't tell what she looked like since she wore a hat and was facing away from shore.

Brianna searched the surface of the water, looking for Nick's snorkel, but it was nowhere in sight. The boat was very near the rocks, and it looked as though the occupant might be trying to land on them. A moment later she could hear the faint sound of the boat's motor as the craft maneuvered in for a safe landing.

Once again, she trained the glasses on the woman who, in shifting her position, now faced toward shore. Her features suddenly came into view, and Brianna's heart stopped. It was the Frenchwoman she had seen in the post office the day before!

"My God," she mumbled and anxiously scanned the surface of the water again, wondering what had happened to Nick and whether he, too, had seen the boat.

Meanwhile the blonde had managed to jump onto the islet. Although the boat was half hidden from sight, Brianna could see her securing the lines.

So she hadn't given up, after all! But what could she want with them now? Obviously the pearl wasn't with them on the beach. And she was clearly unaware that Nick was in the water, near where she had landed.

Wanting to be less conspicuous, Brianna looked around and, seeing some shrubs at the edge of the narrow beach behind her, scampered back into them.

When she had settled into her hiding spot, she raised the binoculars and was surprised to see nothing but barren rock. Were it not for the corner of the boat bobbing behind the barren outcropping, Brianna would have thought the woman had gone. There was still no sign of Nick, and Brianna began worrying that something might have happened to him.

Her anxiety was mounting just as the woman's head reappeared over one of the rocks. The Frenchwoman was scouring the shore with binoculars from her vantage point in the bay. Brianna smiled at the irony of the observer being observed. Still, she worried about Nick. Where was he?

While the mutual observation was in progress, Brianna suddenly saw Nick's snorkel. He was on the side of the islet opposite where the boat was tied up and the Frenchwoman had concealed herself. Brianna saw him lift his head from the water and swim to a low rock.

Moving her binoculars back to the blonde, Brianna could see that she was unaware of Nick's presence. Shifting back to Nick, she saw him climb onto the rock. Brianna's heart began beating wildly. The two people out there were not thirty feet apart but were completely oblivious to the presence of the other.

Nick shaded his eyes with his hand, apparently trying to find Brianna on the shore. He looked directly toward her but apparently couldn't spot her in the undergrowth. She watched as he turned and started climbing to a higher rock, probably to get a better view of the beach.

Meanwhile the Frenchwoman was looking off in the opposite direction, her binoculars to her eyes, still oblivious to Nick's presence. Switching her vision back to the man, Brianna saw that he had nearly reached the highest rock, above and behind the blonde.

By this time Brianna's heart was beating so rapidly she was having trouble breathing. Quickly she switched back and forth between the two unwary actors, knowing that a shocking discovery was about to occur.

Nick was on the highest point of the islet and was just starting to stand upright when he froze. He had spotted the woman behind the rock below him, not twenty feet from where he stood!

Brianna held her breath as she saw Nick squat down, looking for all the world like a cat ready to spring on the unsuspecting woman. He inched his way down the rock. Then, suddenly, the blonde spun around, and Nick leaped down beside her. He grabbed her by the shoulders. She twisted away and began scampering up the rock. He reached for her, but she slipped from his grasp. Then he lunged, grasping her ankle.

The blonde kicked at him, trying to escape, but Nick held tight, crawling up the rock after her. He was hunched over at her feet, ready to stand up and grab her again, when the woman brought her binoculars down sharply on his head. Brianna gasped as Nick crumpled to the rock.

The Frenchwoman bent over the prostrate man, looking at him. Nick didn't move. Then the woman scanned the shoreline again. Could she be looking for help?

Spontaneously Brianna sprang from her hiding place and dashed down to the water's edge, but the blonde was again bending over Nick, examining him. As Brianna watched, the Frenchwoman descended the rock to her boat. A moment later she cast off.

Brianna didn't know what to think. Was he dead? Or was the woman satisfied to leave him alive but wounded? All she knew was that she had to get to him.

She heard the motor fire to life, though at a distance the sound was faint. The boat began moving away from the islet. Lifting the binoculars from her neck, Brianna focused on Nick's motionless body. She couldn't see his face or tell whether he was breathing.

"Nick!" she called, but the sound was swallowed by the sea, her voice no more discernible than the random cry of a gull.

IN THE WATER it seemed a terribly long way to the rocks. Brianna was not a fast swimmer, but she had endurance. She knew she would make it.

By the time she got to the islet, she wasn't sure whether she would find Nick dead or alive. Whenever she had looked up during the swim, she hadn't seen him sitting or standing. She feared the worst.

Fatigued, Brianna climbed onto the rock Nick had first stood on, then hurried on rubbery legs up to where he had fallen. When she got there, he was lying on his back, rubbing his head. Seeing her loom up suddenly, he flinched.

"God, you scared me," he said, blinking.

"Are you all right, Nick?" She bent over him.

He shook his head as though he was trying to clear it. "What hit me?"

"Your lady friend—with her binoculars. I saw it from shore."

Nick was on his elbows, and Brianna slipped her knees under his shoulders to support him. She looked at the lump on the top of his head.

"There's a little blood on your scalp. It looks like a cut."

"I feel like I was hit with an axe."

"What happened out here? I saw you scuffling with her."

"I asked her what the hell she was doing. Obviously, she didn't take kindly to the question." He sat up, rolling his head as if to make sure everything was intact. "If I'd known her binoculars doubled as a tomahawk, I'd have been a little more subtle."

"Did she say anything?"

"Yeah. 'Get your blankety-blank hands off me!'" He grinned through his pain. "Admittedly, a little is lost in the translation."

"At least you haven't lost your sense of humor."

Nick slowly got to his feet, Brianna helping him.

"How am I going to get you to shore?" she asked.

"I'll swim."

"You don't seem in any condition for that."

"I'll be all right. My head's clearing."

"I think you'd better rest first."

He grinned. "I just had a nap. I'm fine."

"Some nap."

"Let me just splash some water on my face."

She went with him back down to the flat rock. Nick bent over and splashed his face with water. Then he dangled his feet into the sea. "Yeah, I'll be okay."

"Maybe it'd be better if I went for help. You can stay here, and I'll have a boat come for you."

"No, I'm okay, Brianna. I really am." He reached up, took her hand and squeezed it. "Thanks for rescuing me."

"I didn't exactly rescue you. I was afraid you were dead. Thank God she didn't try to finish you off or something."

Brianna put her hand on Nick's shoulder, feeling very protective of him just then. He no longer seemed threatening to her. To the contrary, she almost felt like holding him in her arms.

"Maybe it was for a good cause," he mumbled. "At least now we've both had a good look at her."

"She's attractive, isn't she?"

"She has nice ankles. That's what I saw best." He gave a little laugh. "And she sure packs a wallop."

"Why is she doing this, Nick? What's she up to? She didn't come here for the pearl."

"No. That's true."

"This is the second time it's turned violent," Brianna said. "She's deadly serious about whatever she's doing. I think we've got to go to the police."

"On what grounds? Assault? She'd probably accuse me of attempted rape or something."

"You aren't going to just let it go again, are you?"

"I don't know. I'm not sure what I can do. I imagine, though, we won't see any more of her."

"Seems to me you've said that before."

"Well, if she hadn't had those binoculars in her hand, I'd have found out what she's up to. She can consider herself lucky, I guess."

Brianna laughed. "I think you're the one with the luck."

"Well, let's get back to shore before she returns with reinforcements."

Her eyes widened. "You think there might be others?"

"I don't know. The whole business is strange. One thing for sure. If there's a next time, I'm going to get to the bottom of this."

"I still think we should go to the police."

"Naw. It was my head that got bashed. I think we're better off forgetting it." Nick picked up his snorkel and slipped slowly into the sea. He tread water for a moment, then looked up at Brianna. "Come on in. The water's fine!"

AT BRIANNA'S INSISTENCE, Nick agreed to have a doctor in Gustavia look at his head. She went with him, but since the conversation was entirely in French, she couldn't tell what was said. Something told her, however, that the actual cause of the injury was not related. The doctor was most likely left with the impression Nick had slipped on a rock while snorkeling.

"What did he say?" she asked as they walked out.

"To get some rest and take two aspirin. The usual prescription for about anything that's not terminal."

"If you're going to be laid up, maybe I'll do some more shopping. Would you mind if I stayed in town?"

"No, but this time, if you see the blonde, you'd better be prepared."

"Sure. Now that you've softened her up, she'll be no match for me."

Nick laughed, slipped his arm around Brianna's waist and gave her a squeeze. "We make a hell of a team, don't we?"

"Yeah, the Bonnie and Clyde of St. Barts."

He smiled down at her endearingly. "Can I drop you off anywhere?"

"No, thanks. I'll walk."

As she moved along the crowded street alone, Brianna thought about the ever more puzzling situation she found herself in. Nick's fight with the blonde was disturbing, but his reaction to the event was even more disconcerting. When a violent crime occurs, people go to the authorities. What was wrong with him? What was he hiding?

THE CLERK AT THE HOTEL stood up when Nick walked into the office for his key. "Oh, Monsieur Severin, I'm glad you have returned."

"What's up?"

"Two things. First, you had a call from London. A Mr. Havergill. He wants you to call him urgently. And second, the police have been here asking for you."

"The police?"

"Oui, monsieur."

"What did they want?"

"I don't know. For some questions, I believe. They said they would be back later. It didn't seem terribly urgent, but when they asked how long you would stay, I said you could be leaving at any time."

Nick smiled. "You did well." He took a five-hundred-franc note from his wallet and handed it to the clerk. "You deserve a little bonus. I'd like a favor, though."

"Oui, monsieur. À votre service."

"Have a maid pack Miss Wells's things for her and deliver the bags here, to the office. I want to call London, then I'll be checking out for both of us in about twenty minutes. And could we discreetly arrange to switch Mokes? A different color, a different license."

"Bien entendu, monsieur. Please. Use the telephone in the private office."

Nick went into the adjoining room and dialed London.

"Nick, I'm glad you called," Havergill said excitedly. "I think Brianna Wells may be our girl!"

The words sounded strange, somehow unexpected. "Oh? How so?"

"I had a curious phone call from New York this morning. A man named Henri Rosenthal rang up, asking about you."

"About me? Who's Henri Rosenthal?"

"A Frenchman, a dealer in antiquities living in New York."

"What does he have to do with this?"

"That's the point. Out of the blue he asks if I've had occasion to meet a chap named Nicholas Severin. Naturally I was so shocked I was caught sputtering."

"What did you tell him?"

"I said the name was familiar, but I couldn't place you. Then I asked why he was inquiring. He claimed he has a colleague who's involved in a business negotiation with you, and that you were unknown to them. He said you dealt in gems and, since I was familiar with most of the people in the business, I might have heard of you."

"Then what happened?"

"I realized that their side was checking up on you, so I started remembering little pieces of information that would make you look legitimate. Naturally I didn't say anything about our relationship, or our little program. I told him you were a legitimate dealer who ran a discreet one-man operation. I made it clear that so far as I knew you were reputable."

"What do you make of it, Tony?"

"I think it was coincidental that he happened to pick me to call...."

"You're well-known throughout the world. It should be no surprise."

"Yes, perhaps reputation worked to our advantage. In any case, it's beginning to look to me like your Brianna Wells and Mr. Rosenthal are—what is it you Yanks say?—in cahoots."

"Well, what do you know about this guy Rosenthal?"

"He's a fairly small but reputable dealer who's always been around the fringe of the big deals in the industry. Frankly, I don't know him terribly well. I've already made a couple of calls checking up on him and intend to look into the bloke's past pretty thoroughly now. How's the plan going with the young lady?"

"Which plan?"

Havergill laughed. "Our plan, not your personal one."

"I've hit a snag, I'm afraid."

"What's that?"

"Brianna doesn't trust me. I'm having a hell of a time overcoming her doubts."

"It may be her feminine honor she's protecting."

"Unfortunately, it's that, too. But what I'm really concerned about is our scheme. It won't work if she doesn't trust me."

"Have you hit her with the proposal?"

"I'm trying to work up to it carefully, so as not to spook her. The problem is, there's another fly in the ointment."

"What's that?"

"The cops."

"The French police?"

"The local *gendarmes*."

"Whatever for?"

"I don't know, but I think it has to do with a Frenchwoman, the blonde who's been on my tail ever since Brianna Wells showed up."

"The one who took a shot at you?"

"Yeah. This afternoon she was packing a pair of binoculars instead of a pistol. Unfortunately, this time she nailed me."

"Nick, what can I say? There's no allowance for combat pay."

"Believe me, I wasn't planning on it, either. I came here expecting to be dealing with a sweet little white-collar criminal and ended up with this blond bombshell who seems intent on taking my scalp home on her belt."

"Her what?"

"Never mind. She's messing up my job. That's all that matters at the moment."

"What might she be up to?"

"I just don't know. I thought maybe she was with the other side, possibly without Brianna's knowledge, but the involvement of the cops has thrown me for a loop."

"It's risky, but maybe you should cooperate with them. It may shed some light."

"I don't know if I have the time. I'm going to have to speed things up and hit Brianna with our proposal before everything blows up in my face, or she skips on me. She's skittish already."

"Well, she may calm down if this Rosenthal chap puts in a good word. When will I hear from you, Nick?"

"I'm going to have to change hotels because of the cops, so you won't be able to reach me here."

"It's a small island; you won't be able to hide for long."

"That depends upon how badly they want to find me. I don't think they regard whatever they're up to as urgent. I've got a day or two at least, I think."

"Well, hang on, chum."

"Right, Tony. It looks like it's coming down to whether I can get through to Brianna before the police and this crazy Frenchwoman get through to me."

RENIER ET CIE was as cool and inviting as it had been the day before. Fortunately the manager was equally accommodating. Brianna nervously placed her call to Henri Rosenthal in New York.

"Sorry, my dear, but I've made a number of calls, and I haven't been able to turn up a thing on this Monsieur Severin."

Brianna felt her heart sink. "Nobody's ever heard of him?"

"No one that I've spoken with."

"Lord. Do you think he's a phony, a con?"

"That I do not know. I've only begun, though. Perhaps I'll turn up something later. I shall continue to look into it."

"You've already done so much, I couldn't expect to—"

"Not at all, Brianna. I have, shall we say, a personal interest in this. But tell me, have you learned any more about him?"

"Yes, as a matter of fact. The business with the dyed pearl was apparently only a subterfuge. Last night he told me that his real interest is in ancient jewelry, museum-quality pieces."

There was a silence on the line.

"Mr. Rosenthal?"

"Brianna, are you sure about this?"

"Yes. It surprised me, too, considering that's your field and you've never heard of him. I was hoping you would have turned up something—that he was legitimate after all."

"Did Mr. Severin say whether he was in the market to buy or to sell?"

"I asked him that. He said neither."

"Then what does he do as a dealer?"

"I don't know."

More silence. "Brianna, I think it is very important that you find out all you can about this man and his plans."

"What do you mean?"

"If this man is no good, if he is perpetrating a fraud on our industry, I think it is very important that you discover what you can, for the benefit of those of us who *are* reputable."

"Do you think that's what he's up to? Something illegal?"

"I don't know, my dear, but you are in a position to find out. Please discover what you can and let me know what you learn. Will you do that?"

Brianna suddenly felt trapped, frightened. Instead of getting better, things seemed to be getting worse. "Well, I'll try, but Nick hasn't been very forthcoming so far."

"Surely he'll explain his purpose."

"He said he would today. I'll be seeing him soon."

"Excellent. Call me when you learn something."

She sighed. "All right."

"Remember, Brianna, I am a friend."

Chapter Eight

Brianna walked out of Renier et Cie and virtually into the arms of Nick Severin.

"Nick! What are you doing here?"

"There was a little problem at the hotel, so I thought I'd better come and pick you up."

"What sort of problem?"

He took her arm, and they went around the corner to the street fronting the harbor. "There was a mix-up in our reservations. A large group off a schooner was coming in today, and we had to vacate our rooms. I'm supposedly a valued client, so I wasn't terribly pleased."

"How strange. You'd have thought they'd have said something before now."

"Yeah, my sentiments exactly."

"We'd better go pack."

"That's been taken care of. I hope you don't mind, but I had a maid pack your things. I was so angry I just wanted to get the hell out of there."

She looked at him with suspicion and dismay, though Nick didn't seem to notice.

"It's okay, though," he added, "Alain has room for us at the Taiwana. I've called and made arrangements."

They crossed the boulevard to the parking strip along the docks. Nick led Brianna to a blue Moke.

"This is a new car. What happened to the yellow one?"

"It broke down. I had to get another."

"Oh?" She shot him a glance, wondering. New hotel, new car—it all seemed rather suspicious. After Henri Rosenthal's comments, Brianna suspected everything about this man. But now she had another mission: to learn what she could. She gave him a sympathetic look and climbed into the Moke. "What a day you've had. Hit on the head, lost your room, car breaks down. What else can go wrong?"

Nick jumped into the driver's seat. "I'd rather not think about it." He lifted the canvas over the back seat and looked at their bags. "Fortunately everything's still here. You can check over your things when we get to the Taiwana." He started the engine and backed out of the parking space. "How'd the shopping go?"

"Fine."

He glanced at her. "You must be pretty indecisive."

"What do you mean?"

"Two straight days of shopping and not a postcard to show for it."

Brianna laughed, realizing she should have thought to pick up a little something. "When I'm in a place for a few days, I do a lot of browsing, then I buy toward the end."

"I guess that means you'll be around a while longer."

She glanced at him, not liking the way he always seemed to pounce on her mistakes. "By the way, how did you find me? How did you know I'd be at Renier's?"

"It was a guess. I figured you wouldn't be able to resist having a look at the competition. It was the second place I tried."

They had gone through the town and were climbing the hill above the harbor, just passing the spot where Nick had stopped the first day to let her take a picture. What a crazy few days it had been. She looked over at him, studying the handsome visage that intrigued her so. But she was thinking about Henri Rosenthal's request for help in finding out what Nick was up to.

Brianna knew that if it weren't for Nick's enormous appeal, she might already have taken her bag and headed for the airport. Instead here she was, letting the man take her off to still another place under even more bizarre circumstances.

"I don't suppose you saw the little French karate queen?" Nick asked, breaking the silence.

"No, not at all."

"You didn't double-cross me and go to the police by any chance, did you?"

Brianna looked at him in surprise. "No, why would I do that?"

"I just thought you might have taken matters into your own hands."

They had reached the ridge line, and a strong breeze met them, blowing the ebony tendrils of Brianna's hair across her face and fluttering the Moke's canvas top overhead.

"What makes you think I would have done something like that?" she asked.

He gave her his warm, wonderful smile. "I don't know. You seem a little withdrawn, as though something is wrong."

"Nothing's wrong. I've just been thinking."

"What about?"

"Your interest in ancient jewelry."

"Ah. So I've finally piqued your curiosity, eh?"

"Yes," she said, smiling, "you finally have."

"Wonderful. When we get to the Taiwana, I'll have Alain bring us a bottle of his finest chilled wine, and we'll have a long talk."

"Great." Brianna turned and looked at the distant horizon on the sea, sensing that her worst fears would soon be realized.

IT WAS TWILIGHT by the time they had settled into beach chairs at the edge of the sand, as the warm breeze rustled the palms overhead and the first stars began to show in the darkening sky. Brianna looked at Nick. His head was resting against the back of the chair, his expression relaxed as he looked out at the sea. He seemed content, not at all sinister.

She turned her wineglass in her hand and took a little sip from it, feeling nervous, anxious. What was the man up to?

"Let's talk about your proposal," she said, trying to act casual, even though she wanted to blurt out "and get this over with!"

"All right. It's time that I get very candid."

He hadn't yet said anything, but his serious tone gave Brianna a great sense of relief. Perhaps now she would find out what she needed to know.

"I've been playing with you," he admitted. "I couldn't risk coming right out with my real purpose in wanting to meet with you. I had to know the kind of person you were, how tough you were."

She waited, feeling the tension.

"Some associates and I have embarked on a major enterprise involving potential earnings in the hundreds of thousands of dollars." He rolled his head toward her. "Brianna, we'd like you to join us."

"What sort of enterprise?" She heard her voice quiver.

"There is a tremendous market for antique jewelry, especially ancient museum-quality pieces. We intend to supply that market. We have all the elements in place, except one—the master designer. That's where you come in."

"Me?"

"Yes. We need someone with exceptional talent and skill of course, but more than that someone who is both tough and discreet. Discretion is absolutely essential. That's the reason for the business with the dyed pearl. I had to know you had judgment, that you could resist an easy buck, that you could remain coolheaded." He smiled. "Obviously, you passed."

"What is it, exactly, that you want me to do?"

"We're aware of what you've done in your design work—the replication of antique pieces through lost wax castings, your antiquing skills, the use of authentic materials—these are all essential. You're talented, and your skills are both rare and remarkable.

"Museums routinely do replications, but not with the accuracy and precision of your work. There are probably no more than half a dozen people in the world who can do what you do . . . at least with your degree of skill."

"Thanks for the flattering words, Nick, but you still haven't said what you want me to do. If it's restoration, you need a technician, not a designer."

"It's not restoration we're interested in."

Brianna had a sinking feeling. "Then what?"

"We want you to replicate original pieces."

She stared at him, and their eyes locked. Neither moved. "You want me to do forgeries?"

"Rather indelicately put, but that's the gist of it."

Brianna blinked, turning to the darkening sea. She had expected something like this, but now that he had uttered the words, she was stunned. Nick Severin's purpose in asking her to come to St. Barts was to invite her to participate in a criminal conspiracy. She swallowed, the disappointment she felt far stronger just then than her indignation.

"I don't do replicas," she said flatly. "Sure, I copy the elements of original pieces, but my designs are all original."

"I realize all that. But the skill is there. If you can do the elements, you can do the whole."

Brianna didn't respond, she just looked at him, realizing that Nick Severin was in fact too good to be true. He was a con man, a criminal, after all. The handsome face, the seductive charm, even the attention and flattery were directed toward one goal—seducing her into his criminal ring.

Brianna suddenly felt sick, both disillusioned and resentful. She had an urge to jump to her feet and run away.

"I know this is a lot to throw at you," he said calmly, "so why not mull it over, let it sink in? I think it's obvious enough that the money will be astronomical, even by your standards. Hundreds of thousands of dollars will soon become millions. This will make you fabulously wealthy. It will make all of us fabulously wealthy."

She sat listening against her will. She remembered Henri Rosenthal's words: *"If he's perpetrating a fraud, discover what you can for the benefit of those of us who are reputable."* That's what it had all come down to, exposing Nick Severin for what he was.

"Who else is involved in this?" she asked.

"My associates must go unnamed for the time being."

"That's asking an awful lot of me, isn't it . . . joining up with people I don't even know?"

"You know me."

"Do I?"

"Don't you trust me?"

"I've heard so many stories from you in the past few days that it's hard to know which one to believe."

"I had to be careful."

"Isn't that just as true of me?"

"That's why I wanted to be friends, Brianna. This sort of undertaking requires trust." He reached over and took her hand.

She looked down at the fingers caressing hers, repressing the tremor that went through her. Though she didn't want to, she left her hand there, permitted the affection.

For the first time her resentment was tinged with hatred. The man would stop at nothing. Unable to endure it any longer, she finally pulled her hand away. "Somehow I get the feeling," she said bitterly, "that you measure trust by the degree of my physical interest."

"No, it's not a requisite of your participation, if that's what you mean."

"Then why the seduction? You've been coming on to me from the minute we met at the airport."

Nick gave a little laugh of annoyance. "Isn't it possible that my feelings might be genuine? I do like you, Brianna."

She had all she could do to keep from angrily rebuking him. "Well, I've always kept my business and pleasure separate. I see no reason why that should be any different now."

"If that's what you prefer . . ."

Neither spoke for several moments.

Nick turned to her. "When can I have an answer to my offer?"

"You haven't given me much to go on."

"At this stage ambiguity is essential."

"Well, I may as well tell you, then. I'm not interested in your scheme, Nick. Thanks, but I'm going to pass. Maybe things are just too good for me as they are."

"I wish you'd think about it."

"I have."

"Sleep on it."

"Okay," she said, getting to her feet, "I could use some sleep. It's been a rough day." She handed him her glass. "Good night, Nick."

He watched her go, then turned back to the water. The moonlight reflected on the surf, and the sky was nearly dark. It was a beautiful setting, nearly perfect.

Severin felt badly about the conversation, felt like a heel. But his actions had been fated long before she had ever gotten off the plane, and the few days he had spent with her had only made things harder. This deal was a tough one, and staying on track had never been more difficult than with Brianna Wells. The irony was that the only truth he had uttered was the one she least believed—he did in fact like her very, very much.

BRIANNA HARDLY SLEPT. She wanted to get away from Nick Severin as fast as she possibly could. It wasn't simple hatred. It was fear. He was a beautiful, seductive creature, but he was treacherous and dangerous, too. She wasn't safe around him.

She had tried hard to do the right thing. Henri Rosenthal had requested her cooperation, and she had done what she could. In the morning she would call Henri, tell him what she had learned, and leave St. Barts, and Nick Severin, forever. Thank God she had learned what kind of man he was before she had succumbed to him. Thank God she hadn't been weaker.

Although Brianna dozed off and on, it seemed as though dawn came before she had truly gotten to sleep. She thought about calling Henri Rosenthal and realized that getting into town would not be easy. Maybe she would take her chances and call from the hotel.

There were no phones in the room, so it would mean going to the office, which was just a corner of the restaurant building. The important thing was to make the call without Nick's knowledge. Perhaps with the rough day he'd had yesterday, he would sleep in.

She rose, quickly dressed and walked down toward the beach. The sun had not yet risen, and the air was fresh. The only sound apart from the surf was the chatter of birds in the trees.

The sole person around when she arrived at the thatched restaurant building was the young man who had shown them to the room the day they had come for the swim. His English was not good, but Brianna managed to get across her request to use the telephone.

She reached Rosenthal at his home, waking him up. "I'm sorry to call so early, Mr. Rosenthal, but I've got important news." She related the gist of Nick's proposal.

Judging by the silence with which her news was met, she decided Rosenthal was stunned. Recovering, he began a barrage of questions. "Have they begun? How do they propose to operate? Who will they sell to?"

"I'm afraid Nick didn't divulge very much," she explained. "I tried to learn what I could, but he put me off. He said it was a question of trust."

"Did you act interested?"

"No, of course not. I wouldn't get involved with that man for anything."

"That may be the problem. If you're going to find out more, you've got to give him a reason to trust you, Brianna."

"What are you suggesting? That I agree to join his gang?"

"Ma chérie," he lamented, "it wouldn't hurt to give him hope, would it?"

"Mr. Rosenthal, why are you so anxious that I find all this out? Isn't it enough that I learned he's a crook, part of a forgery operation? Isn't the rest a matter for the police?"

"Yes, the police should be informed eventually, but the more you are able to learn, the easier it will be. After all, it is in our interests that this sort of thing be stopped, *n'est-ce pas?*"

"I've already told him I'm not interested."

"That's natural enough. You, too, would be cautious. Perhaps now you can show some interest in the proposal. My guess is that he would be more—how do you say?—forthcoming."

"I was planning on leaving this morning."

"Please, talk to him again. Then return to your home. Call me from St. Thomas, and we will discuss what to do with the information."

Brianna was reluctant, but she could see how important Rosenthal thought it was. "Okay. One more conversation, but that's all."

She hung up, feeling very confused and upset. It was too early for breakfast, so she wandered out onto the sand and slowly began walking up the beach.

NICK SEVERIN WAS AWAKENED by the sun coming in his window. He touched his head, still tender from the blow he had taken the previous day. The night had been a fitful one for him. Guilt and anxiety had been the principal ingredients of his dreams.

Severin expected that Brianna would have come around by now, shown a little interest in his proposal, but she was holding fast to her Little Miss Innocent act. She was either Academy Award material, or something was wrong. Whether it was her suspicion, her fear, or possibly her innocence, Severin wasn't sure, but the answer would come soon enough.

He decided that Anthony Havergill would probably have something on this guy Rosenthal by now. It would be good to find out what he had learned before seeing Brianna again. With luck there would be something he could use.

Severin dressed and went down to the restaurant, telling the young man on duty he wanted to make an overseas call.

"This must be the day for calling abroad, *monsieur*," the clerk said in French. "The young lady has already been down to make hers."

"Oh? Where'd she call?"

The young man checked the register. "New York, *monsieur*."

Probably phoned Rosenthal, Nick thought. He wondered whether her shock at his proposal was so profound that she had to share it with her partner. He smiled cynically and placed his call to London.

"Nick," Havergill enthused, "that call I got from Henri Rosenthal was the damnedest stroke of luck! We've been working frantically on it since I last spoke with you. It seems old Henri is turning up connected one way or another with every forgery we've checked out."

"In what way, Tony?"

"In most cases it's pretty obscure and indirect; that's why we overlooked it before, I suppose. In only one instance did he actually participate in a sale, and then only as a sub-agent. But he is always lurking around in some role, whether as an appraiser, a consultant, a dealer of other pieces in a collection, whatever."

"So what do you make of it? Do you think Brianna is his partner, the master designer of the enterprise?"

"It could well be, but you ought to have a better feel for that than I do."

"I hit her with phase two last night—told her about the scheme."

"How'd she react?"

"Coolly. Gave me the 'I'm not interested' routine."

"I'll wager she's not sure what to make of you. Could it be she's distracted by your amorous behavior?"

"No chance of that. I don't know whether I'm losing my touch, or what."

"Maybe the money you offer will be of greater interest than your infamous charm. Anyway, mate, it's the result that counts."

"The money doesn't seem to be turning her head any more than I do."

"Well, no matter. We've learned a hell of a lot. At least now we have something to go on."

"Looks like she and Rosenthal are in this together," Nick said a bit somberly. "She called New York early this morning."

"They may be concerned about the competition."

"Maybe I've spooked them."

"I don't see how. She has no idea what side you're on—what you're really up to. Rosenthal hasn't rung me up since the first time. I see no reason why he would suspect anything, either, even though he caught me a little flat-footed on that first call."

"What do you think they'll do, Tony?"

"I suspect they'll want to find out as much about you as possible. The main thing is not to scare them."

"Do you think I should continue to try to recruit her? She has no idea who I am or the fact that we're on to them."

"I suppose she'd be suspicious if you didn't keep at it. No doubt you'll find some way to sustain her interest."

"I'll do my best, Tony," Nick said grimly. "I just hope that's good enough...."

Chapter Nine

By the time Brianna made it back to the Taiwana, the sun had already risen above the rocky point of land at the east end of the bay, and Nick Severin was sitting on the terrace having coffee and croissants.

"Well, look who's come in with the tide," he said good-naturedly. "And all this time I thought you were sound asleep in your cozy little bed."

"Morning, Nick."

"Sleep well?" He got up to help her with her chair.

"Not particularly."

"Oh? What's wrong?"

"You and your scheme."

"My proposal?"

"Yes."

Nick rubbed his chin, looking a tiny bit smug, as though he was expecting capitulation.

"I've been thinking about it," she said.

"And?"

"I'd like to hear more."

"I thought you might come to your senses."

Brianna wanted to smack him, but she smiled sweetly instead. "It has nothing to do with senses, Nick. It's just that a person in my shoes can't afford to make the wrong decision."

"Nor can one in mine."

"Yes, I suppose we've got that much in common," she said darkly. "Last night, if I was abrupt, it was because I didn't know whether I could trust you. I still don't, as a matter of fact."

He leaned forward and covered her hand with his. "What do I need to do to convince you?"

"Why don't you begin by laying out the details of your proposal?" She watched him contemplate her, knowing he was questioning whether she was to be trusted.

"There are a variety of things we're considering. In cases where we have access to valuable collections, we'll switch pieces—put the replica in place of the original, then resell the stolen piece. In other situations we might peddle the forgery directly. That would be easier when we're dealing with private collectors, of course."

"You'll need the participation, or at least the cooperation, of legitimate dealers to do that."

"You're right. And we do."

"Who?"

Nick smiled. "Secrets are best kept when the left hand doesn't know what the right hand is doing."

"What happened to trust?"

"Trust is important only when it's relevant. You don't need to know who our marketing people are. Your job would be production. All that matters as far as you're concerned is that we've got the horses to do the job."

"Sounds like you've got it all worked out."

"You're all that's missing."

"If I were to agree to something like this, I'd be taking a tremendous risk. How do I know you're for real?" she asked.

"You don't."

"We've got a dilemma then, don't we, Nick?" She was smiling, but she hated him for disappointing her, for playing so casually with her feelings. At least she'd have the satisfaction of contributing to his undoing. By the time she was finished here, she'd have more than enough information for Henri Rosenthal to make that call to the police.

"This might sound rather unprofessional under the circumstances, but what I said about liking you was the truth."

"I never doubted it," she said simply.

"You say that, but for some reason you're not very convincing," he said ironically.

"First it's a problem when I don't believe you. Now it's a problem when I do."

Nick reached for her hand again, but she pulled it away. She gestured toward the waiter, who was bringing her a cup and saucer, coffee and a fresh basket of croissants. When the waiter had gone, Nick brushed her cheek with the back of his hand.

She eyed him warily. "Don't you think it would be better to keep this on a business plane?"

"I thought now that we trust each other, we can let our feelings show."

She pointedly pushed his hand away. "I don't see what one has to do with the other."

Nick looked annoyed. "Okay, if it's to be all business, that's fine with me." He leaned back, his hands clasped behind his head. He looked as handsome as ever, but there was a trace of contempt on his face.

She hated him for being so attractive, so devious. "Why are you looking so smug?"

"Smug?" he asked with surprise. "I'm not feeling smug at all. Actually, the opposite. I was feeling rather regretful just then."

"What about?"

"About what we've missed, you and I."

"What *have* we missed?"

"Alain asked me last evening if you were my mistress."

"What did you tell him?"

"That we were just business associates."

"At least you don't lie to your friends."

Nick gave her a wry grin. "But it did get me to thinking how unfortunate it was." He looked at her wistfully, his soft brown eyes seductive.

"You never give up, do you, Nick?"

"It bothers me that I was wrong about you."

"What do you mean, that my price doesn't include a roll in the hay?"

He sat upright, his mouth stretching into a hard line. "Is that all you think I have in mind?"

"You're trying to buy my talent. What's the difference—my talent, my body?"

"Maybe you're the one who should answer that question," he snapped.

Brianna's eyes rounded. "You bastard."

He smirked. "Well, at least our views of each other have become clear."

"Yes, well, all's well that ends well, if you get my meaning. Hopefully, the matter of our *friendship* will not be discussed again."

"All right, let's get on with it, then. Are you interested in my proposal?"

Brianna couldn't help glaring. "I haven't decided."

"When, pray tell, will you decide?"

"When I'm good and ready!" She took a croissant from the basket and rose to her feet. "Now if you'll excuse me, I'd like to get cleaned up." She turned from the table.

"Brianna!"

She stopped a few steps away and looked back.

"I'm going snorkeling out by the point this morning," he said in a measured voice. "When I get back, we can have lunch. I'll expect your answer then."

She spun on her heels and headed back to her room.

SEVERIN TRUDGED up the beach, his snorkeling equipment dangling from his exhausted arms. He loved the water, being alone in the sea. This trip to St. Barts was supposed to have been a quick little diversion, a combination of business and pleasure, an opportunity to get away from the chilly damp air of Paris and eliminate another person on Anthony Havergill's list. Instead it had turned into a confounding and frustrating experience.

There had been the wonderful tropical air and water, but Brianna Wells was not at all what he had bargained for. The biggest surprise was that she turned out to be not just a name on a list, but the person he had been seeking. The second surprise was that she was intriguing, fascinating, and had thoroughly seduced his emotions, even as he was discovering her true colors. What a god-awful mess.

"Voilà!" Alain said as Nick came up on the terrace. "It's going to be a lonely lunch today, *mon ami.*"

"What do you mean?"

"Your Mademoiselle Wells packed up and left in a taxi two hours ago. And the *gendarmerie* called about our guest list that was lost. I won't be able to delay for you any longer, my friend. I've got to tell the police you've been here."

"Never mind that. Do what you have to. Where did Ms Wells go?"

"I assume to the airport. She used the phone to call there, I know."

"Damn. Do me a favor, Alain. Call the airport and see if she's booked on a flight. I've got to get dressed and see if I can find her before she goes."

Nick ran to his room, quickly showered and dressed. Alain was waiting when he came out.

"She tried to get on a flight to St. Thomas, but it was fully booked. Then she tried to get on one to St. Martin. They've put her on standby, but the reservation clerk, who's an old friend, told me he thought she was going to try and get the catamaran from Gustavia to St. Martin. It would be the quickest way for her to get off the island."

"I think I'll head for Gustavia then."

"Bonne chance!" Alain called, but Nick was already jogging toward his Moke.

BRIANNA HAD BROWSED through practically every shop in town, nervously looking at her watch, worrying about safely getting off the island. She certainly had gathered plenty of information for Henri Rosenthal. She hoped that he would appreciate it, because there might end up being a price. Since fleeing the hotel, Brianna felt a clear sense of danger.

She had killed as much time as she could in a dress shop just across from the port and was about to go out the door when she saw Nick Severin drive by in his blue Moke. Her heart stopped.

She watched him turn into the dock area. Obviously he had come looking for her. She felt a surge of fear and tried to control the panicky feeling that welled up inside her.

Why couldn't he just let her leave in peace? Then it occurred to her, for the first time, that it might not be so easy for Nick to let her walk away. After all, he had disclosed his plans for a criminal conspiracy. He couldn't feel terribly comfortable having her running around with that sort of damning information.

Too late she was beginning to see it had been a mistake to bolt. She should have played him along until she was able to get safely away. It would have been wiser to have kept his confidence.

But what would he do now? Would he be capable of violence? He couldn't very well use force with her, not as long as she was in public. On the other hand, maybe it wasn't safe to assume anything.

Brianna wondered if she ought to go to the police. But if she did, what story would she give? To accuse Nick of trying to entice her into a criminal conspiracy might create more problems for her than it solved.

She could picture provincial police officials, who probably spoke limited English, listening to her outlandish accusation. It would be easy for Nick to refute her story. And if they did take what she said seriously—and if Nick were held—she, as his accusor, would probably have to remain in St. Barts, at least for a while.

The most telling point of all, however, was that it would be just her word against his. She could almost imagine the story he could make up about a lover's quarrel, and her need for revenge. She really had no proof of his criminal plans.

Brianna decided not to involve the police unless Nick tried to harm her. She would stay in a public place until the catamaran was scheduled to leave for St. Martin. The best place would be somewhere crowded. A few doors down was the Select Café. Every time she had passed by, it seemed to be buzzing with activity. With a cautious glance toward the docks, Brianna headed for the bar.

FOR A LONG TIME she sat at a table under a ceiling fan in the funky old café, its walls strewn with posters, signs, pictures and other memorabilia. The crowd, jammed around the tables and up to the bar, was a mixture of locals and tourists, mostly younger people. The high noise level and jovial camaraderie gave Brianna a feeling of security.

She had been there half an hour, midway through her second soft drink, when Nick Severin suddenly appeared in the doorway, his face grim. Spotting her, he walked through the crowded room toward her table. Brianna's heart leaped.

Steeling herself, she waited, not knowing what to expect.

"That wasn't very polite, running off without saying goodbye."

She glanced up, trying to mask her fear with a show of annoyance. "We both had said what we had to say. I couldn't see any point in waiting around for more of the same."

Nick sat down, not waiting to be invited. "So I take it you're not interested."

Brianna stammered. "I . . . I haven't decided."

"You expect me to believe that?"

"Does it matter what I say? You seem to do what you want, anyway."

"You might be happy leaving things as they are, but I'm not."

"What do you mean?"

"I mean I haven't had my say yet, and you're going to hear me out whether you like it or not."

She looked around, hoping to find a friendly face, someone who might come to her aid if Nick got out of line. But no one seemed to be paying any attention to what was going on.

Just then, over Nick's shoulder, Brianna saw a familiar face. The blond Frenchwoman was standing in the doorway. No sooner had their eyes met than she stepped back, out of sight.

Seeing Brianna's expression, Nick turned around, but the woman had already disappeared. He turned back to Brianna questioningly, but her expression had returned to normal. Perhaps it had been a trick. "I know you're leaving on the catamaran, but before you go, you've got to hear what I have to say."

She waited, seething.

"First, I apologize for the way I acted this morning. I shouldn't have toyed with you. I was being a bastard, and I'm sorry."

"Well, that's an improvement."

"I know you're feeling very hostile right now. And it's obvious enough that you don't care much for me. But I don't want you to miss an opportunity just because of my involvement.''

''I don't consider anything you're involved in to be an opportunity.''

Nick winced at her sarcasm. ''Look, it isn't essential that you deal with me. Your contact can be someone else in the organization.''

Satisfied that he was there to plead his case, not harm her, Brianna decided to lay her feelings on the line.

''Nick, I'm going to give it to you straight, right from the heart. The truth is I'm not interested in you, your organization or your... business proposal. As far as I'm concerned, I don't want to see you again or hear anything about this scheme of yours.''

Nick was surprised at the stinging rebuke. He glanced around, wondering who she was trying to impress. Why the self-righteousness? Was it more acting, or had he misread her? Knowing he didn't have but a few minutes, he decided to pull the last trick out of his bag.

''Listen,'' he said, looking her straight in the eye, ''we've been dancing around each other like a couple of polecats since you arrived. Maybe it's time we both stop dishing out the bull and get down to facts.''

''What's this, a whole new story I'm about to hear? Version of truth number three?''

''Quit being so damned sarcastic and listen to what I have to say. It's no accident that I singled you out and arranged this meeting on St. Barts. And no, it's not your skill alone that prompted it. I would have been a fool to walk in blind and propose what I did.''

''You're right about that, anyway.''

He smirked. ''We chose you, Brianna, because we know you're already doing it. You've been making fraudulent replicas for months. We're also aware that you and your partners have been peddling them as authentic pieces—essentially the scam I proposed to you.''

Her mouth fell open. ''I've what?''

''Oh, come on, you don't have to keep up the act. We've seen your work, and we know you're good. But we also know you've been misused. Whoever handles the marketing in your group isn't worthy of your talent. We can do better; that's why I came to St. Barts. We can make you a much better deal than you're getting now.''

Brianna was shaking her head. ''Nick Severin, you're crazy! I don't know what you're talking about. I'm not a criminal!''

The last words were a good deal louder than she had intended. Nick looked around and saw several heads turned their way. ''For God's sake, Brianna . . .''

''No, I don't care who hears. I want to know where you got this absurd story. First that pearl business, now this. Accusing me of being . . . a crook!'' Her eyes flashed. ''I resent it, Nick. I resent it greatly!''

''Look, let's go somewhere and discuss this quietly.''

''I have absolutely nothing to discuss with you.'' Brianna stood up, her face flushed. ''And I'd appreciate it if you'd leave me alone. I never want to see you again!''

With that she spun around and stepped past the bar to the enclosed patio. Realizing she could not exit that way onto the street, she turned. But behind her the café had fallen silent.

Brianna followed the turned heads to the main door and saw two *gendarmes* standing in the doorway. They walked through the hushed room toward Nick. As they asked him for identification, Brianna shrank behind the other patrons standing at the bar. From her vantage point she could see the police standing over Nick, but she also saw the blonde waiting at the doorway, a hint of triumph on her face.

All at once things began falling into place. The police knew about Nick's criminal plans. The blonde following them had been no accident, she was working with the police. As Nick rose, the officers took him by the arms, and they walked from the café.

Brianna turned to the bartender. "What happened? Did they arrest that man?"

"*Oui, mademoiselle*. He was arrested."

Chapter Ten

Brianna's home was on Water Island, just outside the port of Charlotte Amalie on St. Thomas. The house was little more than a cottage really, with only a single bedroom. But the living room was large and comfortably airy with two ceiling fans always turning overhead. A terrace surrounded the structure on three sides and afforded a magnificent view of the open sea.

The morning after her flight from St. Martin, she lounged around, feeling a tremendous sense of relief, but also a strange sensation of emptiness. She was glad to have the bizarre escapade with Nicholas Severin behind her, but she also felt disappointment.

The man was a low-down crook, but he had been terribly likable despite their conflicts. Even though his motives were bad, even though he was deceitful, Brianna had to admit she'd found him appealing. Nothing in the world could have induced her to join forces with him, either personally or professionally, and yet she felt sorry for him.

The only obligation that remained now was to call Henri Rosenthal and inform him of what had happened. It would be the concluding chapter of the episode, the last thing before she could begin putting Nick Severin from her mind.

For a while Brianna walked aimlessly around her house, wandering out onto her flagstone terrace, which was at the top of a rocky cliff fifty feet above the sea. She stared out at the Caribbean and the familiar vista that she loved. But for some reason it seemed wanting. Though she had happily lived alone for several years, that day Brianna felt lonely. She knew it was because of Nick. It was ridiculous, but it was true.

Though she realized it did her no good to be melancholy, Brianna had trouble getting herself up for the phone call. But she continued languishing on the terrace until she was summoned by the telephone itself, which rang unexpectedly inside.

She went to her bedroom to answer and was surprised to hear Henri Rosenthal on the line. There seemed to be a touch of anxiety in his voice as he explained that he was away from New York for several days and thought he'd best call her, since she wouldn't be able to reach him.

"What did you learn about Mr. Severin's operation?" he asked eagerly.

"He was arrested, Mr. Rosenthal. Isn't that enough?"

"Well, I'm curious. Didn't he relate any more to you?"

Brianna told him about the scheme for marketing forgeries.

"Audacious plan, wasn't it?" Rosenthal said thoughtfully. "Do you think it would have worked?"

"I suppose that would have depended upon the quality of the replicas and their skill in selling them."

"Yes, yes. Amazing what people come up with, isn't it?"

"Well, our interest was in protecting the industry. I guess we accomplished that," Brianna said stoically.

"You think the police were on to Mr. Severin?"

"I assume so. It seems as though he was under surveillance the whole time I was with him on St. Barts."

"Curious they didn't try to speak with you, my dear."

"They probably would have if I'd stayed around. I might even have been arrested, too. It was more important than ever to get off that island. Frankly, I just wanted to come home and forget about the whole thing. Fifteen minutes after Nick was arrested, I was on the catamaran for St. Martin.''

"Perhaps it's just as well. You accomplished what was necessary from our point of view, *n'est-ce pas?*"

"Yes, I guess so."

"In any case, my congratulations to you, Brianna. I am grateful, and I know others in the industry are, as well."

"Thanks."

"You know, I've been thinking, perhaps I ought to buy you lunch sometime when you're in New York. I haven't seen you in quite a while. It would be a way for me to express my appreciation."

"That's very kind, but not really necessary."

"Not at all. I'd like to. It would give us a chance to talk about our work. And you can update me on your collection. We can compare notes. After all, if an outsider like Mr. Severin appreciates your talents, maybe I've been overlooking something. I mustn't be remiss by failing to appreciate what's right under my nose, *n'est-ce pas?*"

"You're very kind."

"I'm serious now. Please call me when next you're in New York. Promise?"

Brianna couldn't help smiling at the man's insistence. "Yes, certainly." She hung up, not feeling notably better despite Henri Rosenthal's compliments.

After wandering around her empty house a while longer, Brianna decided she had to shake free of the funk she had fallen into. Even though she had planned to take the day off before returning to the shop, she realized that the best tonic was work, not rest. After bathing and dressing, she went to catch the ferry for Charlotte Amalie.

Sylvie was happy to see her.

"Brianna, you got some sun. You look wonderful! How was the trip?"

"Don't ask. It's one adventure I'd rather forget."

"The pearl was not good?"

"The pearl was a fake, and Nicholas Severin was a phony."

"What a shame. At least you got to see the French islands. What did you think of St. Barts?"

"The island was beautiful. Fortunately, it wasn't entirely spoiled for me."

"So this Mr. Severin, he was terrible?"

"Yes. Terrible, and wonderful in a way. But in the end a big disappointment."

"Ah," the young woman said, her dark eyes sparkling, "it was one of *those* experiences."

"What do you mean?"

"Oh, Brianna, don't you know I can tell? Was he romantic?"

"Sylvie!"

The girl laughed. "*Mon Dieu*, he was!"

"He might have tried, but I didn't cooperate."

Sylvie was smiling broadly. "Did he kiss you?"

"Well . . . yes, but it was accidental."

The girl giggled.

"It was! We were swimming and a wave knocked me into his arms. That's all."

"And he kissed you before the sharks could get you?"

"Oh, Sylvie, I wish you wouldn't tease me. It was really a miserable experience."

"What happened?"

"I'll tell you some other time . . . when I've recovered." She went behind the display counter and looked in the glass. "How have you been?"

"Oh, fine. Actually, I've met someone, too." Her expression turned coy. "But fair's fair. We'll exchange stories later."

Brianna could see that Sylvie had turned the tables on her. "All right, then. How was business while I was away?"

"Not bad. I sold a necklace and a few smaller pieces."

"Wonderful. Which one?"

"The one inspired by your pre-Columbian collection."

"With the irregular pearls?"

"Yes."

"That style seems pretty popular. Who was the buyer?"

"A couple from a cruise ship. Philadelphia."

Brianna patted Sylvie on the arm and went back into her private office. "Anything else happen?"

Sylvie stood in the doorway. "*Tiens*. I almost forgot. You had a call this morning from a French gentleman. A Monsieur Pillet. He sounded very old."

"Lucien Pillet?"

"Yes, there's a note on your desk."

Brianna picked up the slip of paper. "He's here in St. Thomas?"

"Yes, he said he wanted to see you. I told him I didn't expect you until tomorrow. He asked that you call."

Brianna picked up the telephone and dialed the number of the Frenchman's Reef, where Lucien Pillet was staying.

"Oh, Miss Wells," the room clerk said, "Mr. Pillet is gone for the day, but he asked that I give you a message if you called."

"Yes?"

"He says he will only be in town until tomorrow, and he would like very much to see you this evening. He is having dinner with an old friend from Paris at her home on Water Island and asks if he might come by to see you afterward."

"Yes, certainly. That would be fine. Tell Mr. Pillet he may come by any time this evening." Brianna gave the address and hung up, curious why Lucien Pillet would want to see her.

WHEN CLOSING TIME CAME, Brianna wasn't anxious to rush home to a solitary meal, so she invited Sylvie to go out with her for a quick dinner. The two women walked over to the Twiins Restaurant on Garden Street and had a light meal in the patio garden. While having a drink before their dinner, Brianna told Sylvie what had happened on St. Barts.

"What an adventure you had! *Quelle chance*. Me, I go to the Indies all the time and never do I meet a man like this."

"But you said this morning you have met someone."

"It's a very different sort of relationship. It's a quiet thing. But then you know how strange I am about men." Sylvie looked a little sentimental. "Ones like Nicholas Severin never come into *my* life."

"Be glad, Sylvie."

"Oh, but he sounds so wonderful."

"He's a thief."

"But such a romantic one."

Brianna shrugged. "He's in jail now. And since I didn't know him well enough, it's all the same to me." Even as she said the words, she knew it wasn't true.

Sylvie smiled ironically. "I don't know who is sadder—you or me."

After they had finished and Brianna bid her assistant good-evening, she went to the ferry and headed for home. It was just getting dark when she entered the front door. In a way she was glad Lucien Pillet was coming over. She didn't feel like being alone.

Brianna dropped her purse on a rattan table in the entry and went into the living room that was furnished with twin yellow chintz couches and wicker chairs with plump white cushions. After turning on the ceiling fans, she strolled out onto the terrace to look at the sea and the fading sunset, a favorite relaxing pastime.

Stepping to the railing, she drew in a deep breath, feeling the melancholy return almost immediately. There was sadness in the air, but there was something else, as well, something ominous. Brianna felt a presence, an alien force. Instinctively she turned around.

Someone was standing in the shadows at the far end of the terrace! Brianna clutched her hand to her mouth, letting out a little involuntary scream as the man stepped toward her into the light. It was Nick Severin.

"Nick! My God, what are you doing here?"

"Hope you don't mind," he said, lifting the glass in his hand, "but I fixed myself a drink." He stopped next to her and leaned his elbows on the railing, looking out at the sea. "Nice place you've got here."

"How did you get in? I thought you were in St. Barts. I thought—"

"I was in jail?" He smiled and sipped his drink. "I guess it would be trite to say there's no prison strong enough to hold me. I'm sure it's not true, although I'm not exactly experienced in that regard." He turned toward her, taking in her features that were still filled with perplexity. "The fact of the matter is our conversation was interrupted. I hadn't finished what I'd gone to the café to say."

Brianna weakly leaned against the railing. "Nick, you scared me to death. Why are you here? Did you escape?"

He laughed. "No, I was released as soon as I got things straightened out. It was a misunderstanding."

"A misunderstanding? You mean it wasn't because..."

"I'm a thief? Fortunately it wasn't that. It was the Frenchwoman. She accused me of assault—that incident when we were snorkeling."

"Assault? But she assaulted you! What about that shot, and holding us at gunpoint?"

"She denied all that."

Brianna looked thoroughly confused. "I don't understand. I assumed they arrested you because of your forgery scheme."

"It's plausible, but that wasn't it. Actually, I was lucky. They were following me, but they had no case. Once they realized that, and I cleared up the assault charge, they released me. But if it had happened a few hours later, my goose might have been cooked."

"What do you mean?"

"Brianna, this isn't a social call. I need your help."

She could tell by the weighty tone of his voice that he was serious. "What's happened?"

"After I left the *gendarmerie*, I tried to contact my associates in France. I discovered to my dismay that they had been called in for questioning. I knew it was just a matter of time before the police would be looking for me. I couldn't go back to France, and I couldn't stay on St. Barts. I need a friend, Brianna. So here I am."

"Aren't you assuming quite a bit, Nick?"

"We *are* friends, aren't we?"

"You're asking me to harbor a fugitive?"

"I'm not exactly a fugitive. At the moment I'm an American citizen in American territory, and it's only *possible* they're looking for me in France. There's no warrant or anything of that sort."

"You're quibbling details, aren't you? You and I both know what you were up to."

"It was just a proposal," he said innocently.

"It was a criminal conspiracy."

"Brianna, can't you give me the benefit of the doubt?"

She looked at the handsome face in the fading light, thinking she was done with it forever, and here he was, right back in the middle of her life. "You're asking too much."

He moved nearer. "Am I really?"

"You're a thief."

"A would-be thief."

"What's the difference?"

He eased his arm along the rail behind her. "I've never actually stolen anything."

"You intend to." She felt the warmth of his hand on her waist.

"Maybe if you act quickly, you can save me from a life of crime."

"Oh, it's up to me, is it?"

He was smiling as his mouth drew near hers. "After all, I tried to do you a favor."

"You mean by selling me a dyed pearl..." He was very near. "Or saving me from the sharks?"

In just the passing of a second Nick's lips covered hers, softly, pliantly caressing them. Brianna submitted to his kiss, accepting his affection, realizing how very much she had wanted him, but hadn't admitted it. She moved against him, feeling the length of his firm body along her own, liking his arms wrapped about her slender frame.

When the kiss ended, he looked into her eyes, touched the corners of her wide mouth with his fingertips, then tucked the loose tendrils of her black hair behind one ear. "I'm glad you didn't buy my pearl," he whispered.

"Didn't want it on your conscience?"

"No, that's not it. If you had, there'd have been no challenge left."

Brianna stiffened. "You don't think I still might do business with you?"

"No, that's not the sort of challenge I meant. I'm at your mercy now, don't forget."

"What kind of challenge are you referring to, Nick?"

"Of convincing you how much I really do like you." He kissed her lower lip. "Mmm. You do taste good."

Brianna drew her head back, looking at him. Slowly her face filled with skepticism. She turned away, slipping from his arms. "It would be awfully convenient for you now if I believed you, wouldn't it?"

"Brianna!" He reached out and took her arm. "You don't think I'd say that just because I'm in need at the moment?"

"Your record of credibility is not exactly overwhelming."

"Look, if that's what it comes down to, I'll turn myself in right now."

"Maybe that'd be a good idea. Maybe you should go straight, while there's still time. You do that, Nick Severin, and I might start believing you."

"Don't you think I ought to at least wait and see if I am wanted? I mean, why put people to a lot of trouble if no one is after me?"

"You know, Nick, you ought to sell used cars. At least you probably wouldn't get arrested."

He laughed and reached out, taking her into his arms again, pulling her even closer to him. "I like you a lot," he said, his wonderful mouth smiling, "maybe even enough to go straight."

His mouth was descending on hers again when the doorbell rang. They both turned.

"Are you expecting someone?" There was alarm in Nick's voice.

"Yes, I'd forgotten. It's probably Mr. Pillet."

"Lucien Pillet?"

"Yes. He's a friend of yours as I recall, or at least an acquaintance. Remember? You gave him as a reference."

Nick's face filled with consternation. "Why's he here?"

"I don't know. I had a message he was in town and he asked to see me. I haven't spoken with him yet."

"Look, Brianna. I think it's best that he not know I'm here."

"Why? He'd probably be pleased to see you, an old friend and all."

The doorbell rang again and Nick grimaced. "Please, Brianna. Trust me."

She turned to go inside. "Okay. You can wait in the bedroom."

He followed her through the living room to the bedroom. In the semidarkness Brianna could see a small suitcase—Nick's—on the floor by the bed. She waited until he had stepped inside, then closed the door, noticing that after she had turned away he opened it a crack, leaving it ajar.

Standing on the porch was a little wizened man with thinning white hair and intense, lively blue eyes. He was slightly hunched and carried a stick, but his energy was readily apparent.

"Brianna, *ma chérie*," he said smiling. "How are you? How are you?" His heavy French accent was very pronounced.

"Monsieur Pillet, it's so good to see you." She extended her hand, which the little Frenchman took energetically. "Come in, please."

She led him to the wicker chairs, and they sat, Pillet laying his walking stick on the floor beside him.

"Thank you for seeing me on such short notice, Brianna. I hope it's not an inconvenience."

"Not at all."

"Well, I was in the Bahamas, you see, and spoke with my secretary in Paris. She said you were ... trying many times to reach me. So I thought, Why not come to St. Thomas? I have friends here, and it has been many years since my last visit."

"I hope you came mainly for your friends, because the matter I called you on was not terribly important."

"It was in regard to a gentleman, I believe."

Brianna glanced toward the partially opened bedroom door. "Yes, your name was given as a reference, and I called to check on him. But any dealings we might have had are concluded now, so it's no longer an issue."

"Still, when I spoke with my secretary, I was—how do you say?—alarmed. It seems my name was used improperly."

"Oh?"

"*Oui*, Louise gave you information about this Monsieur ... was it Severin?"

"Yes, Nicholas Severin."

" ... about Monsieur Severin at the request of a police gentleman—or so Louise thought."

"Police?"

"*Oui, ma chérie.* You see a man called who said he was with Interpol. He spoke very good French, but with a slight English accent. He wanted to converse with me, but when Louise told him I was on an extended trip, he asked her to vouch for this Monsieur Severin if anyone was to call for a reference. She was a silly girl to take the word of someone on the telephone."

"Then you don't know Nick Severin?"

"*Pas du tout.* I never heard of him. Obviously this is very upsetting. I asked Louise to call the Interpol headquarters in Paris, to verify the caller, but they knew nothing of it. Naturally I was very suspicious, and I wanted to warn you."

"That's very kind, Monsieur Pillet. But it doesn't matter now. My... business with Mr. Severin is concluded."

"Still I am very curious, Brianna. What kind of business would require such deceit?"

"Since your name and reputation were so wrongly used," she said, with a dark look toward the bedroom door, "I suppose you are entitled to an explanation. Mr. Severin was trying to peddle French-dyed pearls as genuine Polynesian blacks."

"But this is a crime!"

"Well, in fairness, he never actually said they were genuine, but he led me to believe they were."

"But I don't understand. Why he would use my name. I do not deal in pearls."

"I think it was your reputation he wanted me to buy. Because my father had dealt with you, he assumed it would induce trust. He was right," she added ironically, knowing Nick was listening.

"*Tiens, tiens.* What people won't do."

"He definitely was a scoundrel."

"A what?"

"A deceitful man, totally untrustworthy."

Pillet shook his head. "So it seems. So it seems."

"I'm sorry," Brianna said in the silence that followed. "I've been a terrible hostess. May I offer you a drink?"

"Oh, I don't know. I had wine with dinner. But these tropical climates do make a thirst. Perhaps a little mineral water, if you have it, Brianna."

"Yes, certainly." She got up, stepping into the bedroom before heading for the kitchen. Nick was standing behind the door in the dark. "So," she whispered to him, "on top of everything else you arrange your own good references by posing as a cop."

Nick shrugged. "It worked, didn't it?"

She glared at him.

He took her by the shoulders, leaned over and kissed her on the end of the nose. "You're doing beautifully. Thanks."

"Don't get too complacent. I'm not finished yet." With that she stepped from the room and went to the kitchen to get Pillet's water.

In the refrigerator she found a bottle of Bollinger Brut champagne that hadn't been there when she'd left for the shop that morning. Smiling at Nick's audacity, she took a bottle of Perrier and closed the refrigerator door. After pouring Monsieur Pillet's drink, she returned to the living room.

"*Merci,*" he said, taking the glass and sipping the bubbly liquid. "So this Severin's pearls didn't fool you."

"There was more to his plan than just the pearls, Monsieur Pillet. Nick had a scheme in mind regarding ancient jewelry."

"*Ô, c'est vrai?* What sort of plans?"

"It was a forgery scheme to sell replicas as authentic pieces."

Pillet contemplated her. "A daring plan. But not very realistic."

"Oh, it might have worked. The market is very hungry for museum-quality pieces. An accomplished craftsman could have fooled a good many curators."

"You think so really, Brianna?"

"There would be risks, of course, but you know how easy it is to buy stolen pieces. People are so hungry they prefer not to ask questions. Only the best-known pieces would be suspect. But you know that better than I, Monsieur Pillet."

"Perhaps you are right."

"Nick wasn't stupid. That was hardly my complaint. He was deceitful and sneaky. Do you know the man actually thought he could charm me into his little scheme as though I'd just fall for him as easily as all those Parisian women?"

"You knew this sort of thing about him?"

"A woman can tell, Monsieur Pillet. Stolen kisses, bottles of champagne. The mark of a charlatan is easy to spot. Nick Severin was charming, but not charming enough. Maybe he wasn't smart enough, either. The last I saw him the police were leading him away."

"Really? He found—what is it you say?—a just reward?"

"Perhaps that remains to be seen." Brianna smiled devilishly, but the little Frenchman couldn't possibly know why.

Pillet took a long drink of his water and put down the glass. "Well, *ma chérie*, the hour is late for an old man. I have made my explanation, and you also have my apologies. I hope my secretary's mistake did not inconvenience you greatly."

"No, not at all. It was an interesting experience to see a con man at work, close up. It's an education every woman should have. Prevents more serious mistakes later."

"Yes, yes," he said, rising to his feet with the help of his cane, "I am sure you are right."

They went to the door.

"Do you need a ride to the ferry?"

"No, I will walk to the house of my friend. It's not far, and I like the exercise. I may be old, but I am very vigorous. She will see me to the ferry."

"If you're sure..."

"Yes, Brianna. I am sure." He smiled back at her. "We must keep in touch. I always admired your father's collection. Now that it is yours, I think perhaps we should share our appreciation for fine pieces."

"Yes, certainly."

"Bon soir." And Lucien Pillet disappeared up the walk.

Chapter Eleven

When Brianna returned to the living room, she saw that the bedroom door was shut tight. Under it she could see light. "It's safe to come out now," she called.

There was no response. She waited and called out again. "Nick?"

Still no response.

Brianna went to the bedroom door and opened it. Nick was lying on the bed in a silk robe, his bare legs and feet protruding, his furry beige chest exposed through the gap at the top. He was reading a newspaper.

Glancing up, he said, "You did damned well. Thanks. I really appreciate it."

"What do you have on under that robe?"

"Nothing. But don't worry. Since you're on to me, and so alert to my tricks, I knew there'd be no danger in relaxing and just being myself." He glanced again at the paper.

"That happens to be my bed you're lying on."

"I assumed it was. I didn't notice any others in the house, so—"

"If you think I'm going to share my bed with you, Nick Severin, you're sorely mistaken!"

He looked alarmed, but she could tell he was faking.

"You don't expect me to sleep on the couch?"

"I don't expect you to sleep here at all! I didn't blow the whistle on you when Mr. Pillet was here. That's all the generosity from me you can expect."

"Brianna, why do you persist in trying to sound like John Wayne? You might as well tell me you're giving me until sundown to get out of town."

"The sun's already set."

"Then shall we make it sundown tomorrow?"

"Very funny. Isn't your situation a little precarious to be making jokes?"

"I wasn't joking. Actually I was hoping you might let me move in for a while—at least until things blow over."

"Guess again, Nick."

He looked hurt. "Why don't we try and get things on a friendlier footing? You know there's a bottle of Bollinger in the—"

"Yes, I saw it. Thanks for the donation to my wine cellar."

He shook his head mournfully. "You can be so cruel when a guy's down." Tossing the paper aside, he got to his feet. "All right, I'll get the champagne." He walked toward the door, pausing as he passed to give her a little kiss on the cheek. "Where do you keep your champagne flutes?" he called over his shoulder as he left the room.

Brianna followed him. "Nick, you're not staying here."

"Let's discuss it over a glass of bubbly, shall we?"

She stood at the entrance to the kitchen with her hands on her hips, watching him looking through the cabinets. "To the right of the sink," she said with annoyance.

Finding the glasses, he put them on the counter and winked at her. Then he went to the refrigerator and took out the champagne. "Why don't you get into something comfortable while I open this up?"

"As long as you're in my house, I'm keeping my clothes on!"

"Brianna, do I look like a rapist or something? How many crimes do you think me capable of?"

"More than I can conceive of, I'm sure."

He looked thoughtfully at the label on the bottle. "You don't think well of me, do you?"

"Nick, let's stop the games. This is not funny."

He turned to her, put the bottle on the counter and a hand on his hip. The mirth was gone from his face. "Listen, I've tried everything. I've put myself at your mercy. I've begged, cajoled, defied. Everything but threaten. What do I have to do? Tie you up?"

"Why don't you just go away and leave me alone? That'd work. I guarantee it."

"Now *you're* being funny."

"Nick!" she implored.

He walked over to her, taking her gently by the arms. His soft brown eyes settled on her. "Is it totally unbelievable that I want to be with you—that right now all that matters is that I have a chance to make amends?"

"It's difficult to believe anything you say."

"You told Pillet that you understand men. I assume that includes me. But why are you so afraid of me?"

"I don't know."

"Surely you don't think that I'd hurt you."

"Not physically."

"What then?"

"There are other ways."

"You can't get hurt if you know what you're dealing with. Don't you see I'm trying to get to know you? Why do you suppose I came to St. Thomas? You think you're the only person in the world I could go to? No, Brianna, it's because we've got unfinished business that has nothing to do with pearls, ancient jewelry, or anything else."

She looked up at Nick, wanting to trust him, but knowing in her heart she'd be a fool if she did. Then he pulled her against him, and her nostrils filled with his pleasant masculine scent. He felt so very warm as he tenderly touched her, and she knew her resolve was weakening.

Lifting her chin, Nick kissed her lovingly. Brianna felt her insides spark to life, her latent womanly desires stirring. Putting her arms around him, she felt his muscles through the silk of the robe and knew she wanted him.

He reached back to the counter, carefully picked up the glasses and the bottle with one hand, slipped his other arm around her and led her back to the bedroom.

BRIANNA AWOKE EARLY. She was naked and next to a sleeping Nicholas Severin. Her head was throbbing slightly from the champagne the night before, but her body felt wonderful, exquisite. Nick was even a better lover than he was a salesman. Somehow she'd known it would be that way. Maybe that's why she had been so afraid.

She lay for long minutes, thinking about her situation. What should she do now? Fabulous as Nick was, the previous night hadn't really changed anything. He was the same man he had been before—at least as far as the rest of the world was concerned. He couldn't stay with her forever, pretending it wasn't so. They both would have to face facts.

Crawling carefully from the bed, Brianna slipped into the bathroom to take a shower. She wanted to be dressed when Nick awoke. To talk seriously with him about the future, she wanted to be the old Brianna, the one he had known before last night.

SEVERIN HEARD THE SHOWER running as he blinked awake. It took him a moment to figure out that Brianna was not beside him, that she was in the other room, bathing. He was alone.

Reaching for his watch on the bedside table, Severin saw that it was late. It was unlike him to sleep in. But then the previous night had not exactly been your typical evening. Now that it was morning, though, he felt uneasy about what had happened. He put on his watch, thinking about Brianna.

Things had gone according to plan—better even than he had hoped. And although seducing her had not been essential, he had done it, not for the gratification, but because he had wanted her. Ironically, last night he'd been the real Nick Severin, but she would never know.

Severin rose, slipped on his bathrobe and went into the kitchen. He didn't want to encounter her in the bedroom. Better he stay in here. Again he looked at his watch. They wouldn't have to spend much time trying to cope with what had happened the night before.

He wouldn't have to deal with her joy, recrimination, or embarrassment, whichever tack she chose to take, for long. He was grateful for that. He'd lived with about all the duplicity he could take for a while.

Severin found some instant coffee in the cupboard and put the teakettle on to boil. It had just started to whistle when Brianna came out, dressed in white pants and a lavender silk blouse.

"Morning, Nick," she said shyly.

"Don't you look beautiful! You put me to shame. Sleep well?"

"Yes. How about you?"

"Wonderfully. Care for some coffee?"

Brianna's eyebrow lifted as she sat at the table. "You'd think this was your place and I was the guest."

"I'm sorry. I didn't mean to be . . . presumptuous."

"Oh, that's all right. I'm not used to having anyone around in the morning. It's been a while since men have been a big part of my life."

Nick smiled at her warmly, but inwardly he winced. He sensed she was going to be sentimental, fragile rather than combative as he'd hoped. "I don't know why that is. I'd think you'd have to beat men off with a stick."

"Oh, I'll admit there is no dearth of opportunity. I guess I'm just particular."

He felt a sudden urge to apologize, but he held his tongue. No sense getting sentimental himself. After all, this was what he was paid to do. Severin glanced up at her from the coffee he was preparing on the counter. Seeing her pretty face and large trusting eyes, he felt miserable.

The doorbell rang, and he gave an inward sigh of relief.

"I wonder who that could be?" Brianna said, getting to her feet. She glanced at Nick, who shrugged, though there was, it seemed, a funny look on his face.

Brianna went to the door, opened it and was shocked to find three men in business suits standing on the porch. Behind them was a uniformed police officer.

"Brianna Wells?"

"Yes . . ."

The man nearest the door flipped open a leather wallet, revealing a badge. "Federal Bureau of Investigation, ma'am." He took some papers from his inside coat pocket. "We have a federal search warrant and a warrant for your arrest. May we come in?"

"My arrest?" Brianna took the papers, glancing down incredulously. She saw the official seal of the federal court in Puerto Rico and her name filled in on the form. The search warrant listed her address and the address of her shop in Charlotte Amalie.

"May we come in?" the agent repeated.

Brianna stepped back. "But for what reason? What have I done?"

"Grand larceny, fraud, criminal conspiracy, and so forth. The charges are listed there." The first man walked past her, and the second took her by the arm.

"Please step into the front room, Miss Wells."

Brianna dumbly went with the agents into her own living room. Nick was standing at the doorway to the kitchen.

"Are you Nicholas Severin?" she heard the first agent ask.

"Yes," he replied.

"You're under arrest, too. You'll have to get dressed and come with us for questioning."

Brianna looked at Nick. "What's this all about? Why are they arresting me?"

He looked at her glumly. "I hope you know a good lawyer. It looks like we'll need one."

"I can't believe this," she said mournfully, turning to the agent beside her. "I've done nothing. I've committed no crimes."

The man didn't reply. He stood stony-faced beside her, his hand firmly on her arm.

BRIANNA SAT in an interrogation room at the Government Building in Charlotte Amalie, her stomach in a knot, her brain a swirl of confusion. The principal agent, a man named Quillan, had been questioning her. Another man sat quietly nearby. She looked up at her interrogator.

"I've told you," she lamented, "I don't know anything about a forgery ring, except what Nick told me in St. Barts. That was the first time I'd ever heard about it. Talk to Henri Rosenthal in New York. He knows. I called him for advice. He knows all about it."

"Why would you call somebody in New York? Why not go to the police in St. Barts? Isn't it normal when people learn a crime has been committed to report it to the police? If you weren't involved, why didn't you go to the authorities immediately?"

"Well, I considered it, but I wasn't sure what Nick was up to. I didn't know for sure he was part of a forgery ring."

"But he said he was authorized to recruit you."

"He said that, but he said a lot of things. I didn't know what to believe. Besides, if I had gone to the police, it would have been just his word against mine. And I had no proof."

"Come on, Miss Wells, how do you expect us to believe a story like that? We walk in and find you with the man this morning. You spent the night with him, you've admitted that. If you suspected him of being a criminal, why not just call the police? I'm afraid your actions speak louder than words, Miss Wells."

Brianna lowered her head. "Perhaps I should have called the police. Maybe I did make a mistake. But Nick said he hadn't yet done anything. Maybe I was a fool to believe him, but that's no crime. You have no proof I've done anything."

"Maybe not in this particular incident. But we have a number of cases of theft and fraud under investigation, both in the U.S. and in Europe. We're aware of your involvement in those cases."

"But how could you be? I've done nothing, other than let Nick Severin stay at my house last night. He told me he might be wanted in France, but he said nothing about the States. Even the police in St. Barts let him go. I had no reason not to believe him."

"When your home and shop have been searched, there'll be more to talk about, Miss Wells."

"What? I have nothing that would incriminate me. I'm innocent. You've made a mistake."

Brianna could tell by the expression on the man's face that he didn't believe her.

"What will it take to convince you?" she pleaded.

There was a knock at the door, and another agent entered the room. "Mack," he said to Quillan, "Severin broke. He's admitted his involvement."

"Well, he didn't say anything about me," Brianna interjected, "because there's nothing to say."

The man looked at her. "That's not the story I'm getting, miss."

"Then Nick's lying!" She shook her head incredulously. "I can't believe this."

Quillan turned to the other man. "Get her a cup of coffee, Jerry. I'm going to talk to Severin."

NICK SEVERIN WAS SITTING on a desk with a cup of coffee in his hand when Quillan entered the room. "Are you sure you're right about this broad, Nick? She's showing no signs of bending. Chrisakes, she didn't even want a lawyer."

"We know she's talking to Rosenthal. She's got to be in on it. Did she deny that?"

"Hell, no," Quillan replied. "*She* brought his name up first, like that's supposed to exonerate her."

"Did you tell her we've got the goods on Rosenthal?"

"No, I was hoping she'd break when Don came in to announce the news about you, but she jumped on it like that ought to prove her innocence. I think you're wrong about her, Nick. I think she's clean."

"Damn. I don't understand it."

"Maybe it was just a coincidence she called this guy Rosenthal. I mean, he's in New York, and there can't be that many people she'd go to for advice or information about you."

"No, that's true. And she did try and reach the old French guy, Pillet. Of course, that's because I gave his name as a reference."

Quillan shook his head. "If you don't mind me saying so, I think you've screwed up, Severin."

"Hell, Mack, it all adds up. I gave you everything Tony Havergill and I had on her."

"Granted, it made sense."

"Maybe something will turn up in the search. She might just be tougher than any of us think."

"I hope you're right. But if you don't mind me asking, what are you going to do if the house and shop are clean?"

Severin sat rubbing his chin. "Maybe if we've got lemons, we can make lemonade."

"What are you talking about?"

"Assuming for the moment she is innocent, Rosenthal's aware of that too, right?"

"Yeah. So?"

"So maybe we can use Brianna to get to him."

"How do you mean?"

"We know that she's perfectly capable of making this fake stuff, right? And she does have a wonderful collection at her disposal. Hell, this old guy, Pillet, even commented on it last night."

"And?"

"If we're aware of it, Rosenthal has to be aware of it, too."

"Yeah, but what makes you think he'd want to involve her?"

"I don't know that he would," Severin admitted. "But, on the other hand, maybe Brianna could convince him. Maybe she could approach him with the idea."

Quillan shook his head. "For that you'd need her cooperation. I don't think she's very pleased with us at the moment. And you, I'm sure, she'd kill in cold blood."

"I don't doubt that, but things are a little different now. I'm a good guy, not a bad guy."

"Are you sure you understand women, Nick? She's got blood in her eye, and I don't think she'd walk across the street for you right now if you were the president of the United States."

Severin shrugged. "It's worth a try. Anyway, I look better in police blue."

"Let's don't get too highfalutin. You're just a private dick, remember?"

"Sorry, didn't mean to offend your federal sensibilities."

The agent smiled. "Go on in and talk to her if you want. But remember, if she assaults you, I'm going to look the other way. I may be facing a false arrest charge as it is."

"Mack, you'd sell my hide just to protect yourself?"

"Severin, if you've got the nerve to walk in and tell that girl the truth, you're either braver than hell or nuts. I'd tend to go with the latter."

Severin laughed and got up. "Wish me luck."

BRIANNA WAS ALONE in the interrogation room. The agent with her had been called out. What were they up to now? How long would this nightmare go on?

She rested her head in her hands, thinking of Nick. She couldn't believe that after the night they had had together it had come to this. Nothing made sense anymore—not since he had come into her life.

Brianna rubbed her head. Maybe the truth wasn't enough, maybe she ought to get an attorney. Obviously someone was trying to hang her. There had been lies, facts had been twisted. No telling what they might do, how far they'd go. It didn't seem likely she could go it alone any longer.

The door to the interrogation room opened, and Brianna looked up. She was shocked to see Nick Severin step in. He was alone. "What are you doing here, Nick?"

He sat across from her at the table.

"Why did they let you come in here?" she asked, searching his face.

"Brianna," he said somberly, "I'm not a thief, I'm a private investigator. I'm working with the police."

"A private investigator? You?" She stared at him incredulously. "I don't believe you."

"It's true."

She looked at the door. "I don't believe any of this. Tell that FBI agent to come back in here."

"Please, just listen to me. I'll tell you exactly what's been going on."

Brianna laughed derisively. "What's this going to be, version of the truth number twenty-three?"

"I know this has been like a comedy of errors, but you're going to hear it straight this time. I swear it."

She glared at him. "Very convenient that you come out with the truth now, isn't it? What was wrong with last night? That wasn't a very opportune time for you, was it? There was something you wanted first, wasn't there?"

"Please, Brianna, that wasn't it at all."

Her laugh was scathing. She rose and paced back and forth across the far side of the room, her arms folded across her chest. "If there's a lawsuit in this, I'm going to squeeze every drop of blood out of you, Nick Severin."

"Will you listen to what I have to say?"

"Why should I?"

"Because I want you to. I care what you think."

She laughed again.

"Last night it was me in bed with you, not a detective, not a thief. Just me, Nick Severin."

"And what was Nick Severin doing? Having his pleasure before poor little Brianna Wells was locked up and sent off to prison?"

"It's true I thought you were guilty. And I was trying to gain your confidence. Making love to you wasn't part of the plan. . . . It just happened."

"You poor boy. Just lost your self-control, huh?"

"Please don't deride me that way. I care for you, that's why I made love with you."

"Love 'em and arrest 'em? Is that it?"

Nick lowered his eyes. "Okay, I was wrong. I was weak. I was a fool. I was selfish. I took advantage of you. I deserve whatever you're going to dish out."

She gave him a weak smile. "Perhaps you are beginning to see the light."

He sighed. "Right now I'm not the issue, Brianna. I came in here to ask your help."

"Help? You have the nerve to ask for my help? All I want is my freedom." She put her hands on her hips. "May I go now?"

"Not until I tell you what's happened."

Brianna returned to her chair and sat down. "All right, but make this fast."

"Over the past year or so there's been a spate of thefts, switches, forgeries and other crimes involving ancient jewelry and artifacts in museums around the world. We don't know for sure how long it's been going on because bogus pieces have been turning up regularly. It's hard to know when switches were made."

"What's this got to do with me?"

"Whoever is behind it is operating worldwide. We're pretty sure it's a ring, involving several people. I was hired a few months ago by Anthony Havergill, the executive director of the International Association of Fine Art Museums in London, to help in the investigation. The various national police agencies were concentrating on the actual thefts. Tony Havergill's idea was to track down the craftsmen and work backward."

"And you thought I was the one?"

"Well, you were on a list Tony had drawn up. My job was to check out everybody he had identified. Frankly, you were one of the last people I investigated. There were a couple of suspects with criminal pasts, records. I started with them, but to no avail. I doubted you were the one until you started talking to Henri Rosenthal. Then I was sure we'd cracked the case."

"Henri Rosenthal? You think he's involved in this?"

"We've got a lot of circumstantial evidence, but we'd like something a little more substantial. We thought a confession from you would start the ball rolling."

"Sorry to disappoint you."

"Having been mistaken about you, we're at a bit of an impasse. The FBI and local authorities are investigating

Rosenthal thoroughly at the moment, but he's covered his involvement very well.''

Brianna was shaking her head in disbelief. "You mean all that business in St. Barts was trumped up to make me think you were a thief so I'd trust you? That woman, the police—all of that was a hoax?"

Nick laughed. "No, not exactly. It was a surprise to me, as well. For a while I thought the blonde was working for your side. I didn't know her."

"Who was she?"

"That's the funny part. Her name is Marie-Claude Tissot. She's a private investigator from Marseilles who had been hired by a consortium of international insurance firms to conduct an investigation very similar to the one Havergill hired me to do. As it turned out, she spotted me with a suspect in Milan and, not knowing me, thought I might be involved. She followed me to St. Barts and, when I met with you, she thought she'd cracked the case, just like I had."

"So she thought we were involved in this business together?"

"Yes. She was the one in my room that night, just as we thought. She was looking for evidence to use against me. Then, when we surprised her, she was afraid she'd blown the whole thing. But the fact that I didn't go to the police immediately convinced her she had the right guy. So she pressed ahead with her investigation."

"It never occurred to her you might be on the same side?"

"Apparently not."

"After the incident on the rock she decided time was running out on her, so she had the police pick me up for assault—to see if anything turned up in the interrogation. By the time she got around to looking for you—you were gone. It was an unfortunate case of the left hand not knowing what the right hand was doing."

"The police are prone to that as much as the thieves, I see," Brianna said sarcastically.

"We both felt pretty foolish by the time we got it worked out. She agreed to let me have the case, including you, which did give me a rather good excuse to come to St. Thomas."

"And complete your business?"

"Brianna, I told you what happened last night had nothing to do with this case."

"Better that it did. At least then it would have been for a good cause."

"But it *was* a good cause."

"Nick Severin's gratification?"

"It was wrong of me to let my personal feelings dictate my behavior; I've already admitted that."

"There'll never be enough contrition for that, Nick."

"Can't we think of the future and forget the past?"

"What future? Obviously not that of the dyed pearl merchant, he's gone. The forger? No, he's gone, too. The fugitive? No, he got what he wanted and dropped out. Let's see, all that's left is the detective. What does he want?"

"There is something that the detective wants, that's true. But Nick Severin is interested in something, as well."

"Nick Severin has had his. What does the detective want?"

"I'd rather talk about me first."

"Sorry, Nick, but I'm not terribly interested in you."

"What are you saying?" he said irritably. "That as a crook I was acceptable, but now that I'm a good guy, you're not interested?"

"Yeah. Maybe you blew it, Nick."

"You're never going to forgive me, are you?"

"What does the detective want?" she replied, ignoring his question.

There was a tense moment of silence.

"We'd like your help with Rosenthal."

"We?"

"Quillan, Havergill, me, the museum people, the insurance companies—everybody who's trying to put a stop to this thing."

"What do you want me to do?" Brianna heard the cooperation in her voice and realized Nick was in the process of getting his way with her again. She studied the face, trying to see him in the new light, to think of him in his new role. It did set a lot better with her that he was innocent, but she still doubted his motives, especially about what had happened the night before.

"We want you to infiltrate Rosenthal's ring, Brianna. Or at least get them to solicit your involvement. We've got to wedge an opening, break their shell."

"You're saying you want me to become a crook, or at least act like one."

Nick nodded. "Yeah, that's what it amounts to."

Brianna looked at his handsome face, the one that had seemed so deceitful and sinfully appealing from the day they had met. She couldn't help laughing.

"What's the matter?"

"Don't you see how funny that is, Nick? Things have come full circle."

He grinned, then reached over and touched her hand.

Brianna pulled it away. "But some things haven't changed."

Chapter Twelve

Brianna shifted in the soft leather chair. Mack Quillan was on the edge of the desk in front of her. Nick sat in another chair to the side.

"Miss Wells," the agent said apologetically, "we're deeply sorry about the mistake, and about the inconvenience to you. Obviously, nothing incriminating was turned up in the search of your home and shop. In our defense, however, it was not an unreasonable mistake."

"Considering the source of your information," she replied, "it's understandable."

Quillan glanced at Nick, though Brianna didn't bother.

"Mr. Severin tells me you want my help with your investigation," she continued. "But I don't know why Henri Rosenthal would be interested in recruiting me. He knows I'm not a criminal."

"Involvement in this sort of thing has a funny way of occurring sometimes, Miss Wells. People occasionally ease into these things, at first only peripherally, later more directly."

"What do you mean, Mr. Quillan?"

"Henri Rosenthal must know about your collection of jewelry and your skills as a designer...."

"Yes, he expressed an interest in getting together to discuss our work the next time I'm in New York."

"Excellent. There's your entree. You see, it's possible he might regard your pieces as potential stock."

"You mean to steal?"

"More likely to copy so he could peddle the replicas to the hungry market as authentic merchandise. It would be much easier to do with your cooperation. Under those circumstances your participation would be rather passive. But I doubt Mr. Rosenthal would be content to stop there.

"You have talent they could undoubtedly use. I'm not knowledgeable in such matters, but I'm told by the experts this group's workmanship varies. The more sophisticated the buyer, the better the work has to be. At times they've been a little shoddy. That's when we first got on to them, and that's where your expertise would come in."

"But how can you be sure Henri Rosenthal is involved in this? You thought I was, and you were wrong about me."

"What damned you in our eyes, Miss Wells, was your apparent involvement with Rosenthal. We've traced a close connection between him and many of the cases under investigation around the world. But we don't have enough yet to convict him."

"Yes, that's what Nick said. What, exactly, do you have on Mr. Rosenthal?"

"I'll need to know you'll keep any information I give you in the strictest confidence."

"Of course." She glanced at Nick, who sat quietly listening.

"It was almost accidental that we connected Rosenthal with the case. Actually, it was because of you."

"Me?"

"Yes. Apparently you contacted him to check up on Nick Severin. Rosenthal's suspicions were aroused over a dealer he'd never heard of before."

"That's true. Mr. Rosenthal told me as much."

"Yes, but he may not have told you that he contacted Anthony Havergill in London to check up on Nick. You see,

Tony is like the dean of the business, he knows everyone. When Rosenthal called, Havergill figured the two of you had to be working together.''

"And Tony related this to me in St. Barts," Nick interjected. "When they started checking up on Rosenthal, they found he was involved in some way in virtually every theft, usually in some remote capacity so that he wasn't at all obvious. Naturally, I assumed you were in on it, too."

"Mr. Rosenthal never told me he'd talked to anyone about you, Nick. Every time I spoke with him, he said he couldn't get confirmation you were legitimate."

"That's not too surprising. If you told him about the scheme I'd proposed to you, he was probably very curious who else might be getting into the business. He probably wanted to keep you suspicious of me. The odds of his getting good information from you were better so long as you were kept in the dark."

"That's probably true. He did keep after me to find out more and was always full of questions."

"You see, he didn't have just a casual interest in what I was doing."

Brianna shook her head incredulously. "So Rosenthal is up to the same thing you'd proposed to me in St. Barts?"

"What we think they're doing," Quillan continued, "is getting their hands on pieces from various museums, duplicating them and switching the real piece with a replica.

"For example, an Egyptian necklace was stolen from a museum in Britain. Although Rosenthal never dealt with the piece, he did handle a swap with a Japanese museum for another item in that collection.

"In the process of working with the objects involved, we speculate that he managed to get access to the necklace long enough for his craftsman to examine it, take measurements, match materials and so forth. The whole thing may have happened in a hotel room over a weekend."

"And that's only an example," Nick added. "In some cases he may have been called in for an appraisal. But he's been careful not to steal the item he was commissioned to work on. That would be too obvious. It's always something else he manages to get ahold of."

"Incredible," Brianna said. "I don't know him well, but my father always considered him reputable."

"In his direct dealings he is," the agent replied. "He's able to do this because of his stature and reputation, so he's very careful. He'll slip up one day, and we'll catch him, but we'd like to hurry the process along if we can. That's why we'd like your help, Miss Wells."

"I really don't think he'd believe me if I went to him with some kind of proposal."

"But it does make sense," Nick said, "that you'd go home after your experience with me and think about the scheme, knowing you could make a lot of money with comparatively little risk."

"Won't he wonder why I'd go to him? After all, I supposedly don't know he's a crook."

"You'll have to be subtle. Plus there's a good possibility he's already thinking of you in those terms himself. Look how hard he has to work to get his hands on good pieces to forge. You're a potential gold mine, and your willingness to be involved would be awfully hard to resist."

Brianna looked at the two men.

"I know it's a lot to ask after what we've put you through," Quillan said.

"So now that Nick's charm has run its course, you're appealing to my patriotic duty?"

"You have no obligation, Miss Wells, of course. If you need some time to think about it, that's fine. We just ask that you not discuss this with anyone else. We don't know who all might be involved. It could be anyone."

"Okay, Mr. Quillan, I'll think it over."

"If you have any questions, don't hesitate to contact me."

"Am I free to leave now?"

"Yes, certainly."

As they rose, Nick took Brianna's arm. "I'll walk you out, if I may."

She went to the door after giving him a cursory look. They walked down the corridor together.

"Well, Nick, congratulations on your innocence. Your skills of deception were even more remarkable than I thought."

"You don't know how badly it tore me up to think you were in on this."

"I wasn't exactly thrilled with the notion of you being a criminal, either."

They came to the front door of the building. Nick smiled at her. "Look how much we have to be glad of. Don't you think we ought to try and be friends?"

"That sounds suspiciously like something you said to me once before."

Brianna knew he was watching her. He looked sexy, provocative, just as he had from the day they met. But despite the revelation of his innocence, he was the same man, and Brianna felt leery of him.

"How about dinner tonight, so that I can make my full apologies?"

"You've already apologized, so dinner's not necessary."

"I've got reservations at the 1829."

She regarded him. "You must have a pretty liberal expense account."

"This is on me, not my employer, Brianna."

"A gumshoe with champagne tastes?"

"I'm really a collector. Paris, art and unraveling baffling swindles are all part of my life. Art theft investigation is as much a hobby to me as it is a vocation."

"What you really ought to be is an actor."

"Why?"

"Because your story—whatever story you're telling at the moment—is always convincing."

"Why don't we discuss this over a bottle of wine at the 1829?"

Brianna considered his invitation. "If I had any sense, I'd say no."

"Come on and have dinner with me. How else can you get your revenge?"

"That's the first thing you've said that appeals to me."

Nick grinned. "Will you be at your shop?"

"Yes. I won't need to go home before dinner. I've something there I can change into."

"Great. Shall we say six?"

WHEN SHE RETURNED TO WORK, Sylvie Voirin was full of questions about the visit of the police and the search of the shop. Brianna dismissed it as a mistake resulting from her unfortunate encounter with Nick in St. Barts, telling her assistant that it had all been straightened out. She withheld the details out of courtesy to Mack Quillan, though she knew it would be safe enough to tell Sylvie.

At five-thirty her assistant left for the day, and Brianna closed up the shop. She changed into a periwinkle-blue silk dress and took a necklace from the safe to wear for the evening. It was one of her personal favorites—black pearls interspersed with cylindrical gold beads.

Nick arrived promptly at six, and they walked to an outdoor café-bar in one of the nearby alleys that was lined with boutiques. It was a pleasant balmy evening, and they sat sipping tropical drinks in the shadows under the large potted plants and small trees that adorned the café.

"I realize you're not the man you said you were at first," she said after a while, "but how did you come to be an art collector and gumshoe?"

"You ask about my past?"

"Yes."

"I was in the service in Europe as I told you—an intelligence officer to be exact. I stayed on after being discharged, but did investigation work for U.S. companies in Europe—industrial espionage and security work.

"When my parents died, I inherited some art and a considerable amount of money, much of which I used to buy more paintings. Contrary to what I told you before, I did not have a particular interest in jewelry, but I do have a substantial collection of canvases, statuary and artifacts."

"How did you get involved in this case?"

"Because of my interests, and shall we say a certain expertise, I became fairly well known as a specialist in art fraud. The combination of the subject matter and the thrill of the chase have always appealed to me. When this ancient jewelry thing grew to epidemic proportions, Tony Havergill and his cronies called me in as a consultant."

"I take it the thrill of the chase, as you put it, doesn't refer exclusively to the pursuit of criminals?"

The corners of his mouth twisted in amusement. "Whatever do you mean, Brianna?"

"I was thinking of the ladies' boudoirs you undoubtedly manage to traipse through on your chase."

"What gave you that idea?"

"Personal experience."

"Surely you aren't going to hold one little incident against me."

"What bothers me, Nick, is not so much that I went to bed with you, but rather that I'm not fully confident of your motives—even now." Brianna reached for her drink as the face of a man walking down the alleyway caught her eye. As she looked at him approaching, her mouth dropped open in surprise.

Seeing the expression on her face, Nick turned and looked back. "What is it?"

"My God, I don't believe it!"

"What, Brianna?"

"That man walking this way, the one in the blue suit . . ."

"What about him?"

"That's Henri Rosenthal."

Nick slowly turned again. "Are you sure?"

"It's been a while since I've seen him, but that's either Rosenthal or his twin brother."

The man, in his late fifties or early sixties, had dark hair liberally streaked with gray that was combed straight back. He was broad-shouldered and very neatly dressed. Though he was too far away for Brianna to see clearly, she remembered his pale blue eyes that were nearly expressionless.

As Brianna watched him over Nick's shoulder, he wandered into the café, which formed an island running down the center of the broad alleyway. Rosenthal sat at the far end, some distance from where they were. She shrank farther into the shadows, glancing at Nick with alarm.

"Mack had said something about Rosenthal dropping out of sight in New York a few days ago," Nick said. "Now I see why. I wonder what he's doing in St. Thomas."

"He's probably here to see me."

"You could be right. Your appeal may be even stronger than we realized."

"Remind me to change perfumes."

Nick grinned at her, seemingly amused. He looked back again just as the dealer glanced at his watch then turned to peer up the alley in the direction he'd come.

"I'd say he's here to meet somebody," Nick said casually.

"Who?"

"I don't know. Shall I go ask him?"

She gave him a dirty look. "What are we going to do?"

"Nothing, for the moment. Let's wait and see what he's up to."

"What if he sees me?"

"Just keep behind me as much as possible. It's beginning to get dark, and he's not expecting to see you. Just don't get up and go to the ladies' room."

Brianna looked at the wry grin creasing Nick's smooth tanned skin. "I don't think you're taking this seriously at all."

"What do you expect me to do, go over and arrest him?"

"It seems like we ought to do something."

"No need to do anything for the moment. He's fallen into our lap. Let's just sit tight. Tell me what he does, so I don't have to keep turning around."

Brianna watched Rosenthal. "He's lighting a cigarette...now the waiter's going over to the table...they're talking...the waiter's pointing out something on the drink menu...."

"What's he ordering? Very important that you see what part of the menu he's pointing to."

She looked at Nick with surprise; then, by the big smile on his face, she could see he was teasing her. "You're incorrigible. I ought to get up and join Henri for a drink. He'd probably be better company."

"That might not be a bad idea. But let's wait awhile first." Nick sipped his drink. "The old boy didn't say anything to you about coming to the Virgin Islands?"

"Not a word."

"Something obviously caught his imagination."

"Well, it wasn't you or Mr. Quillan."

"That's probably true," he replied. "Ironic, isn't it? What's he doing now?"

"Just sitting there. Every once in a while he glances back up the alley."

"Hmm. Curious turn of events." Nick studied Brianna's face, liking in particular her wide mouth, which fascinated him all the more for having tasted it. Her eyes kept shifting back and forth, and he could see the excitement on her face that the situation had generated. Unconsciously she swept

her hair behind one ear, and the gesture brought back rec-
ollections of St. Barts.

Looking at her, it seemed absurd now that he had actually suspected her of being in league with Rosenthal.
Maybe he never truly believed it, but only wanted to as a
way of protecting himself. But from what?

"The waiter's bringing him the drink...it has a little
umbrella and a straw sticking out the top," she said slyly,
giving Nick a little smile. "If you'll slip me your miniature
camera, I'll take a picture of it for you."

"Now *you* aren't taking this seriously," he replied in
mock protest.

"It must be your corrupting influence."

Grinning, Nick contemplated her beauty and its effect on
him. The thick, glossy black hair, and the mouth—especially the mouth.

Then, as he watched, her mouth dropped slightly open
again. Nick couldn't resist turning around. Everything
looked the same to him. "What, Brianna?"

"Farther up the alley...that woman in the white blouse
and black pants..."

"What about her?"

"That's Sylvie, my assistant."

Nick saw the attractive mulatto with the cocoa skin and
pretty face walking slowly along the pavement, looking into
the café as she approached. Brianna leaned into the fronds
of the large plant next to her.

"Maybe she's the one Rosenthal's been waiting for,"
Nick said in an offhanded way.

"Why would Sylvie..."

Nick watched Brianna lift the drink menu up to her face
and peer over the top of it.

"Yes...that's it; she's going to Rosenthal's table. I can't
believe it."

"It looks like you're not the attraction, after all. What's
happening?"

"He stood up to greet her . . . good heavens! He's kissing her on the cheek . . . now Sylvie's sitting down." Brianna stared at Nick. "What do you think it means?"

"That we're going to have to check up on Sylvie."

"She can't be involved with him. Not Sylvie. It must be something else."

"I wish we could hear what's going on." Nick rubbed his chin, thinking. "Is there an empty table near them?"

Brianna looked over her menu. "Not real close."

"I suppose I could move down there and try to eavesdrop. Neither of them know me."

"What about me?"

"You'll have to fade farther into the jungle."

"Lord, I already feel like a cockatoo."

Nick smiled at her and signaled for the waiter. "Incidentally, I like your necklace. One of yours, I take it."

"Yes, from the shop."

"Genuine Polynesian blacks?"

"No, French-dyed. Of course they're genuine. You know better than anyone that I never settle for second best."

The waiter arrived.

"Will you bring the lady another drink?" Nick said to the man and laid a twenty-dollar bill on the table. "I'd like to take care of the check now. I'm going to have to leave."

"Yes, sir." The man took the bill and withdrew.

Nick got to his feet and stepped around the table to stand next to Brianna. "I'm going out down here and then circle around and reenter at their end of the café. When they leave, I'm going to follow Rosenthal. I'll meet you at the 1829 for dinner at seven." With that he leaned over and kissed her sweetly on the lips.

When Nick was gone, Brianna looked at the couple at the far end of the café, but was relieved to see that they were too engrossed in conversation to have noticed what had happened at her end of the terrace. She stared at Sylvie from her shadowed vantage point, wondering what mischief and deceit could be at work under her very nose.

Chapter Thirteen

Over the tops of the trees across the street, Brianna could see the lights of a cruise ship anchored in the harbor, looking for all the world like a great floating carnival in the blue-black tropical sea. A soft breeze drifted across the veranda of the hotel-restaurant 1829, caressing her face, carrying with it a mélange of incredible scents—tropical blossoms, aromatic sauces from the kitchen, the colognes and perfumes of diners, but above all the smell of the warm, wet sea air.

It was seven-twenty, and there was no sign of Nick. Brianna began to worry. She had last seen him at the café-bar where he had gone to the empty table nearest Sylvie and Rosenthal, just as he said he would. She had watched the three of them, wondering what Nick was hearing, wondering what her trusted and valued employee was up to.

Sylvie, the daughter of a white Frenchman and his black wife from Martinique, had left the French island hoping initially to find fame and fortune as a model in New York. One day, nearly destitute and discouraged, she had come into Brianna's Manhattan shop looking for work. Her exotic image, pleasant personality and lovely accent seemed well suited for the sort of thing Brianna sold, so she was hired as a clerk.

Sylvie learned quickly, and her value to the business grew right along with her personal friendship with Brianna.

When the woman who had previously managed the shop in Charlotte Amalie quit to have a child, Sylvie was offered the job and took it, finding the American Virgin Islands a comfortable compromise between Martinique and the States.

Sipping her drink and waiting for Nick, Brianna dreaded the thought that her friend might be involved with Rosenthal in some illicit activity, and what's worse, that she might be doing it at Brianna's expense. She racked her brain, trying to think what Sylvie had access to, which of her things might be compromised, what the possibilities were that some pieces from her own collection might have been stolen.

Perhaps the meeting with Rosenthal was innocent, perhaps Sylvie wasn't involved in any criminal activity. Brianna knew she could only pray that it was so and hope that Nick would show up soon with some news that would answer her troubling questions.

When he still hadn't come by seven-thirty, she was sure that something had gone wrong. Surely, though, Nick wasn't in any physical danger. Rosenthal might be a thief, but he couldn't be dangerous. On the other hand, there had been so many surprises. Nothing was certain.

Brianna wondered whether she ought to try to reach Mack Quillan. Perhaps he should be aware of what Nick had undertaken. But Nick hadn't asked her to contact the FBI or anyone else. If he had wanted her to secure help, he undoubtedly would have said something. After all, he was the expert in these matters, not she.

The waiter came, and Brianna ordered a second drink, knowing she was tying up the table, though the maître d' assured her there was no problem. For a while she listened to a young couple at an adjoining table who were in St. Thomas on their honeymoon. The innocence of their situation made Brianna feel a little sad, a little out of touch with the important things in life.

Brianna's mood and her concern for Nick invariably brought her thoughts back to the previous night. She had tried to dismiss it from her mind, to keep it in perspective, to protect herself from disappointment. But her fatigue and the drinks had softened her defenses. She didn't want to admit it, but she cared a great deal for Nick Severin, and the love they had shared in her bed made denying it virtually impossible.

But Nick's motives were more of a mystery. Somehow the line between what he felt and what he did had become blurred. There was a pattern to his behavior, a well-intended duplicity. He was charming as could be, but everything he did was for a purpose—to accomplish a goal. Even their lovemaking had had a function in the greater scheme of things.

Brianna was sure Nick enjoyed being with her, and even felt that he liked her in his way, but she had no doubt he was driven by considerations having nothing to do with her. She was being used. No matter how it was carved and served up, that's what it amounted to. And Brianna knew she was a fool to hope for anything more.

At quarter to eight she ordered dinner, ate leisurely and, when at half past the hour Nick hadn't arrived, paid the bill. She took a cab to the ferry and went home to Water Island, deciding that if she hadn't heard from him by nine the next morning, she would call Mack Quillan.

BRIANNA DIDN'T SLEEP WELL and rose with the sun the next morning. After fixing herself some coffee and toast, she went out onto her terrace overlooking the sea. Nick was in her thoughts, just as he had been much of the night.

It was irrational, she knew, but she almost had the feeling she'd never see him again. Was it because she cared too much?

She sat thinking for a long time, letting her cup of coffee grow cold, changing it for a fresh cup, taking a few sips before letting it turn cold again. She thought about her mother—something she hadn't done for a long time—and then about her father as she often did during difficult times. Brianna wished he were there to turn to for advice.

As she watched an early-morning sailboat struggling a half mile offshore to make headway in an indifferent breeze, Brianna noticed a rowboat bobbing in the swells off the point to the north of her house. At first she assumed it was a neighbor out for exercise, but then she saw that the boatman was making a purposeful effort to move along the shoreline in her direction.

Curious, she moved to the edge of her chair and watched. When the boatman had drawn within a hundred yards of the house, she realized that it was none other than Nick Severin. She was at the railing when he finally managed to pull within shouting distance of her.

"Ahoy, there!" he called. "Will you give a weary seaman refuge?"

"Nick, you didn't row that thing all the way from Charlotte Amalie, did you?"

"Could you spare a cup of water?" he called again as he bobbed in the swells near the rocks below.

"Tie up, you scoundrel," she replied, suddenly feeling buoyed by his unexpected appearance. She watched as he maneuvered to the dock. Then she made her way to meet him down the steep stairs carved into the rock.

When she got to the lower steps, Nick was tying up the rowboat, his brow saturated with perspiration.

"After all those hours at sea, you look like an angel of mercy."

"You didn't *really* row all the way out here?"

He grinned. "I couldn't wait for the first ferry."

Brianna could see she wasn't going to get a straight answer out of him. "What happened to you last night?"

"Sorry I missed our engagement. I was . . . otherwise detained."

"Come on upstairs," she said, taking his hand. "I've been worried about you, and dying to know what happened."

They reached the terrace, and Nick followed Brianna into the kitchen.

"What were Rosenthal and Sylvie talking about? Could you hear their conversation?"

"Not well," Nick said, mopping his brow with his handkerchief. "My impression was that it wasn't the first time they had met."

"Oh, no. I can't believe Syvlie is mixed up with that man."

"Apparently she is."

"What happened after you left the café? Why didn't you come to the 1829?"

"I was following Rosenthal, who himself had a busy night. I would have called you, but I never had a chance."

Brianna had the refrigerator door open. "Orange juice?"

"I'd love it."

She got a glass from the cupboard. "So what happened?"

"I followed him to the Frenchman's Reef, where he was staying. The first thing he did was check out."

"Check out? In the evening?"

"Yeah. The bad news was he went to your friend Sylvie's place. I think the conversation in the café was a seduction. My theory is he propositioned her."

Brianna wrinkled her nose. "Henri Rosenthal?"

Nick shrugged. "Maybe his Gallic charm appeals to her."

"Poor Sylvie."

He took a long drink of juice. "I don't know what happened, of course. It all may have been an act, but I'm pretty sure he spent the night. I hung around her place until after midnight. He never came out."

Brianna looked sick. "What do you suppose it means, Nick? That she *is* involved in his ring, or that she isn't?"

"I don't know. How's her love life? Is it probable that she might get involved with this guy romantically?"

"Come to think of it, she did say she'd met someone. But never in my wildest dreams would I have thought of Henri Rosenthal. Of course, she's kind of funny about men. Sylvie was very close to her father, who died when she was a teenager. I think she's attracted to older men, but . . ."

"Well, Rosenthal qualifies in that regard," Nick said, and followed Brianna out onto the terrace where they sat.

"Sylvie has always had this thing about success and money. I think she may regard men as a form of financial security."

"That all fits. Maybe she thinks of this guy as a meal ticket."

"Sylvie's not *that* mercenary. I know there must be something more to it than that, Nick."

"It can't be just a coincidence that Rosenthal shows up in St. Thomas and picks up your assistant."

"No, it has to be intentional as far as he's concerned. Hopefully Sylvie's innocent, though."

"I don't know, but I imagine we'll find out soon enough. Quillan's got some people on Rosenthal."

"And Sylvie, too?"

Nick nodded.

"The poor thing. I'm sure she doesn't know what she's got herself into. I feel like I ought to warn her."

"You can't, Brianna. We've got to play this out."

She looked at him, knowing what he said made sense. But even though catching Henri Rosenthal was important, Sylvie was important, too. If she weren't involved in the man's crimes, she didn't deserve what was happening, and Brianna was determined to find out one way or the other, no matter what the consequences.

"She's my friend, Nick, not just an employee."

"Nobody forced this on her. She let that guy into her apartment last night of her own free will."

"How do you know that? You didn't hear what was said."

"I didn't hear their words, that's true, but I've got pretty strong feelings based on what I observed . . . the way they reacted to each other."

"Yes. And you were sure of me, too, remember?"

"That was an unfortunate mistake."

"This might be also. Henri Rosenthal's using that girl."

"Perhaps."

She stared at him, seeing the determination on his face. "All you care about is this damned case, Nick You don't care about the people involved—who might get hurt."

"That's not true."

"It was true of your dealings with me. It's true with Sylvie. You do whatever you have to, whether it's letting an innocent bystander get hurt or going to bed with someone yourself just to prove a point."

"Now just a minute," Nick said, showing his annoyance. "I didn't push that girl into bed with Rosenthal, and I didn't force you, either."

"You weren't honest with me, though."

"Brianna, I thought we were going to forget the past. I've apologized for my mistakes."

She could see things had gotten off on the wrong course, but it was almost too late. She was angry now, and her indignation was out of control. "It's not me I'm concerned about, it's Sylvie."

"There's nothing that can be done about her at the moment."

"Perhaps you can't do anything, but there's no reason why I shouldn't."

"Yes, there is," he said angrily. "You could mess up everything. Rosenthal's given us a golden opportunity. We can't blow it."

"I'm not part of the 'we' in this case. And the more I see of the way you operate, the less inclined I am to help."

Just then the doorbell rang.

"Who could that be this time of the morning?" Brianna mumbled, getting to her feet.

"Probably Quillan."

"To put me under protective arrest this time?"

Nick smirked at the sarcasm and got up to follow her into the house. When Brianna opened the door, the FBI agent was standing there.

"Good morning," he said cheerily. A look at their faces turned his own expression sober. "Can I come in?"

Brianna stepped back to admit him. Quillan looked at Nick. "I take it she didn't care for our plan."

"I hadn't gotten that far, Mack."

"What plan?" Brianna asked.

The agent's expression was woebegone. "Could we talk for a moment, Miss Wells?"

She gave Nick a suspicious glance. "Yes, I think that might be a good idea."

They went to the couch and chairs. Quillan cleared his throat. "We want to set up a sting operation," he said simply. "With the apparent involvement of your employee in the case, it seemed the right time to press ahead, possibly while Rosenthal is here in the Virgin Islands."

"You mean you want me to help catch Sylvie right along with Rosenthal?"

"It does appear that she's mixed up in it."

"Sylvie's my friend."

Quillan and Nick exchanged glances. "People have a way of disappointing us sometimes," the agent said stoically.

"There's no need to be patronizing, Mr. Quillan," Brianna said. "What is it you want me to do?"

"We can't be sure at this point why Rosenthal is here in St. Thomas, and what Miss Voirin's involvement is, but our hunch is that you'll be in a position to find out before very long."

"You want me to encourage them? Is that it?"

"That might be a little strong. We'd like you to . . . shall we say . . . be the bait. You may very well be the object of his visit, anyway. It's difficult to tell."

Brianna looked at Nick. "That's why you came out here? To put me up to this?"

"Mack and I discussed it, yes."

She glared at him. "That cute little trick with the rowboat. How did that come about?"

"Mack's people dropped me off around the point."

Her eyes narrowed. "Couldn't resist making a game of it, could you, Nick?"

"That wasn't my intent."

"The truth is you think my friend is a criminal, and you want me to help you catch her. But instead of coming right out with it, you figure you have to charm me into it."

"No, Brianna . . ."

She turned to the agent. "Listen, Mr. Quillan. If in the future you expect me to help, I would prefer that you just ask me rather than sending Romeo with the invitation."

The agent had to force back a smile. "All right, Miss Wells, whatever you like. I take it we can expect your cooperation in our investigation, then?"

She shot Nick Severin a glance. "I suppose so."

Quillan moved to the edge of his chair. "That's terrific. We really appreciate it."

Brianna felt miserable, knowing what she was getting into. "What do I do next?"

"I think the first order of business is to spend some time with Miss Voirin, see if she and Rosenthal wish to involve you or if they intend to work independently."

"And at my expense?"

"And at your expense, yes. It should be clear enough very soon. Also, I think it would be a good idea to check over the pieces in your collection to see if anything is missing, has been replaced with a replica, that sort of thing."

"Yes, certainly. Anything else?"

"Let us know immediately if Miss Voirin proposes something, or if Rosenthal himself makes contact with you. Of course, it's very important that you not let them know you're aware of what they're up to. Don't confront either of them, whatever you do. Just get to us as quickly as you can. Once we get a handle on their scheme, we can react accordingly."

"What if they do or say nothing to me?"

"It's possible. I've got people following both of them, and we're doing what we can to unravel this thing independently of you."

Brianna turned to Nick, who sat dolefully watching her with his soft brown eyes. "And what about you? Headed back to Paris?"

"No, I thought I'd stick around for a while. Since my excellent relationship with you no longer seems to be a factor, I suppose it will be more as an observer than a participant."

"We're very grateful to Nick and Tony Havergill for their contribution," Quillan interjected.

"I'll be at the 1829 for at least a few more days," Nick added. "I thought maybe when you have the time we could share the dinner we missed."

Brianna smiled at him stiffly. "It appears I'll be pretty busy."

"Call me after work one of these evenings, anyway."

"I'll consider it."

Quillan got to his feet, taking a card from his pocket. "Here's a number where I can be reached at any time of the day or night, Miss Wells," he said, handing it to her. "A message can be gotten to me if necessary. I take it you're going to your shop now?"

She looked at her watch. "Yes. If I hurry, I can make the next boat."

Nick stood up with her, his expression regretful. Brianna could see there was something he wanted to say, but he didn't. Instead he turned and followed the FBI agent to the door.

SYLVIE VOIRIN WAS ALREADY at the shop when Brianna arrived. She was sitting on a stool behind a display case, staring wistfully out the window. She smiled weakly at Brianna, her pretty cocoa face tinged with uncertainty.

"Good morning, Sylvie."

"Hi, Brianna."

"Nice sunny day."

Sylvie nodded.

Brianna stepped behind the partition and set her purse down on the desk, opening it to remove the pearls she had taken the night before. She went back to the safe and carefully replaced the necklace, glancing up at her assistant. "Borrowed it for a dinner date last night."

"Oh?" Sylvie said vacantly. "Somebody new?"

"Truth of the matter is, I was stood up. He was detained on business, though, so I suppose I should forgive him."

Brianna felt very uncomfortable and could see the pretense would be difficult. She didn't know whether she should be feeling compassion or betrayal. Was Sylvie deserving of her sympathy or her resentment? Frustrated, she wanted to take her friend by the shoulders and give her a good shaking until the truth came out.

"How was your evening?" Brianna asked.

"Okay...fine."

Sylvie hadn't met her eyes, and Brianna could see the conversation was troubling her, as well.

There was an uncomfortable silence, then the young woman blurted out anxiously, "Brianna, before things get too busy, could we talk?"

Sylvie's tone, the unexpected desire to communicate took her by surprise. "Sure. What do you want to talk about?"

The girl took a deep breath, lowering her eyes. "I'm going to have to quit the store, leave you."

Brianna was stunned. "Leave? What for?"

"It's personal, but I want to go back to New York. I have met someone, an opportunity..." Her eyes were almost pleading. "I must go."

"I don't understand. You mean you've had a job offer?"

"*À peu près.* Yes, sort of."

"You don't know?"

The pretty young mulatto gave a Gallic shrug. "The truth is I have met a man, a wonderful man who has talked of fabulous opportunities, and he cares for me very much."

"What sort of opportunities, Sylvie?"

She hesitated. "Work like I do for you, only with more responsibilities."

"Who is this man?"

Sylvie bowed her head, shaking it slowly. "I cannot say."

"Cannot say? Why?"

"He asked that I not tell you. He asked that I not even say why I wanted to leave—not the truth—but I couldn't be dishonest with you."

Brianna's mind began spinning, trying to discern what was happening, Sylvie's motives. "I don't understand. Why wouldn't this man want you to tell me? People leave jobs all the time to take another."

"*Je le sais,* but this is different."

"Why is it different?"

"Because... because I have become his lover."

"Sylvie! What are you saying? When did you meet this man?"

"Only days ago, Brianna. It has happened very fast, but I know that what I do is the right thing."

"But it's so sudden. How can you be sure?"

"I am. I know in my heart."

Brianna contemplated her friend, trying to decide whether what she said was in defense of Henri Rosenthal's web of deceit, or if Sylvie was being victimized by him. "I still don't understand why this must be so secretive, if his intentions are good. Doesn't it make you wonder about him, Sylvie?''

"No, he is a wonderful person. He is French, and we understand each other well.''

"But you hardly know him!''

"It doesn't matter. I'm sure he is honorable.''

Brianna could see she was getting nowhere, but she was also getting the impression Sylvie was more Rosenthal's victim than his accomplice. Despite Mack Quillan's warning to keep a low profile, she couldn't stand idly by while her friend was ruined. "Listen, you're a grown woman, you can do what you want. As your friend my only wish for you is happiness. But this whole thing sounds crazy to me. I don't want to see you hurt.''

Sylvie walked around to where Brianna stood and took her hands. "You *are* a good friend to me. And I feel so badly about leaving you. You have helped me so much. But this is not just a job. This man is so wonderful. You cannot know.''

"Yes, I can, Sylvie. I met a man recently, too, remember? He turned out to be someone different than I expected. I was very fond of him also, but he disappointed me. Several times.''

"Perhaps I will not be so unfortunate.''

"Honest people—good people—don't have to hide behind lies and deceit.''

"But he *is* a good man! Henri would never...'' Sylvie gasped, covering her mouth with her hand.

"Henri? From New York? Is this man—''

"No, Brianna! *Je t'en prie!* Please. I am a fool. I have said too much. Please don't—''

The bell over the door jangled just then as two tourists, elderly women, came into the shop. Brianna and Sylvie looked at each other.

"Don't worry,'' Brianna whispered, "you wait on them, and we'll talk later.'' She touched her friend's arm reassuringly. "Don't worry." Turning away, she saw the trepidation on Sylvie's face, knowing instinctively the girl was innocent, though how innocent, she wasn't sure.

BRIANNA SAT IN THE BACK listening to Sylvie talking with the customers, who had become very interested in a ring. The sales talk sounded much as it always had, the young woman patiently explaining the story behind the black pearls.

But Brianna wondered if under the gentle, patient veneer there wasn't a hint of anxiety in Sylvie's voice. Or was it wishful thinking on her part—a desire that her friend not conceal her feelings too easily.

As the conversation in the next room drifted in and out of Brianna's consciousness, she glanced at the telephone, remembering Quillan's request that he be kept informed, that she do nothing to spook Rosenthal. She considered retreating to her private office to call him but knew how the conversation would go. He would want her to wait. He would put no stock in her judgment of Sylvie's innocence. He'd want to play it out. Like Nick, he'd be willing to sacrifice Sylvie in order to get Rosenthal.

But Brianna knew that the young woman's innocence now wouldn't necessarily protect her later. Rosenthal obviously was a viper. He'd drag her into his scheme, and she'd eventually go down with him.

It was clear enough that if Sylvie were to be saved, Brianna couldn't leave it to the authorities. It would be up to her. Once again, she was stuck in the middle.

As she wrestled with the problem, Brianna considered the possibility of going to Nick for advice. His capacity was only semiofficial, so he might help. On the other hand, he had not proven to be terribly reliable.

It seemed this was something she'd have to handle alone. But before Brianna could say or do anything, she had to know how deeply Sylvie had become involved, whether Rosenthal had already got her to help him with his mischief.

Mack Quillan had advised her to check over her collection, so Brianna went into the back room and opened her private safe to examine the many pieces of ancient jewelry her father had left to her.

Taking each piece in turn, she examined the collection carefully, looking for bogus pieces or replicas that might have been switched for her originals. Nothing suspicious turned up. Checking and double-checking the inventory, she found that every item was accounted for. For the moment, nothing was amiss.

Brianna wondered if Henri Rosenthal might eventually show up and ask to see the collection. That would be the time wrongdoing was most likely to occur. After locking everything securely in the large safe, she returned to the outer office, her thoughts and concerns turning again to Sylvie Voirin.

Brianna sat at the desk, thinking about the conflicting loyalties tugging at her. After a few minutes the sound of the bell ringing over the front door brought her back from her reveries, and she realized that the customers had left. A moment later Sylvie came back, leaning against the door frame. She looked dispirited.

"I'm sorry," she said apologetically. "They wanted the ring, but I didn't do a very good job. I guess I was distracted. But they said they would come back this afternoon."

"Don't worry about it."

They looked at each other for a long time.

"Sylvie, I know that the man you've been seeing is Henri Rosenthal. And I also know that his interest in you is not just as a woman. I'm aware of the kind of work he has in mind, and it's not what you think."

"Brianna, what are you saying?"

"Come on," she said, pointing at a chair, "we have to talk. I think you'd better sit down."

Chapter Fourteen

After they had locked up the shop for the evening, Brianna and Sylvie stood at the door. "Give me at least ten minutes," Brianna said under her breath before bidding her friend farewell. Then she turned and headed up the alley toward Main Street.

As she walked away, she felt eyes on her, though she knew that there was no reason Quillan's men would be following her. Still, she couldn't be too careful, and she knew Sylvie would be followed.

Brianna walked purposefully along, turning down a side alley to Storetvaer Gade, where she went around the corner and ducked into a doorway. Waiting, she held her breath anxiously, expecting a man to come by at any second. If someone was following her, he'd have to come by soon. When no one suspicious appeared, she stepped out of her hiding place, satisfied she wasn't under surveillance.

Feeling more at ease, Brianna walked down Main Street to Strand Gade where she began looking for a taxi. After a few minutes she managed to flag one down. Jumping in, she instructed the driver to go to the Waterfront Highway, where she had him turn east and then stop in front of an emerald shop at the Royal Dane Mall. After a few minutes Sylvie came running up to the taxi and climbed in.

"Anyone following you?" Brianna asked.

"I don't think so. I'm sure they're still waiting around outside the linen shop."

Brianna smiled, thankful now about the incident six months earlier when she had been followed from her shop by a man who had been lingering around out front most of the day. Going into a nearby linen store, she had asked for help. The proprietor had ushered her out the back door, enabling Brianna to escape into the adjoining mall undetected. At her suggestion, Sylvie had used the same ploy to elude the FBI tail.

Giving the driver the name of a small Creole restaurant in Frenchtown, Brianna eased back in the seat, knowing that she had solved only the first of her problems. Now she had to contend with Henri Rosenthal.

Next to her, Sylvie Voirin fidgeted. "Are you sure this is right, Brianna?"

"If Henri's intentions are good, we'll know soon. I only hope he's cagey enough to get away from the hotel without being followed. It won't do us much good to lose the FBI if they follow him to our meeting."

"I don't know if he believed my story about a jealous ex-boyfriend lying in wait for him. I hadn't said anything about another man before today."

"I'm sure Henri gave it some credence. The last thing he wants is to run into an angry young man with blood in his eye. We can only hope he was clever enough to evade the agents assigned to follow him."

"And what if he wasn't?"

"Then let's hope they lie low and don't interfere."

"Oh, Brianna, it is so crazy to trick him like this."

"It's the only way to keep you from falling into their trap right along with Henri."

"I still can't believe what you say about him. He is such a kind man."

"I wish I was wrong, but I know I'm not."

After the short ride to Frenchtown, a small settlement at the edge of the waterfront consisting primarily of restaurants and bars, they decided to get out of the taxi and walk through the twisting congested streets. They arrived shortly at a small restaurant in a remote corner of the district where they were to meet Henri Rosenthal.

Christmas lights adorned the front window of the place regardless of the season, giving the restaurant a strange appearance. It wasn't the most likely meeting place, but that's what made it seem so good.

The rendezvous was early enough that there would be privacy at a back table. They were late, according to plan, thus enabling the maximum element of surprise when they walked in.

Henri Rosenthal was sitting at a corner table at the back of the room, bent over a menu. He glanced up as the women approached, his mouth slowly dropping open at the sight of Brianna. He looked at Sylvie questioningly as he got to his feet.

There was laughter and loud talk in the native patois coming from the adjoining bar as the three stood looking at one another.

"Well, Brianna," Rosenthal said a little self-consciously, "what a surprise."

"Hello, Henri."

He gestured for the women to sit, glancing uncertainly at Sylvie Voirin. *"Tu es méchante, ma chérie,"* he chided.

"I'm sorry, Henri," Sylvie said mournfully, "I had no choice."

"I'm afraid I did threaten her, Henri," Brianna said, "if she refused to cooperate."

"What sort of threat?"

Brianna looked at him evenly. "I told her I'd expose you unless she brought me with her."

"Expose me?" He gave her the condescending laugh of a disdainful Frenchman. "What's this about?"

"After that business I went through on St. Barts, our conversations on the telephone, and this coincidental visit of yours to St. Thomas, I figured out what you're up to."

"Oh? What's that?"

"You're planning the same thing Nick Severin had in mind when he approached me."

Rosenthal looked back and forth between them. "This is ridiculous. Whatever made you think this?"

"Come on, Henri, there's no point in being coy. I'm no cop. I'm a business person just like yourself. I'm interested in making money, same as you."

He smiled cagily, glancing at Sylvie. "What are you saying? That you are interested in doing what you accuse me of?"

"Why not? It made sense to Nick Severin, why shouldn't it make sense to me?"

"Aren't you assuming that I myself have an interest in this scheme, Brianna?"

"Why else would you be here?"

He laughed again. "America is free like France, no? I came to the Caribbean for a few days' rest. I met this lovely creature, and now all of a sudden I am accused of plotting crimes!"

Brianna shot Sylvie an anxious glance. "You're trying to say it's just a coincidence that you happened to meet my assistant?"

"No, it's not a coincidence. I was in Charlotte Amalie, and I thought I would drop by to say hello to you. I went into your shop, and I find instead this lovely young lady. I am captivated by her. I learn of her talent, and I wish for her to work for me. Is this so unusual?"

Brianna was beginning to see that she had overplayed her hand. Either that or Henri Rosenthal was being very cautious. The bastard! "Why did you tell Sylvie to keep your identity a secret?"

Rosenthal shrugged. "Isn't it obvious that you should hear this from me and not her? Of course I was planning on telling you, but not until we had come to an agreement, Sylvie and I."

"You see, Brianna," the young woman interjected. "I told you Henri is an honorable man."

The Frenchman reached over and patted Sylvie's hands. "I am sorry, *ma chérie*, this is all my fault. I should never have put you in this position."

"Oh, Henri, it is I who is wrong, not you!"

"Tiens, tiens," he said benevolently. "But Brianna is right: I have wronged her, as well. Better that I spoke to her about this before making you any offer. We are confreres and we have certain responsibilities, one to the other." He looked at Brianna. "I know you have this wild story about some scheme because you are angry with me. Perhaps I deserve it. But believe me, I am innocent. We all have contributed to this misunderstanding. I think it would be best if we forget that it has happened."

Brianna could see that Rosenthal hadn't gone for the bait, and that the whole thing was in danger of blowing up in her face. She had bungled it and was sure that Mack Quillan would kill her. What's worse, now Sylvie didn't believe her, either, and would probably tell Henri everything. It had been a terrible mistake to bring her here.

"Perhaps I did jump to conclusions," Brianna admitted, trying to make the best of a bad situation. "Maybe I *was* angry with you, Henri."

"Well, it's understandable. The main thing is that you both realize that I have no ill intentions." He took Sylvie's hands again, squeezing them. "I am sorry for this, my pet."

"I'm the one that owes you both an apology," Brianna said, feeling even more sorry than she sounded. "You're right, Henri. It's best if we forget this conversation even took place." She turned to Sylvie, hoping to get her out of the restaurant where they could talk again. "Will you ride with me back into town?"

"Yes, of course."

The two women rose. Henri Rosenthal stood as well, taking each of their hands in turn and kissing them. Sylvie he kissed also on the cheek.

"What was this business about an old boyfriend, little one? Was that a story, too?" he asked, still holding her hands.

Sylvie glanced at Brianna. "No, it was the truth. I worried he might hurt you, Henri. He did not follow you, did he?"

"No. I may be older than the young men, but I have the cleverness of years."

Sylvie smiled uncomfortably.

"May I call you later, *chérie*?"

"*Bien entendu*, Henri. Of course." Sylvie looked at Brianna, and they turned to leave.

Rosenthal watched them walk from the restaurant, then sat again at the table.

BRIANNA AND SYLVIE made their way back toward the main street of Frenchtown in silence. "I don't know what happened," Brianna said. "He was lying, I hope you believe that."

"I don't know what to believe. I'm totally confused."

"He must have been suspicious—that's all I can figure."

"Perhaps you are mistaken about him."

"No, I—" Brianna looked up to see four men step into the narrow street in front of them. She gasped with fright until she recognized Mack Quillan, wearing the same expression he had worn that first day when he had come to her house. In his hand he carried his wallet, which as before was flipped open, revealing his identification.

"Miss Wells, Miss Voirin, FBI. Please come with us."

Sylvie, who had frozen, cried out with fright. "Oh, Brianna!"

But Brianna was searching Quillan's face incredulously. As they stood immobile, agents stepped to either side of them and, taking their arms, walked them to two nearby automobiles. They were hustled inside and moments later were being driven away, Brianna in one car, Sylvie in the other.

Brianna, her heart hammering, turned and saw Quillan beside her.

"I hate amateurs," he groused.

"What are you going to do, shoot me?"

"We're going to see if we can salvage the mess you've made."

"Why am I under arrest?"

"You aren't. We needed an excuse to keep Sylvie from talking to Rosenthal."

"Then you knew about what we were doing—you followed us, after all?"

"Our people in New York advised us Rosenthal had slipped out of sight, so we considered the possibility that he might eventually make contact with you. During the search of your shop listening devices were installed, just in case."

"And in my home, too?"

Quillan nodded.

"You mean you listened to everything Sylvie and I said?"

"Yes."

"Good Lord, there's no privacy left in the world."

"Why didn't you just play it as I had suggested, Miss Wells?"

"Why didn't you tell me my place was bugged, Mr. Quillan? At least then I'd have known you were aware that Sylvie is innocent."

"We figured your acting would be better if you were unaware of an audience."

"Thanks for the vote of confidence."

"You think you deserve it after tonight?"

"No, I suppose I was pretty foolish. What are you going to do with me?"

"Nothing. We wanted to get Sylvie out of circulation until we get a reading on Rosenthal. We couldn't very well have taken her into custody without arresting you. There was a palpable conspiracy being discussed back there in the restaurant. That gives us something legitimate to talk to her about. I'll have Miss Voirin questioned for as long as it takes to get a fix on Rosenthal."

"You mean you knew what we were talking about in the restaurant?"

"You didn't give us much time, so the bugs we installed there were a hit-and-miss proposition. But we heard enough to know what went on."

Brianna shook her head with amazement. "Is Nick Severin in on this?"

"No. He's a private citizen, as you know. We kept him involved as long as it appeared he'd be helpful. When your displeasure with him became evident, I asked him to move to the sidelines."

"So he's not aware of the bugs, or what went on tonight?"

"No. Why?"

"I was just curious." She looked over at the agent's implacable face. "So what happens now? Do I get moved to the sidelines, too?"

"You're free to do as you choose. We'll drop you off wherever you wish."

"Really? Just like that?"

Quillan gave her a sardonic smile. "Well, after this evening's fiasco, I sort of feel like you owe Uncle Sam a favor."

Brianna gave a little laugh. "That sounds suspiciously like you're saying I owe Uncle Mack a favor."

"If Rosenthal doesn't panic and bolt, and we figure out a way to use you, will you stay on the case?"

"Either I wasn't as bad as you made me out to be, or you're desperate," she joked. "Which is it?"

"No comment."

"Gestapo!"

Now Mack Quillan laughed. "Where to, Miss Wells?"

"Just let me off at the ferry, please."

THE USUAL SORT OF CROWD was at the docks waiting for the ferry to Water Island when Quillan dropped Brianna off. She bid him goodbye and wandered into the covey of passengers. Making her way to the railing, Brianna absently watched the lights of boats out in the bay, thinking about the disaster she had caused that evening and feeling rather foolish.

After a few minutes she sensed someone nearby. Out of the corner of her eye she saw the figure of a man move to the railing next to her. He seemed uncomfortably close, and Brianna turned to view the imposing presence. It was Nick Severin.

"Hi," he said, smiling.

She stared at him for a moment, gathering herself. "Why so cheerful? Did you hear about my big gaffe this evening?"

"What gaffe?"

Brianna gave him a brief account of her encounter with Rosenthal.

Nick shrugged. "I've made a few mistakes myself in this case."

"You aren't upset with me? After all, you've been working a long time to catch him."

"Yeah, it doesn't please me. But it's Quillan's baby now. I'll let him worry."

The champagne-beige of Nick's hair and mustache contrasted nicely with the rich dark tan of his skin, and Brianna grew increasingly aware of the energy that his presence always seemed to generate. His eyes were smiling, friendly.

"I must say, I admire your tolerance," she said casually.

"I figure I still owe you a few after the trouble I've caused."

She smiled wryly. "I admire your contrition, as well."

"Had dinner yet?"

Brianna chuckled. "Did I sound like I admired it that much?"

"I have a rain check."

She looked at him sympathetically. "I would, Nick, but I'm a little tired after all the excitement."

"How about a relaxing dinner at home?"

The corners of her mouth twitched mischievously. "Is there a Concorde leaving for Paris?"

"I was thinking about your place."

"Haven't lost any of the old presumption, have you?"

"I thought you could use the commiseration."

The ferry approached the dock out of the darkness, its engine lumbering wearily. Brianna observed their progress for a moment, then looked at the man beside her, his face full of the charm that had become his trademark. He waited, having tossed the ball clearly into her court.

Brianna's failure earlier in the evening had sapped her confidence, and she felt more in need of a friend than an adversary. Besides, she enjoyed his company, and something deep inside her longed for the intimacy they had shared the night before her arrest. She vacillated.

"I'll cook," he volunteered.

"*That*'s beginning to sound irresistible."

Nick grinned and took her by the arm. "Done," he said and led her toward where the boarding ramp had been pushed from the ferry onto the dock.

NICK HAD MANAGED to whip together a pretty decent meal with the odd assortment of ingredients Brianna had on hand, and she sat back, enjoying the last of her wine, trying to divine his intentions for the balance of the evening. She knew there wasn't much fight in her, but she didn't want it to end in bed, either. The ambivalence she felt was disconcerting.

Nick contemplated her as he had so often before when they were together. Sitting across from him, she had, by force of events, regained much of the innocence he at first associated with her. His suspicions of the past, always more intellectual than emotional, had evaporated, leaving only the vulnerable woman behind.

Now there was really nothing standing between them but a few uncomfortable memories and the nagging discomfort of unfinished business. He felt it and was sure she did, as well.

He smiled as she tucked her silken tresses behind an ear.

"What's so funny?"

"Nothing. I like your mannerisms, that's all."

Brianna thought, then realized what he was referring to. "My ears," she said dolefully.

Nick considered her mouth, liking the way it dominated her face, remembering the taste of her kiss. "You're really very attractive," he murmured as much to himself as to her.

Brianna played the words over in her mind, considering his meaning, his intentions.

"Come on," Nick said, scooting his chair back, "let's go out on the terrace and get some air."

She let him lead her out, his strong hand clamped on hers, his physical presence more and more overpowering. It was hard to resist him because there was no longer a specific danger. And, his underlying motives were no longer suspect.

They sat side by side in deck chairs looking out at the moonlit water, Nick toying with her fingers. Brianna watched him for a minute. "Why are you here?" she asked, transposing her thoughts into words. "Is it for sex?"

"Do I strike you as that mercenary?"

"I don't know. I suppose I don't feel as though I really know you—whoever you are."

"I'm the same man underneath. Why can't you believe that?"

"I want to. I'm not sure I trust you enough yet."

"We're both guilty of past crimes, even if they were only illusion."

"So where does that leave us?" Brianna asked, not really sure she wanted to hear the answer.

"You tell me."

She looked out at the moonlight on the water, shining silver in the deep plum of the sea, aware of Nick's touch, neither fighting nor submitting to it. "When are you going back to Paris?"

"When I've finished here."

"Finished what?"

"I don't know. But things aren't complete, I'm sure of that."

"You're an elusive man, Nick Severin."

"How so?"

"I'm trying to figure out your intentions, and you're not being very cooperative."

"What I want is to get to know you better, Brianna."

Feeling suddenly overwhelmed, she pulled her hand free and got to her feet, walking slowly to the railing. Below, the waves crashed ghostlike against the rocks, silver froth rising from the black before melting again into the obscurity of the night sea.

A moment later Nick was beside her. She turned and blended almost instantly into his waiting embrace, his mouth descending to cover hers, her senses roiling within seconds like the churning sea below. They kissed hungrily, and Brianna was a prisoner of her desire.

In the midst of their passion the doorbell sounded, and she stiffened as though having been struck. She looked into Nick's eyes. He shook his head.

"I have no idea who it is this time. Honest."

"Lord..." she muttered warily, and began moving uncertainly toward the door.

Nick was walking with her but stopped in the middle of the living room. "Maybe I'd better wait in the bedroom," he whispered.

Brianna nodded and stepped toward the entry as the bell sounded again.

Chapter Fifteen

"Mr. Rosenthal!" He was the last person on earth Brianna had expected.

"Sorry to come to your house without an invitation," he said easily, "but I wanted to speak with you, Brianna. May I enter?"

"Yes." She stepped back. "Come in. Please."

He gave her a sly look with his flat blue eyes and walked through the entry hall into the living room, glancing around as he did. "It is a nice home you have."

Rosenthal turned slowly to face her, and Brianna noticed how his face sagged. *How could Sylvie find this man attractive?* she wondered.

"I am certain you didn't expect me," he said, "but I like surprises. You'll learn that about me when we get to know each other better, my dear."

Brianna glanced toward the bedroom door that Nick had left ajar, just as when Lucien Pillet had visited. "Sit down, please."

He did, smiling slightly as he looked at her. It was evident that the man was there for a purpose, and she was reasonably sure it had to do with her proposition. Brianna decided to challenge him.

"Think better of my proposal, Henri? Is that why you're here?"

"You're really serious about what you said at the restaurant, aren't you?"

"I can't believe you flew all the way to St. Thomas to pay a social call."

"And why would I necessarily have a forgery scheme in mind? Do you take me for the criminal type?"

Brianna could see that he was playing with her, perhaps even having a little fun at her expense. "Maybe it's my own interest in the idea talking. Maybe I'm projecting, Henri."

"Rather—what's the word?—rash, *n'est-ce pas?*"

"Rash?"

"Yes, my dear. I'm not a lawyer, but if I'm not mistaken, you proposed a criminal combine to me earlier at the restaurant. Isn't it *rash* to suggest such a thing without knowing how I'd react? What if I took the matter to the police?"

"You're too smart to go to the police, Henri. Besides, I only suggested something that you yourself had already considered. Isn't that why you came to St. Thomas—to enlist my services?"

"You give me too much credit, my dear. But to eliminate any doubt, I will tell you that was not my purpose in coming."

"Oh? I'm surprised."

His little smile bordered on a smirk.

Brianna wondered whether Mack Quillan's bugs were still working, whether by any chance someone besides Nick was listening to the conversation. Rosenthal's visit was an opportunity to redeem herself. She decided to press ahead.

"Now that Sylvie's not here, there's really no reason to be coy," she said, trying to combat his arrogance with some of her own.

"Yes, Sylvie," he said thoughtfully. "I'm surprised you decided to involve her in this."

"Me? Don't you have that backward, Henri? You're trying to drag off one of my employees to make fraudulent replicas, and not so much as a word with me."

He grinned, running his fingers through his hair. "Why do you persist in this story about fraud? I am truly surprised you would accuse me of this."

"I don't know whom you're trying to impress, but if you want it that way, so be it. I would like to know why you're here, though."

"*Bien*. The truth is that I have come to discuss a business proposition with you."

"What sort of proposition?"

"It involves a very clever and very profitable money-making idea. It's a wonderful scheme."

"Yes, I'm listening." Brianna glanced quickly in the direction of the bedroom, hoping Nick was listening, too.

"There is a matter I would like to clear up first."

"What?"

"My little friend, Sylvie."

"What about her?"

"You truly misunderstood my motives regarding the girl. I am very fond of her, Brianna."

"She seemed to think so, yes."

"I would like for her to come to New York to work for me. I'd appreciate your cooperation in that matter."

"What do you want her to do?"

"Am I obligated to tell you everything?"

Brianna studied him. "Sylvie's my friend, Henri. I regard her almost as a little sister. I'd hate to see you take advantage of her."

"Again, you attribute me with bad motives. I wonder what you must think of me."

"What I think is not important. But Sylvie is. I thought you were using her to get to me, and I didn't want to see her hurt."

"But I've already told you, I'm very fond of the girl."

"Then it was coincidental that you became friends?"

"Yes. I swear it."

Brianna smirked, not quite sure what to think, not sure what Rosenthal was up to.

He saw her skepticism. "She's young, but she's not a child."

"Yes, I suppose you're right."

"Then you have no objection to her joining me?"

"I can't stop her. Ask her."

"I had planned to. I was hoping I could discuss it with her tonight, telling her I had your blessing. Unfortunately, she has disappeared. She wasn't at her home. I thought perhaps she was here with you." He glanced around as though some trace of Sylvie might be lying about.

Brianna fidgeted, worried that Henri might spot evidence of Nick Severin's presence. "No, Sylvie and I parted back in town. I don't know what she had planned, unless perhaps she's visiting friends."

"She knew I wanted to see her."

"Maybe you should call her now." As soon as she said it, Brianna remembered that her phone was in the bedroom, where Nick was hiding.

"Would you mind?"

She cringed inside but tried to act indifferent. "No, but the lines off the island weren't working earlier when I tried to make a call myself. Let me go check. The phone's in the bedroom."

Brianna got up and walked to the bedroom door. Nick was waiting inside. He took her by the shoulders, grinning from ear to ear.

"You're doing terrific!" he whispered. "See what you can do to find out more about his business proposal."

"Maybe there is no business proposal. Maybe he made the whole thing up to get me to cooperate and let Sylvie go."

Nick was shaking his head. "I doubt it. He came to St. Thomas for a reason. It had to be this deal with you he mentioned."

Brianna looked anxiously at the phone on the night table. "I've got to get back. What shall I tell him?"

"Let him come in. I'll hide in the bath. He might really think you've got Sylvie in here. That could explain why he's being rather coy."

"All right, you go hide. I'll tell him."

She started to turn, but Nick stopped her. Taking her by the shoulders again, he leaned over and kissed her. "Keep up the good work."

She turned to the door, feeling pleased at the compliment, but unsure whether she liked the idea that Nick was getting back in the middle of things. When she returned to Henri Rosenthal, she found him with a trace of suspicion on his face.

"Phone's fine now if you want to use it."

He stood. "Forgive my impertinence, Brianna, but while you were in the bedroom, I went to the kitchen for a drink of water. I noticed you hadn't yet cleared your dinner service."

Brianna felt the color rising in her neck. "You don't approve of my housekeeping skills, Henri?"

"I noticed you didn't dine alone this evening."

"So?"

"Considering you must have gotten in late from Charlotte Amalie, isn't it unusual to have a dinner party?" His flat blue eyes narrowed.

"If you must know about my personal business, it was a friend . . . a delicate friend who happens to live nearby. We occasionally share a meal."

Rosenthal's thin mouth transformed into a smug grin. "As when his wife's away?"

Brianna gave a silent sigh of relief. "Remind me not to invite you to any of my cocktail parties, Henri." She pointed toward the bedroom door. "The phone's in there if you care to call Sylvie."

"Merci," he said and strode across the room.

Brianna sat nervously waiting. He seemed to be taking an awfully long time. Anxiously she glanced toward the door that Rosenthal had closed behind him. Still he didn't reappear. She began to worry.

Just as she was about to get up and check on him, she heard the toilet flush, and her heart nearly dropped to her toes. What about Nick?

A moment later Rosenthal appeared, his face betraying no indication anything was amiss.

"I hope you don't mind, but while I was in there, I used the facilities."

Brianna swallowed the lump in her throat. "No, of course not." Her mind raced over the possibilities. Who was this guy Nick Severin—Houdini?

Rosenthal took his place.

"I take it Sylvie was pleased to hear from you?"

"Still no answer," he said with consternation.

"She's young. Perhaps the incident tonight upset her more than I realized." She looked at him, trying to project sympathy. "I *am* sorry, Henri."

He shrugged.

"Okay," she said, making the word sound like a sign of surrender, "you've piqued my interest. What is this business proposal you're talking about?"

His expression turned smug again. "You, Brianna, are quick to trust. I less so."

"Meaning?"

"I won't disclose the details of my idea tonight, but I'd like for you to come to New York where there can be serious discussions."

"You're saying you don't trust me, but you expect me to get on a plane to hear what you have to say? Why be so coy? We're both sitting here. Why not tell me now?"

"Because I'm not the only one concerned. There are others. More specifically, a significant other."

There was a weightiness in Rosenthal's voice that made Brianna's stomach tighten. "Henri, why the mystery?"

"Let's say I have my reasons."

"Why should I go all the way to New York on the strength of that?"

"If my assurances aren't enough to entice you, then let me utter three words that I think will."

"What three words?"

"My dear, I want you to come to New York to hear about . . . *a black pearl*." His grin turned demonic. "A fabulous black pearl!"

"Henri, is this a joke?"

He shook his head. "No, Brianna, I swear it. I would give up little Sylvie if that's what it took to induce you to come and hear the story. I believe when you've had a chance to think it over you will agree. So sure that I will call to confirm your answer very soon."

Henri Rosenthal's words sent her mind spinning. She had been lured to an exotic island by a story about a black pearl, and now this.

Was her Achilles heel that widely known, or was there something behind it all, perhaps an invisible hand? And what about Houdini hiding in the other room? Or had he, too, disappeared, like the flame of a candle extinguished by the wind?

BRIANNA WATCHED Henri Rosenthal disappear down the walk. When he was gone, she closed the door and returned to the living room. "Nick! You can come out now!" she called. She waited, but nothing happened. "Nick?" She headed toward the bedroom.

Opening the door, she found the room dark. She turned on the light switch and peered inside. The bedroom was empty. She went to the bathroom door and knocked. "Nick? Are you in there?"

No answer.

Slowly she entered. No one was there. Turning, she spied the closet and marched over, but he was not inside. The bedroom window was closed and locked. Brianna glanced at the bed, then broke into a broad smile. Getting on her knees, she looked under it. Still, no Nick.

"Lord," she mumbled as she got to her feet. Then she returned to the bathroom. He was not behind the door. Seeing the shower stall, she stepped over and pulled back the curtain. Nick was standing inside, his arms folded across his chest. Seeing her round eyes, he broke into laughter.

"You sneaky bastard!" she said over his mirth, but Nick was enjoying his joke too much. When he doubled over, roaring, Brianna couldn't resist. She reached in and gave the faucet a turn, sending a stream of water over him.

Nick shouted with surprise, and Brianna retreated quickly. She was lying on the bed when he appeared at the door a few moments later, dripping wet.

"You know what this means," he said, wiping his face with a towel. "I have no choice but to spend the night."

MACK QUILLAN WALKED back and forth in front of the window, his fingers steepled before his face. Outside the Government Building horns sounded as traffic squeezed through the narrow streets. He turned to look at Nick and Brianna seated across the desk.

"It's a shame we'd turned off the surveillance equipment. I'd like to have heard that conversation."

"I, for one, am glad it was off," Nick said with an ironic grin.

Brianna elbowed him, but Quillan didn't see.

"Why's that?" the agent asked, turning to him.

Nick shrugged his shoulders. "Well, like they say, two's company, three's a crowd. I'm useful again—as a witness, if nothing else."

Quillan smiled slightly. "Perhaps you have enjoyed a renascence."

Brianna ignored the innuendo. "What do we do now?"

"You'll have to keep that engagement with Rosenthal in New York," Quillan replied. "I don't know what he's up to, but it has to be something significant."

"I've been racking my brain, trying to figure out what scheme he could have in mind regarding a black pearl."

"Nick used the ploy successfully to lure you to St. Barts. Perhaps Rosenthal decided to borrow a leaf from his book."

"Maybe. But I had the feeling he was being sincere. And I can't believe he would be into dyed blacks, too."

"We'll have to wait and see, I suppose. When was it he wanted you to come again?"

"Sometime in the next week or so. He said he'd call with specifics."

Quillan dropped into the desk chair. "I think, Miss Wells, we'd better give you a short course in the use of listening devices. And we should go over some of the legal pitfalls involving entrapment. There's really a lot to do."

"What about Sylvie?"

"She's a problem. We convinced her to stay overnight, for her own protection, but we can't really keep her. I'm reluctant to give her too much information for fear she won't keep it in confidence. I know you've already told her quite a bit, but coming from us it's official, and I just can't risk blowing the case."

"I didn't tell her as much as you might think. Actually, little more than that you were investigating Rosenthal for theft and fraud. No real details."

"If he were to get wind of just that much," Quillan said dryly, "it'd be all over."

"What did you tell her about me?" Brianna asked.

"Nothing. But we'll have to come up with a story of some sort this morning. I really can't justify holding her any longer."

"Maybe if I talk to Sylvie, I can convince her not to see Rosenthal, or at least to give us a few weeks to make a case against him."

"Do you think you can trust her?" Nick asked.

"If we get her away from the Virgin Islands, she'll cooperate. Maybe I can convince her to go back to Martinique for a few weeks."

Quillan shook his head. "If Rosenthal is as keen on her as you say, it might not set very well with him that she's disappeared."

"He knows she's feeling confused. It makes sense that she might want to go away for a while. I think the most important consideration is going to be how strongly he feels about her. If she doesn't mean all that much to him, he'll probably let it pass."

Quillan sighed. "I still don't like it."

"The whole thing's my fault," Brianna said dolefully. "If I hadn't tried to save her from him, none of this ever would have happened."

Nick reached over and patted her hand. "If Rosenthal was going to bolt, he would have done it after your meeting at the restaurant. Obviously his proposition was pretty important. If you can convince Sylvie to lie low for a few weeks, everything should be all right."

"Yes," Quillan said, "I agree."

"How much can I tell her?"

"I'd prefer you not say anything about our plans. Just tell her an intense investigation is underway and that Rosenthal's guilt or innocence will be apparent within a few weeks. Hopefully she'll accept that."

SYLVIE WAS SITTING on a chair in a small, dingy room with a cot and little else when Brianna entered. She rose, her eyes round with surprise. They embraced.

"Brianna, what have they done to you? I've been so worried."

"They've done nothing, Sylvie. I'm fine. Are you okay?"

"Yes, just a little frightened. But I'm confused. Why have they done this?"

"I think so we wouldn't talk to Henri anymore. They're afraid we'll ruin their investigation."

"Do you still think he's done these things?"

"Yes, Sylvie, but we'll know for sure in a few weeks."

"Was Henri arrested, too?"

"No."

"I want to see him, Brianna."

"You can't. Not until later."

"But why?"

"It's important that the investigation continue without Henri knowing. That's the only way we'll ever find out the truth. You're going to have to leave St. Thomas, Sylvie. I want you to go to Martinique for a few weeks and visit your mother. Then, when you come back, we'll know about Henri."

The young woman looked very sad. She went to the cot and sat down. "There's something I must confess," she said solemnly.

Brianna went to the chair beside her. "What?"

"I didn't tell you this before, but Henri asked something of me that I didn't like."

"What sort of thing?"

"He asked me to show him some of the pre-Columbian pieces from your collection. I felt terrible about it and couldn't do it. I told him I had no way to get into the safe." Her eyes filled with tears. "I lied."

"You did the right thing, Sylvie."

"Yes, but I like Henri so much. I didn't want to disappoint him, so I showed him photographs of the collection."

"The entire collection?"

"No, he was only interested in the pre-Columbian—especially the Inca pieces. He was very excited about them and asked many questions. I didn't tell you this before because I knew you didn't like him. I didn't want to make it worse. But last night on this cot I thought about you, and I worried. I was afraid what you said about him was true."

Brianna moved over to sit next to Sylvie. She put her arm around her. "Don't worry. It's almost over now."

"I was so afraid you'd be angry with me because of the pictures."

"Of course I'm not."

"What does it mean, Brianna? Why were the pictures so important to him?"

Brianna held the young woman against her and thought. "The Inca pieces were what he cared most about?"

Sylvie nodded.

"I don't know. It seems very strange. What did he ask?"

"Whether you often used the beads and other parts from them in your designs."

"And what did you tell him?"

"I said that you did. And I showed him some of the necklaces from the display. He was very, very pleased. But I don't know why. He never said. Oh, Brianna, did I do something very wrong?" she asked bleakly.

"No, Sylvie," Brianna said slowly. "You didn't do anything wrong." Now if she could only convince herself that was true.

Chapter Sixteen

Just as Brianna was closing up for the evening, Nick came by. They walked through the shopping district toward the 1829 where he had insisted they would have dinner. They climbed the hill up Kongen's Gade and stopped at the foot of the stairs leading up to the hotel-restaurant. Standing there, they looked back over the harbor.

The sun had set, and the sky had turned orange and coral beyond Hassel Island. Lights were beginning to show onshore and on the boats and ships in the bay. The breeze was cooler than it had been.

"Do you know what tomorrow is?" she asked.

"What is it?"

"Thanksgiving."

Nick chuckled. "You know, it's been years since I've even thought about turkey day. We don't have it in France, you know."

"Don't you miss it?" She looked into his soft brown eyes.

"It's a family day. I have no family."

"I don't either now, but I try not to let that be an excuse. I managed to scrounge a small turkey. Would you care to join me tomorrow for a little nostalgia?"

"That's awfully sweet," he said, taking her arm as they started up the steep flight of stairs, "but I've got a plane to catch."

Brianna looked at him with alarm. "You mean you're going back to Paris?"

"Yes."

The maître d' greeted them on the veranda and showed them to a table in the dining room near a large stone fireplace. Brianna had been thinking about Nick's announcement, and her disappointment had grown to the point of sadness.

"So this is our last supper," she said glumly.

"Not necessarily."

"Not if we happen to take vacations in St. Barts at the same time. Is that what you mean?"

"No, I plan on being in New York in a week—about the same time you'll be there."

She brightened. "You will?"

Nick nodded, taking her hand. "Quillan invited me to be there for the sting."

"Then why are you going to France?"

"Late this morning Rosenthal returned to New York, then got on a connecting flight to Paris. Mack has been in contact with the French police and is sending an agent over tomorrow to help in coordinating investigations. He asked me to go along. Tony Havergill will be flying in from London to get briefed, as well."

"I see. From the way you said it, I thought your involvement in the case was over and you were saying goodbye." She looked down at the hand resting on hers, suddenly feeling a little emotional. Even if this were not going to be their last evening together, it would come soon enough. Brianna could tell it was time to begin preparing for their eventual separation.

"I've gotten rather wrapped up in this case, and I want to see it through," Nick said. "I'm glad Mack's letting me stay on it."

"He should. You initiated the investigation, and you've devoted a lot of time and effort to it." She looked up at him, expecting him to look as sad as she felt. He did.

His mouth was twisted in a frown under the fringe of his mustache. "The case is not the only consideration."

"What do you mean?"

"I like the idea of seeing you again."

"Do you really?"

He nodded. "And I'd like to have Thanksgiving dinner with you, if I could."

"When's your flight?"

"Early evening."

"We could have an afternoon meal."

Nick smiled at her, watching her heavy lashes drop shyly over her wide-set gray eyes. "I'd like that, if it wouldn't be an inconvenience."

"No," she said, feeling somewhat cheered, "we'll make it like a real family celebration, even if there's only the two of us. Is that okay with you?"

"Couldn't be better," he said.

She could hear a touch of *tristesse* in his tone and wondered why it was there.

THE CLOUD COVER extended far out into the Atlantic from the European mainland, and Nick Severin couldn't tell from his view out the window of the plane when they had passed over the Normandy coast. After the Caribbean the somber gray of the approaching European winter looked a little dreary, yet familiar. France, after all, had become his home.

Anthony Havergill was waiting for him outside customs.

"Tony, what a surprise! What's the matter, couldn't you wait until I got home?"

Havergill, a reedy man in his fifties with thinning, brownish-blond hair, laughed good-naturedly. "Not at all, mate. After your commendable effort I thought a proper welcome was in order."

They walked through the crowd toward the cabstands outside the terminal building.

"I don't know how commendable my effort was, Tony. As a matter of fact, Brianna Wells did more to crack this case than I."

"Well, in a way you were responsible for her. That qualifies you, I'd say."

"You put her on the list, not I. My crowning achievement in the case—if you'll pardon the pun—was getting clunked on the head by friendly forces."

Havergill laughed. "I'm afraid I owe you an apology for that one. Sloppy work in coordinating with the insurance people. We were chasing our own tail."

They came to the cabs, and Severin handed his case to the driver at the head of the queue. While it was being placed in the trunk, he and Havergill climbed into the taxi.

"You're looking fit, Nick," the Englishman said cheerily. "Got some sun, I see."

"A little."

"Things right with the young lady?"

"That was the best part of the job, Tony. You guarantee a subject like her each time, and I'll do more of these things for you."

Havergill laughed. "She must be smashing."

"Hell of a nice lady, as a matter of fact. We had Thanksgiving dinner together yesterday."

"That's the business with the pheasant, squash and Indians, isn't it?"

Nick chuckled. "Turkey, pumpkin and football, but you were close."

They rode in silence toward the city, the leaden sky and barren trees in stark contrast to the weather and scenery Severin had enjoyed over the past weeks.

"What's Rosenthal been up to in Paris? Do you know?"

Havergill shook his head. "Strange bird, that one. We haven't quite figured out what's going on. My friends among the police tell me he managed to elude the tail that picked him up at the airport and had several uncharted hours in Paris before they managed to catch up with him.''

"Hope nothing significant happened in the interim.''

"My sentiments exactly. Bloody Frenchies don't screw up often, but when they do, it always seems to be at the wrong time. We haven't a clue what he's up to.''

"Anything interesting turn up in your investigation of the thefts?''

"We've been working night and day since the Rosenthal connection was discovered, trying to find some hard evidence to use against him. Unfortunately, most of it seems circumstantial. We've had bits and pieces from Paris, Amsterdam, Munich, Tokyo and London, but nothing really solid that'll hang him. Brian Grimsley's heading up the investigation in London, and he's developed an interesting hypothesis.''

"What's that?''

"Brian's opinion is that Rosenthal is not the leading actor in this scenario. That in fact, he's working as a sort of front man for someone else. He thinks the pieces of the operation are divided between several individuals. That way no one person has too many fingers in the biscuit bowl at the same time.''

"Or cookie jar, for that matter.''

"What?''

Nick laughed.

Havergill caught his meaning. "You Yanks and your damnable corruption of the language.''

"Any ideas on who else might be involved?''

"No, not a clue. My own theory is that if there is someone else, he's even better placed than old Henri, someone with access, but also above suspicion.''

"It does fit with the impression Rosenthal gave when he propositioned Brianna. I happened to be at her place when he came by. . . .''

"My, isn't love fortunate as well as grand?" Havergill smiled wickedly. "Sorry, old chum, you were saying..."

"I was saying he spoke of others being involved. A significant other was the expression he used, as I recall. And there was a note of deference in his voice when he said it."

"Hmm. That does seem to fit all right. The problem, it seems, is determining who the chap might be."

"I have a hunch we'll be finding out in New York in a week or so. Rosenthal wouldn't tip his hand to Brianna in St. Thomas, so I imagine they're saving the details for New York."

"Is the young woman up to all this, Nick? Even if these people aren't particularly dangerous, the pressure on her must be considerable."

"She's done a hell of a job so far."

Havergill grinned. "Yes, I suppose any woman that can handle you could handle just about anything—from wild boars to jewel thieves."

"Tony, your charitable spirit never ceases to amaze me." Severin looked out at the bleak industrial suburbs of Paris and felt a sentimental twinge go through him as he thought about being with Brianna Wells in the surf at Anse des Flamands and holding her in his arms.

FOR BRIANNA the days passed slowly. She spent most of her time in the shop and on the terrace at her home. With Sylvie gone and Nick in Europe, she felt lonely. Mack Quillan called at least once a day, but she had nothing to report. Henri Rosenthal hadn't contacted her, though she was told he had returned to New York. She wondered if the whole thing hadn't fallen through.

Leaving nothing to chance, Quillan had left the bug on Brianna's telephones both at home and at the shop, so she knew when Henri called they'd have company. But he didn't call. The FBI agent counseled patience, but Brianna was sure Rosenthal had been spooked.

During the week she was invited to a dinner party that she gladly accepted, happy for the distraction and the prospect of companionship. Loneliness had never been a problem before—her time had always seemed to be filled—but the anticipation of the sting and the vacuum left by Nick and Sylvie had changed that.

Another of the guests, a woman of about fifty who was a well-known painter in the Virgin Islands, also lived on Water Island, so they went together, taking the ferry to Charlotte Amalie and a taxi to Cache Point, where their hosts lived.

The dinner party did prove to be a welcome distraction, and she managed to forget her situation for a few hours. But the long trip home plunged her back into her solemn mood. The uncertainty, she realized, was the problem—uncertainty over Henri Rosenthal and Nick Severin. Brianna had just climbed into bed when the telephone rang. It was Nick.

She was surprised to hear his voice. "It must be the middle of the night there, Nick."

"It is," he admitted.

"What's happened?"

"Nothing. I was just lying here listening to the wind in the eaves, thinking about that water at St. Barts, and decided your voice might help bring it all back."

"It was nice there, wasn't it?"

"Nice isn't the right word. I think it was wonderful."

She heard the emotion in his voice, and it pleased her. "Yes, you're right."

"You know what I liked best?"

"Uh . . . Nick . . . you know we've got company, don't you?"

"On the line? You mean Mack? Oh, that doesn't matter. He could use a little stimulation."

"Nick!"

"All right. I'll save it for later. Any word from New York?"

"No, I'm beginning to think I've heard the last of Henri. He was either playing games with me or he's panicked."

"It's too soon to tell."

"But what if he doesn't call?"

Nick gave a little laugh. "Then maybe I could interest you in a fabulous black pearl...."

"It seems to me we've tried that already."

"Yes, and as I recall, you didn't like my paint job."

Brianna laughed. "You silly goose."

He sighed. "I miss you."

She felt a little surge of happiness go through her. "Uh... Mack and I miss you, too."

"I can see this collegial thing has gotten out of hand."

"It's hard to be romantic under the circumstances."

"Yes, and I realize how anxious I've become for the circumstances to change."

"Have you?"

"I'm as disappointed as you that Henri hasn't called. Let me put it that way."

Hearing his voice made her feel much better. And she sensed genuine emotion in Nick, as well. "I'll let you know if I do."

"I'm sure I'll hear right away. There are a lot of people on this side of the Atlantic who are sitting on the edge of their chairs, too."

"I'm glad you called." She would have liked to have been in his arms just then, but she knew she couldn't be. The conversation ended unfulfilled in that respect.

Brianna had hung up the receiver and had just turned out the light when the phone rang again. Groping in the dark, she picked it up.

"Brianna, Henri Rosenthal here."

"Oh, Henri, how are you?"

"Fine. I am sorry to call so late, but I've been trying all evening. I assumed you were out, and I wanted to speak with you tonight."

"It's no problem. I was at a dinner party."

"I thought perhaps it was something of that sort. *Alors.* Have you thought about my little proposal?"

"There wasn't much to think about, Henri. You hardly told me a thing."

"Then we must talk. Will you come to New York?"

"I could arrange to, yes."

"Would a week from today be convenient?"

"I suppose so."

"*Bien.* That would be perfect."

"Would you like to come to my flat? I'm on the East Side," she asked.

"No, no. That would not be convenient. Could we meet somewhere instead?"

"All right. Where?"

"How about in front of the Ritz Carlton?"

"In front?"

"Yes. Stand right next to the doorman at two o'clock sharp. You will be picked up."

Brianna remembered how Mack Quillan had encouraged her to arrange the meeting at a place they would have control of in advance, if at all possible. "But isn't that a little inconvenient?" she protested.

"You won't have to wait long. Wear a fur so you'll be warm." He laughed a little. "Next Saturday, two o'clock, in front of the Ritz Carlton. Good night, Brianna."

She heard the phone click in her ear and then the bland hum of the dial tone.

BRIANNA SAT IN A ROOM on an unknown floor of an undistinguished building in New York City. Her attention was on an FBI technical specialist who was explaining the operation of the listening devices arranged on a gray metal table. Mack Quillan sat nearby.

"It seems from the suspect's comments," the technician was saying, "that your interview will take place in a moving vehicle, or at some remote location after being transported there. This will make live audio surveillance difficult. We can try to monitor your conversation by radio transmission, but the most reliable method would be to use a midget tape recorder that would be concealed on your person."

"A tape recorder?"

"Smaller than a pack of cigarettes," the man replied, picking up a tiny rectangular instrument. "On a man we frequently strap it to an ankle under a pant cuff. On a woman it's a little more difficult."

"Why not in my purse?"

"You can be separated from your purse, but not so easily from a leg or arm." The man smiled. "Particularly in cases not involving organized crime."

"Let's keep the jokes to a minimum," Quillan said dryly.

"It's all right," Brianna assured him. "We have to keep our sense of humor."

The FBI agent shrugged. "As long as you see it that way."

"What do you plan on wearing, Miss Wells?" the technician asked.

"A dress, I suppose. Or a suit, if that's better."

"But not a pantsuit?"

Brianna smiled. "No, not in Manhattan."

"If you're wearing a skirt, it'll have to be strapped to your thigh, or if you prefer, we can hide it in your blouse. Comfort will have to be considered."

"Thank goodness for small favors."

The man chuckled. "I had to fix up a guy with one of these things for the beach once. All I had to work with was a pair of swim trunks. Fortunately, he left me a little room to work."

Quillan cleared his throat.

The technician held up the recorder and began explaining how it was activated. Brianna turned and winked at the agent.

"HOW ARE YOUR NERVES holding up, Miss Wells?" Quillan asked as they drove across town.

"I'm a little jumpy, I must admit."

"Well, it'll all be over in a couple of days."

"I certainly hope it works, since I bungled it for you in St. Thomas," she said, fidgeting.

"I'm sure you'll do fine."

"I had nightmares about that incident for a week, so I hope I've gotten all my mistakes out of the way."

They were nearing Brianna's place.

"Have you heard from Nick? He told me he was going to be here for the sting," she said.

"Yes, he's due in. Apparently he got involved in some sort of negotiation with the French government—an art deal of some kind. It kept him in Paris longer than expected."

"I see."

"He knows your meeting with Rosenthal is tomorrow, so I expect he'll be arriving at any time."

"I hope so."

"Incidentally, the French have been very cooperative in keeping an eye on your friend, Miss Voirin. The authorities in Martinique say she's been staying close to home and has made no attempt to contact Rosenthal that they're aware of."

"Good. I just hope that she's holding up emotionally. Learning his true colors was a big shock to her."

"It's a shame she fell for a guy like that."

"She was vulnerable. And I suppose Henri's a bit exotic in his own way. Sylvie had a weakness for older Frenchmen, I'm afraid."

"Well, none of us are without our vulnerabilities."

"No," Brianna replied, thinking of Nick, "I guess we aren't."

The car pulled up to the curb, and she got out. "Thanks for the lift, Mack," she said, looking in. "Guess tomorrow is the big day."

He nodded.

Brianna gave a weak little smile and turned to go inside.

"Sleep well," he said.

"I wouldn't count on it," she told him before she walked away.

Chapter Seventeen

It was still dark when Brianna awoke the next morning. She was sure she would hear from Nick, but he neither came to her flat nor called. Perhaps the negotiations in Paris had turned out to be more important than the sting. Perhaps during their separation his feelings for her had cooled.

Brianna knew she couldn't expect much, for he really owed her nothing. There had been no commitment, no guarantee. He would probably turn out to be just another person who had passed through her life, a man with whom she had shared a little emotion, a little sentiment, a little love.

But thinking about Nick Severin could wait. Henri Rosenthal was a thief, and today he was waiting for her with some sort of criminal scheme, and *she* was in a position to catch him red-handed.

Brianna glanced at the darkened window blinds, knowing daylight was still half an hour away. She would have liked to go back to sleep, but her brain was already racing, and the adrenaline flowing; it was too late.

She thought about the meeting that afternoon. What Henri would be proposing remained a mystery. His black pearl story had to be a hoax. It didn't fit into his forgery operation in any way she could see. And his interest in her Inca pieces made no sense, either, though it had served to rekindle memories of her own, memories of her father and his profound interest in the subject.

Feeling more fatigued than when she had gone to bed, Brianna rose, went to the window and opened the blind. It was still dark outside, the city lights cool gems on a drab backdrop of concrete, steel and glass. To the east the first hint of dawn began glowing through the late autumn haze lying over the city.

A horn sounded in a nearby canyon, a muted echo dying quickly before another followed it in some still more remote quarter. Unlike the islands, the city never slept, it just paused before surging recklessly forward with the first light of day. Brianna liked both places, perhaps because of what they said about each other.

Retreating to the bathroom, she showered, shampooed her hair and mentally ran over the instructions Mack Quillan and the others had drilled into her over the past few days. As the hot, soothing water ran over her naked body, she thought about Nick Severin and decided he wouldn't show up.

Perhaps it was just as well. There was no real prospect of a future relationship with him. After all, he lived in Paris, and she split her time between the islands and New York.

Quillan had asked her to be at the federal offices at eleven for a final briefing and to get wired with the listening devices. There would be a quick lunch, then she would take a taxi to the hotel. Afterward, win or lose, Brianna decided she would get on the first plane for the Caribbean.

MACK QUILLAN PERCHED on the edge of a table and looked at Brianna, who wore a plum wool suit that was loose fitting enough to conceal the array of devices they had selected.

"We've decided to go with live audio plus a recorder," he said. "A mobile unit will follow you at a distance to maintain maximum reception. You'll also have to wear a small tracking device, in case we lose you.''

"Let's hope Henri doesn't try to get fresh," Brianna said dryly. "If he touches me, he's likely to get electrocuted."

Quillan smiled. "Rosenthal's clever, but we have no reason to believe he's sophisticated in these matters. The people in the drug business, who so often have to deal with strangers, are the astute ones."

"Remind me not to go into drug smuggling."

"The main thing, Brianna, is to remain calm. If something unexpected occurs, try not to panic. You'll have support nearby at all times, though you won't *see* us. There'll be four teams of agents in unmarked cars in your vicinity continually. I'll be in one of the cars. We'll constantly be monitoring what goes on in your vehicle."

"I'll probably be safer than if I were walking down the street alone," she said, wanting to believe her own words.

"That's the idea. Any questions?"

"No. Let's just get it over with."

The FBI agent got to his feet. "We've got a little luncheon planned. Are you hungry?"

"My final meal? I suppose I should eat. Not advisable to do this sort of thing on an empty stomach, is it?" Listening to her own chatter, Brianna could tell she was nervous. She rose and followed Quillan down the hall.

He opened the door to a small conference room with the table already set for a meal. Stepping in, Brianna saw a man in a dark brown business suit looking out the window. He turned at the sound of her entering. It was Nick.

"Hi, Brianna."

She was caught speechless for a moment. "Nick, I didn't expect you."

Behind her Quillan withdrew and closed the door.

"I couldn't miss your big day," he said, slowly walking toward her.

She waited until he was before her, pleased at the sight of him. When he was just inches away, Nick lifted her chin and kissed her softly on the lips. Then he took her, gathering her protectively into his arms.

"I'm glad you're here," she mumbled, pressing her face against the warm, aromatic flesh of his neck. His masculine scent enveloped her.

"I would have been here sooner, but I got tied up."

"That's what Mack said. I hope you didn't leave anything important for this. It wasn't really necessary for you to come."

"I concluded my business. Besides, this is very important to me."

They turned to the table that was set for two.

"A luncheon *intime*," he said, holding a chair for her. "It was Quillan's idea, but I readily seized the opportunity."

"They still have you assigned to the hand-holding duties, I see."

"No, this is one of my rewards for spotting your innocence so quickly."

"And trying to undo it just as quickly."

Nick chuckled. "I didn't make a point of including that in my report."

"How very cavalier of you."

Nick took her fingers, pulling them to his lips. "Henri is going to get his this afternoon, but I do owe the old boy a debt of gratitude."

"Don't count your chickens yet," she replied, watching him kissing her fingers, liking the sensation it created.

There was a slight knock at the door, and a waiter in a white jacket wheeled in a serving cart, quickly filling the room with mouthwatering aromas.

"My, I didn't know the government was capable of such savoir faire," Brianna said with a little laugh.

"It's not. This was my idea. Quillan wanted to send out to the deli for sandwiches."

When the waiter had served them, he left the room. Brianna looked over the tempting meal, then at Nick, who looked so very different from that first day on St. Barts at the airport, though no less appealing. The combination of the suit, the hair and mustache, made him seem so debonair, so sophisticated. And yet beneath it all the raw sex appeal was there.

"Bon appétit," he said, giving her his wry, irresistible smile.

Brianna picked up her fork but looked up at him again, beginning to realize that she was hopelessly in love.

DURING THE FINAL PREPARATIONS for her mission Nick stayed in the background. He was there at the sufferance of Mack Quillan, and perhaps because of the agent's insight into their feelings for each other, but he had no official capacity. But Brianna felt better because he was there, and that undoubtedly was the point.

The plan was for Brianna to ride to the Ritz Carlton alone in a taxi, operating on the theory that Rosenthal might have someone watching the hotel before his arrival. If she were seen in the presence of another person, they might panic.

Nick was going to be with Quillan in one of the four vehicles, monitoring the operation.

The unmarked government cars were at the curb, lined up behind the cab when Brianna, Nick and the agents went out onto the street. Nick squeezed her hand, Quillan wished her luck, and she got into the back of the taxi.

The two men got into the car behind her, Nick in the back seat, Quillan in front with the driver.

"What do you think, Mack?" Severin asked, leaning forward. "Is this going to work?"

"God, I don't know. I just hope somebody shows up at the hotel."

"What do you mean?"

"Just before we left the office, I got word that Henri Rosenthal is in a taxi headed for Kennedy International."

"You're kidding."

"Nope. Either poor Brianna is going to stand out there until her feet get cold, or somebody else will be coming by to pick her up."

BRIANNA WAITED NERVOUSLY in the lobby of the Ritz Carlton. It was quarter of two. She would go out a few minutes early, but there was no reason to stand outside in the cold any longer than necessary. Though she was alone, and nobody paid any particular attention to her, she felt very much on stage, knowing that at least a dozen people were listening to every sound around her. She wondered if they could hear the anxious thumping of her heart.

After pacing back and forth in the lobby for several minutes, Brianna made her way toward the hotel entrance. Peering out, she saw the doorman at the curb, trying to hail a cab.

"The doorman's tied up," she said under her breath to the agents listening from their remote stations. "As soon as he returns to his post, I'll go out."

Brianna glanced around to make sure no one was near in case she wished to make another announcement. After a minute the doorman had secured a taxi, had put his passengers safely inside and stepped back to his place.

"He's back," she said to her invisible audience. "Here goes."

Brianna went through the revolving door and walked to where the uniformed doorman, a large man, stood.

"Taxi, ma'am?"

"No, thank you. I'm waiting for a ride."

"I can call you, if you'd prefer to wait inside."

"They'll be along any minute, but thank you." She glanced at her watch. It was two minutes till the hour.

Brianna stared across the boulevard at Central Park. It was a brisk autumn day. A stiff breeze kicked up leaves from the lawn and sent them tumbling into the street. The trees were mostly bare, and the sky was overcast. The doorman next to her slapped his gloved hands together then rubbed them vigorously.

"Cool day," he said cheerfully.

"Yes, it is."

"Don't look forward to the snow, though. No ma'am."

Brianna wasn't in the mood for small talk and almost felt guilty that the doorman was ignorant of how many people were listening to their little exchange. She looked again at her watch.

A moment later a taxi pulled into the circular drive, and the doorman stepped down to assist the passengers. Brianna peered into the cab to see if Henri Rosenthal was inside, but he wasn't. Two women got out and walked into the hotel.

As the taxi moved away, Brianna noticed that a long black limousine with darkened windows had pulled up in the drive. The doorman went to the vehicle and opened the back door, leaning over to look inside. He turned to Brianna.

"Miss Wells?"

"Yes."

"This is your ride, ma'am."

Brianna felt her heart lurch. "Oh." Her head cleared, and she remembered the instructions she had been given. "It's a long black limousine, New York plates," she said under her breath, her hand shielding her mouth. "I don't know what kind." Giving a little cough to cover her action, she walked to where the man stood holding the door.

Bending over, she peered inside and saw a small wizened man with white hair sitting in the corner of the rear seat. "Monsieur Pillet!"

"*Bonjour,* Brianna. Won't you join me?"

"I was expecting Henri Rosenthal."

Pillet smiled through the deep wrinkles on his face. "Henri was occupied with other matters. He asked if I would come in his place."

She climbed into the limousine with the help of the doorman, settling on the wide seat at the opposite end from Pillet. Then, remembering what she had been told, Brianna casually scooted toward the middle, as the Frenchman moved his cane aside.

"What a surprise," she said, hoping the expression on her face didn't reveal too much.

Lucien Pillet chuckled, but said nothing. He tapped on the glass separating them from the driver, and the limousine started to pull away.

"PILLET?" QUILLAN SAID with surprise. "Who the hell is Pillet?"

Severin was at the edge of his seat, leaning forward to hear the crackling transmission coming over the radio. "Lucien Pillet is a notable French dealer, now semiretired," he explained, his eyes filled with surprise. He shook his head in disbelief. "I'll be damned. He's the guy Havergill and I used as a reference with Brianna."

He paused to listen, but the radio was silent. "I tricked his secretary into thinking I was with Interpol so she'd vouch for me."

Sound again came over the radio, and the men in the car fell silent, listening.

"I take it you and Henri are involved together in whatever it is that I've come to hear about," Brianna said.

The Frenchman's voice came clearly over the radio. "My dear young lady, let's say for the moment I have an interest in talking with you."

"What's this all about?"

"In due course, in due course."

"Easy, Brianna," Quillan said. "Take it easy, baby."

The agent at the wheel, wearing headphones for separate communication with the tracking team, started the engine and the unmarked car moved out onto Central Park South. Severin looked up the street in the direction of the hotel, but had only a brief glimpse of the limousine as it, too, moved into the flow of traffic.

"I hope this isn't some sort of joke," Brianna said, the weariness in her voice coming through.

"*Tiens, tiens.* I am an old friend of your father, my child. You must trust me, just as I must trust you."

"Henri invited me to come to New York to talk about a black pearl. Are you aware of that, Monsieur Pillet?"

"Of course."

There was silence. Brianna wasn't pushing.

"Thata girl," Quillan mumbled as he minutely adjusted the radio control knobs.

Severin was nodding his head. "It was no accident Rosenthal and Pillet were in St. Thomas at about the same time. God, why didn't I see that before?"

He craned his neck to see up the street, but the limo was out of sight. The driver of their car, receiving directions through the headphones, moved to the left and at the corner turned into Central Park. They had a brief glimpse of the long black vehicle before it disappeared around a curve ahead.

"Brianna," Pillet said, his voice cracking through the faint static of the radio, "I am an old man, but still a man of vision, imagination. I have a very great project in mind, and I want you to be a part of it."

Severin leaned forward on the front seat, listening intently.

"What sort of project?" she asked.

"You and I together can discover some of the most wonderful treasures known to the world of archaeology."

"What treasures? I don't understand."

"Before your father's death we spoke of his wonderful collection of Inca relics and ancient jewelry. He told me about his theories of the many pieces that must have been lost over time, items the world will never see. Did you ever discuss these things with him?"

"Yes, we talked about his work."

"Recently it occurred to me that it would be fortunate if some of these lost items were found. Do you realize what a wonderful and valuable discovery that would be?"

Pillet's laugh echoed through the government car.

"Where do you propose to find them, Monsieur Pillet?"

"Perhaps right here in New York, my dear. Perhaps they are right under our very noses. Brianna, they could even be here with us now, in this very car."

Severin and Quillan waited, staring at the radio.

"Please, say what you mean," she said.

Quillan shook his fist excitedly, urging her on.

"I mean that there are countless gems right in the mind of a creative artist," Pillet continued. "I have the vision to know that they could exist, and how to find them. You have the ability to create them, just as the Inca craftsmen did hundreds of years ago."

"You want me to make replicas? Is that what you're saying?"

"Not replicas, no. I want you to make originals!"

Both Quillan and Severin gave a little cheer.

BRIANNA LOOKED at the little Frenchman and smiled wryly. "So, Henri and I were thinking along the same lines, after all. He was just afraid to admit it."

"No," Pillet said, gesturing with his hand, "my dear friend Henri was not afraid. He was under instructions not to discuss anything with you until he spoke first with me."

"Somehow I knew there was a greater talent behind all this, Monsieur Pillet."

He grinned. "If that is flattery you give me, I will take it as such."

"There's one thing I don't understand. If you've been so successful switching replicas and then reselling the originals, why are you interested in a totally new scheme?"

"It's not a totally new one. It's—how do you say it?—a variation of the theme."

Conscious of her instructions, Brianna tried to get Pillet to be as explicit as possible, to make him state things in his own words. "Why do you say it's a variation?"

"We have been duplicating known pieces. What could make more sense than to create totally new ones? Of course, I mean by that ones which are newly made but ancient to the rest of the world." Pillet gave her a sly little grin. "It makes perfect sense, no?"

"I suppose so, but why Inca?"

"Because there is much interest now in South America, and the market is hungry. Also, we must have access to a collection with considerable resources. Finally, we need a designer who knows our target market very well."

"And you thought of my father's collection and me."

"I must say the idea didn't fall into place until you discussed with Henri the possibility of working with us. When I saw that your mind was, shall we say, on our wavelength, I decided to visit you in St. Thomas."

"I take it, then, that I passed your scrutiny."

"*Oui, ma chérie.* I see in you the same cunning and creativity that I myself have."

Brianna looked out the window of the limousine. They had been driving through Central Park and were nearing the Hundred-tenth Street boundary. She wondered what Nick, Mack Quillan and the others were thinking, whether she was doing all the things she was supposed to do.

"And what about this black pearl? What does it have to do with your idea, Monsier Pillet?"

"Ah. That, my dear, is the stroke of genius. If we are to discover spectacular new finds, they must capture the imagination of experts and the public alike. Our first piece must be the envy of the world. It will be scrutinized minutely by the experts, so on this, the first one, we must use authentic elements from genuine artifacts."

"What do you mean?"

"Isn't it obvious? We will take several minor pieces and use their parts, reassembling them into one dramatic masterpiece. It will be the necklace of a queen, a magnificent creation that we will call the black pearl necklace."

"An ancient necklace with a black pearl?"

"The pearl will not be there, of course, but the center place, where it once hung, will be evident. You see, it was your own interest in black pearls and an amusing little story once told to me by your father that gave me the idea. There is a story that natural blacks from the South Seas once made their way to South America...."

"Yes, I remember that story from when I was a girl."

"*Bien.* Then you know it is magical. We will not be able to prove the pearl existed, of course, but it will be a wonderful story to release with the discovery. The publicity and interest in that alone will increase the value of the piece incalculably."

"Do you really believe we can deceive the experts?"

"We must take great care, of course. But I have seen your work. I know that the necklace will succeed. The lesser pieces that come later can be made of beads and gems that you reproduce. But this first one must be made with authentic elements. I am very confident. And there is much talent and knowledge looking over your shoulder."

"Who all is involved?"

"Brianna, Brianna. You ask many questions. Now is not yet the time."

"But, Monsieur Pillet, you ask a great deal of me. There is much that I must trust."

He gave her an amused smile. "Think what I have disclosed to you. I would be a fool to tell you the things I have unless I was willing to make good my word. I have taken much risk just meeting with you."

"How much fraudulent jewelry have you and Henri moved?"

Pillet shook his head. "Always questions. Hundreds of thousands of dollars' worth, Brianna. We are experienced. We are good."

Her mind was spinning. What other information should she wring from him? What other admissions should she attempt to get? She looked out the window again and saw that they were circling back toward the south end of the park. Perhaps Quillan would be satisfied with what she had done. She would go through the scenario that had been planned and see.

Brianna took a deep breath and groaned. Then she put her head in her hands, bending over.

"What is it?" Pillet asked.

"I'm suddenly not feeling well. Perhaps it's the excitement, or the drive. I sometimes get carsick." She clamped her hand to her mouth as though she were about to be ill and groaned again. "Could we stop for a moment? Perhaps if I stepped outside for a breath of air . . ."

Pillet leaned forward and pushed an intercom button to indicate to the driver he wanted to speak with him. Through the glass separating them, Brianna saw the chauffeur take the microphone.

"Yes, sir?"

"Pull over where you may, please. We want to stop for a moment," the Frenchman replied.

"Yes, sir."

Brianna waited until they stopped at the edge of the park near a busy boulevard. "I'll just be a minute," she said as she slid to the edge of the seat, opened the door and climbed out. With her back to the passing traffic she stood watching the oncoming cars, waiting to see if it was time—if she had gotten enough information.

Soon she saw the signal, a brief flash of headlights in the traffic. Waiting until the lead car was near, Brianna began walking briskly back in the direction they had come, just as Quillan had instructed.

"Brianna!" Pillet called to her from inside the limousine, but she didn't look back.

More headlights flashed on, and an FBI car in the far lane swerved over just as a cab was changing lanes in the opposite direction. Brianna watched in horror as the vehicles collided.

Another FBI car, its lights on, was behind the taxi and tried to avoid the collision, but it, too, skidded into the pileup. Other vehicles slammed on their brakes, and soon half the parkway was jammed. People began getting out of their cars, including some of the agents. There were shouts and general confusion.

Finally, out of the turmoil, Brianna saw Nick making his way toward where she was waiting at the side of the road. He arrived at a run.

"Brianna, are you all right?"

She melted into the protective embrace of his arms. "Yes, I'm fine."

Nick was looking back to where the limousine had stopped. The driver had gotten out and was standing by the vehicle, surveying the scene. The rear door on the passenger side, which Brianna had exited, was still open. Because of the darkened glass they couldn't see Pillet inside.

"I'd better check on our boy," Nick said, and jogged back to the limo.

Just then Mack Quillan ran up to Brianna. Nick was leaning over, looking inside the vehicle. "Mack!" he shouted back. "He's gone."

"Damn," the agent muttered and headed for the limo. Brianna was right behind him.

Nick had turned and was looking up and down the boulevard and at the gathering crowd. "There he is!" he shouted, just as Quillan and Brianna arrived. He was pointing across the wide street where the old man stood on the far corner, waving his cane to flag a taxi.

Nick and Quillan sprinted to the corner, but the traffic was whizzing by so quickly that neither of them was able to cross. As they looked at the oncoming traffic, watching for an opportunity to dash to the other side, Brianna saw a cab pull up in front of Pillet.

Quillan shouted at the driver but couldn't be heard over the roar of the traffic. Nick edged into the street, ready to make a dash as Pillet was struggling into the back seat of the taxi.

Brianna looked up and saw the light change, but it was too late. The cab had started through the intersection on the caution light. Before she realized what was happening, Nick dashed across the intersection in front of the traffic. He closed in on the accelerating taxicab and dove for the hood just as the driver saw him and threw on the brakes.

As Quillan and Brianna watched, Nick's flying body landed on the hood and slid across it, falling onto the pavement on the far side. The driver jumped out immediately, and Quillan ran to the cab in the middle of the street. Pillet was getting out just as the agent came around to intercept him.

Brianna stood frozen, her hand to her mouth, when Nick's head finally reappeared from the far side of the cab. He slowly got to his feet and waved. She sighed in relief. Instantly a couple of uniformed police officers arrived on the scene and began directing traffic.

When he was able, Nick made his way back to Brianna, a little smile on his face.

"Bravo!" she exclaimed.

The smile grew larger.

"Are you all right?"

Nick looked down at the tear on his trouser leg. "I'll live."

She put her arm around his waist. "When you didn't come up right away, I was afraid you'd been hurt."

"You mean fallen down a manhole or something?"

Brianna laughed. "Oh, sure, make jokes, but he wasn't worth the risk."

"After all the clunks on the head and other tribulations I've been through, I couldn't just stand there and watch him drive away." He put his arm around her shoulder, and they walked back toward the limo and the other vehicles that were now at the side of the road. A team of agents passed them on the way to assist Quillan.

"You were fabulous," Nick said, kissing her forehead. "Between what we got on tape and the other evidence, Mack thinks he's got a tight case."

"Thank goodness. I was worried I'd forgotten something."

They stood surveying the scene.

"I hope nobody was hurt," she said with concern.

"It doesn't appear any serious damage was done."

Moments later Quillan arrived with Pillet, who was escorted by two other agents. The old man, his face ashen, glanced up at Brianna as he was led past her to a government car.

"Pourquoi?" he said. "Why? It was such a wonderful idea."

Brianna watched in silence as the Frenchman was hustled into the back seat. She shivered, and Nick squeezed her more tightly.

"Come on," he said. "Let's go some place and have a cup of coffee."

Chapter Eighteen

Brianna wanted to be out in the air, so after a technician had disconnected and helped her remove the listening device, she and Nick walked across Central Park, arm in arm. The blustery wind gusted, whipping her ebony hair about her face. She pulled it away, smiling up at her companion, who leaned over as they walked and kissed her on the temple.

"Imagine what it would be like to be in that balmy air on St. Barts right now," he said wistfully.

"Nick, you're a hopeless romantic."

"No, I'd just like to be there with the Brianna Wells I know now."

"Would it be all that different?"

"You couldn't captivate me any more than you did."

She laughed happily. "And if it had been me who was arrested today, you'd be saying 'I knew from the minute I saw her.'"

"Well, I did, as a matter of fact."

Brianna looked at him questioningly. "You knew what?"

"That you wouldn't easily escape from my life."

"So that's why you hunted me down at the Select Bar that last day? You couldn't bear to see me go?"

"Yes, as a matter of fact."

"Had nothing to do with wanting to put me behind bars?"

He pulled her hard against him. "Not a thing."

They had come to the edge of the park, crossed over the boulevard and began walking down a side street.

"Nick, did you know Lucien Pillet was going to be in that limousine?"

"No, it was a total surprise. Although we did find out at the last minute it wasn't going to be Henri Rosenthal. We just didn't know who it was going to be."

"You mean you and Quillan let me get in that car not knowing who was there?"

He shrugged sheepishly. "We figured Jack the Ripper was dead by now, and buried in England."

Brianna gave him a jab in the ribs with her elbow.

"Whoever it was, he was bound to be the one we were after. The last person I suspected was my very own character witness."

She laughed. "I suppose that's a comment on your character, isn't it?"

"He was your friend, not mine."

"He wasn't a friend, but it's no less disappointing. My father knew him well."

"A shame, actually. But those boys were turning millions."

"What about Henri? What's happened to him?"

"He was on his way to Kennedy. Quillan said he wouldn't be permitted to leave the country, so he's undoubtedly under arrest by now."

They walked for a few minutes, and Brianna thought about the surprising turn of events. The wind whistled down the street, and she shivered. "Brrr."

"St. Barts air starting to sound better to you?"

"I *am* getting a little chilly."

Nick spotted a small coffee shop across the street, and they dashed over and went inside. The clean but simple little place was deserted, except for a single customer and the proprietor who stood talking with him.

They went to a booth at the back of the café. The warm, dry air stung their cold skin. Nick vigorously rubbed Brianna's hands between his own as the counterman came ambling back, his white jacket snug about the belly.

"Two coffees," Nick said, barely glancing up.

The man retreated without a word. Nick still held her hands in his. They silently observed each other until two steaming cups were placed on the Formica tabletop in front of them.

Brianna took hers greedily, wrapping her hands around the cup for warmth. She smiled at Nick before taking a sip. "What happens now?"

He silently reached into his coat pocket and pulled out a small velvet pouch, putting it on the table in front of her.

Brianna put down her coffee. "What's this?"

"A token of my love."

She looked at him, questioning his meaning.

"Go ahead. Have a look."

With her fingers still numb, Brianna nervously opened the pouch. Inside was a cloth folded into a tiny bundle. Carefully she unfolded it to discover a deeply lustrous black pearl.

Brianna stared at it. "Nick, it's gorgeous!" She looked up at him, her wide mouth smiling impishly. "I can tell already it's not dyed."

"It's not cultured, either."

Her jaw dropped. "A *natural* black? My God!" Then, with quivering fingers, she picked up the pearl, examining it minutely. "This is the rarest gem on earth," she said, barely above a whisper. "Where did you get it?"

"Believe it or not, the French government was kind enough to give it to me."

"*Give* it to you?"

He nodded. "Of course they had two, and gave me the smaller."

"Why would they *give* it to you?"

"Oh, it wasn't free. I had to part with one of the two Renoirs my mother left me. She had these two canvases, both rather undistinguished by all accounts, but the Ministry of Culture has been salivating over them for years. Frankly I never cared much for the paintings, and it seemed a propitious moment to make them an offer."

"Nick, you gave up something like that in order to give me a natural black pearl?"

He ran his fingertips over the back of her hand. "I had to make sure you'd go back to St. Barts with me."

Brianna felt tears begin to well in her eyes.

"The only remaining question is whether you'd go as my wife, or my friend."

She blinked back the tears, biting her lip. "Do I have to choose?" she whispered.

"I'd like it to be both." His soft brown eyes were misty.

"But you live in Paris . . ."

"Shouldn't somebody as notable as Brianna Wells have a shop in Paris, as well as New York and St. Thomas? I could certainly find a way to spend part of my year in New York and the Caribbean, if you could join me for a few months in France."

She shook her head, disbelieving. "Oh, Nick . . ." The tears overflowed and began running down her cheeks.

He took her hands again, and Brianna stared down at the pearl lying on the cloth.

"What are you thinking, darling?" he asked after watching her for a long moment.

"How I feel like an Inca queen."

"An Inca queen?"

She smiled at him, bemused. "Strangely enough, Lucien Pillet would understand."

"I'd like to understand."

"You will. It's a long story. Maybe I'll tell you when we take a walk some moonlit night on the beach in the Caribbean."

"All right," Nick said. "Then I'll wait." He contemplated her for a second, then reached over and tucked her hair behind her ear. "I love you."

ATTRACTIVE, SPACE SAVING BOOK RACK

Display your most prized novels on this handsome and sturdy book rack. The hand-rubbed walnut finish will blend into your library decor with quiet elegance, providing a practical organizer for your favorite hard-or soft-covered books.

Only $9.95

**Approximately
16" x 8"
when assembled**

Assembles in seconds!

To order, rush your name, address and zip code, along with a check or money order for $10.70* ($9.95 plus 75¢ postage and handling) payable to *Harlequin Reader Service*:

Harlequin Reader Service
Book Rack Offer
901 Fuhrmann Blvd.
P.O. Box 1325
Buffalo, NY 14269-1325

Offer not available in Canada.

BKR-1R

*New York residents add appropriate sales tax.

Take 4 best-selling love stories FREE
Plus get a FREE surprise gift!